My Odyssey

My Odyssey

Short Stories from the
Life of Paul Straub

*to Jim Ashford, who
I greatly admire.
from Paul Straub*

Paul Straub

Outskirts Press, Inc.
Denver, Colorado

Outskirts Press, Inc.
http://www.outskirtspress.com

ISBN HB: 978-1-4327-4470-0
ISBN PB: 978-1-4327-4786-2

Library of Congress Control Number: 2009935021

Outskirts Press and the "OP" logo are trademarks belonging to Outskirts Press, Inc.

PRINTED IN THE UNITED STATES OF AMERICA

Contents

Introduction

Originally, the idea for this book was to illustrate for my children the principles which have given me great happiness in life. Among these are to live and enjoy each day at a time. The most important moment is the present, not the past or the future. Other standards are always to be honest and to treat every person with respect.

A small portion of the book, which was written at the time it occurred, is written in *italics*. Much of this was written in flight under unusual conditions. Very little editing was done on these parts in an attempt to transmit to the reader the sensation of being present at the time.

To write a book about yourself is an act of vanity, but I think you will take pleasure in some of the extraordinary stories.

Paul Straub

Casablanca — 1957, Saturday

Everybody said it was not safe to go into the medina—especially at night. It was about midnight when I staggered out of the tiny bar deep in the native section called the medina. The natives couldn't have been more hospitable. I could hardly pay for a beer; everybody wanted to buy the young American a drink. And they kept presenting me with strange things to eat and drink. One after another, I was brought small plates with food that I did not recognize. In Arabic and with hand signs, they would indicate that I should eat their offerings. I knew that it would be an insult not to eat the food that these poor people gave me, and I certainly didn't want to insult them since every man wore a fez and carried a long curved knife in his belt.

The narrow curved streets in the medina were pitch-black. There are no street lights there. Fortunately I knew that the medina was up on a hill, and, if I wanted to find my way back to my room in the Seaman's Hotel at the port, I would have to go downhill. At every corner, I chose the downhill direction and eventually I broke out of the darkness of the medina to a broad street with a few street lights, which I recognized as the street which I had taken from the port to the medina. All I had to do now was follow this street downhill to the port and my hotel. Not a soul was to be found on the street, and barely a sound. For safety, I walked down the middle of the fairly broad street and avoided the doorways where someone might hide. The cool desert air had cleared my head by now, and I began to think that I had accomplished my adventure into the medina at night without incident, and later I could gloat to my friends that the only thing which one has to fear is fear itself.

I was almost to the water by the port. If I had walked a short block further and turned right, it wouldn't have happened. I would have come to the Seaman's Hotel on main streets with streetlights. But as I passed a narrow passage to the right, I saw the neon sign, "Seaman's Hotel," a few hundred yards down a narrow dark passage. I decided to run the short distance through the passageway and arrive more directly to the hotel.

About two running steps into the alleyway and three men jumped simultaneously on my back. The weight of the three brought me immediately to the ground, and one of them stuck the tip of his razor sharp knife into the side of my neck. With split-second timing, the point was placed precisely on my carotid artery and jugular vein in such a manner that a slight movement of his wrist, requiring no more energy than a finger pulling a trigger, would cleave both vessels. Clearly this young chap was the master of his chosen profession. I was wearing a washable sport coat with my wallet in the inside pocket. I had very little money, and to lose that would not have been a tragedy, but I had to protect my military identification or I wasn't getting home. I doubled up in the fetus position with both hands protecting the wallet. My parents had given me a watch seven years previously for high school graduation, and this watch was prominent on my wrist in this position. They removed the watch; this satisfied them and the three ran away. I sprinted the rest of the short distance to the hotel, where there was a French gendarme. Breathlessly I informed the policeman that I had just been robbed and there go the robbers around the corner. Did he try to catch the thieves? Did he blow his whistle and order them to stop? No, he looked sternly and berated me with, "And what were you doing walking around Casablanca by yourself at night?"

Each of the parties was left with a souvenir of our encounter; the thieves with my watch, and I with a petite crimson mark which vanished in a few days.

Morocco — 1957, Wednesday

No foreigner ever hitchhikes in Morocco, but if you don't have any money, what are you going to do? I had hitchhiked via MAT, military air transport, from my base in Frankfurt, Germany, to Casablanca. I wanted to visit my brother, who was serving as a dentist in the United States Navy in Port Lyautey. Port Lyautey, also known as Kenitra, lies about ninety miles northeast of Casablanca on the coast. Since I had very little money, I had hitchhiked from Casablanca to Port Lyautey. I had been extremely fortunate on my way northward because a United States military truck had picked me up and taken me the entire way from Casablanca to Port Lyautey.

My brother Rand and his new wife Marcie enjoyed living in Morocco. The military provided them with a house with a garage. The navy had also shipped his car, a powder blue Pontiac convertible, to Morocco. But Rand couldn't keep his car in the garage because a family had moved into it. With no prior permission or discussion, the family—a man, wife, and children—had moved in. He couldn't force them out because then they would vandalize the house. As long as he let them live in his garage, he was protected from other vandals and thieves because they wanted to protect their own home site. But they did none of the work around the house; that was delegated to the maid.

In Morocco you don't lock your car. If you do the windows will be broken to enter it. The trick is to leave nothing in your car and leave it unlocked. Most people coming upon a parked car open the door and search the car for anything which is of value to them, and if they find something, take it. They don't steal the car because not very many people know how to jump the ignition or drive a car. If they find nothing, they continue on their way. If you park your car, you expect a dozen people to have been in your car while you were away.

After a couple of very pleasant days with Rand and Marcie, I departed to hitchhike back to Casablanca, where I hoped to catch a military hop back to Frankfurt. Rand and Marcie were appalled that I was hitchhiking but could find no other transportation which would get me back before my leave was up. I wore a wash-and-wear seersucker suit and a tie and carried a brown cardboard suitcase so I would look presentable, and hopefully somebody would pick me up. Rand took me to the edge of town, left me by the roadside, and wished me luck. He said I was going to need it.

I always walked on the right side of the road, then paused and put out my thumb when a vehicle came by. I had the opinion that a driver would perhaps think better of a hitchhiker who walked rather than just stood at one place and stuck his thumb out. Any foreigner alone in Morocco will be surrounded by children and adults begging for money or anything that you might give them. With my outfit, I stood out like a sore thumb. I could have doubled as the pied piper. Eventually a young man joined the group and took over. He shooed the children and other men away and walked alongside me. Passing traffic was rare, and he had plenty of time to tell his sad story. He wanted to carry my suitcase but I refused. I had been told that they can run faster with a suitcase than I could run without one.

He told me of his need for money. His family needed money to eat. He had many sad reasons why I should give him money. He began asking for five dollars. I sympathized with him but explained that that was impossible. He gradually reduced his request to two dollars and eventually one dollar. Finally he said he would accept any amount which I would give to him. Sadly and politely, I explained that if I had any money I would not be hitchhiking. He then, in a normal conversational tone, said, "Then I will kill you." In a matter of fact way, he explained. Morocco had just in the past few days gotten its independence from France. I was a foreigner here, and whether I lived or died was a free choice of his. We were walking down a straight two-lane road with rare traffic. In the distance there was a tree, and the road curved to the left. He said, "See that tree out there? When we get there the road curves; they can no longer see us from the town. After we go around that curve I am going to cut your throat."

He was shorter than me and I had not seen a knife. I kept my bravado up. I pulled back my shoulders and continued walking. With a firm voice I said, "The minute I see a knife you are done for." I listened for a quiver in my voice which might betray the fact that my heart was pounding, but I didn't hear it. It appeared that my act was working.

For about a quarter of a mile, we continued to walk side by side. Usually in silence, but he repeated his statement several times that he would kill me when we rounded the bend in the road, and I repeated that he was done for the minute that I saw a knife. About fifty feet from the bend in the road, in a strong, very determined whisper, he repeated that he was going to kill me as soon as we turned this corner.

When we went behind the tree and around the corner, there was a gas station about 200 feet away. I walked up to the attendant and asked, "Do you mind if I stay here a bit? This man says he is going to kill me." My companion complained that he had carried my bag and I now refused to pay him. The station owner said no, I have been watching you with binoculars for miles because this is a strange procession on this road. He always carried his own bag. The station owner was French, and the French were at great odds with the Moroccans at this time. He said you hold him; I will call the police. I grabbed him with both arms from the back. He struggled to get away but I found that I could hold him; however, after a short time I elected to weaken my grip and he appeared to escape from my grasp and ran away. A short time later a truck headed for Casablanca stopped for gas, and I was again fortunate to get a ride back.

Haiti

I had filed a flight plan from Fort-de-France, Martinique, to Grand Turk Island, where I planned to refuel before flying to Nassau, a distance of about 870 miles when following the island chain. It was the end of April 1973. Pat and I had spent a pleasant few days on the French Island of Martinique and were now returning to Johnstown, Pennsylvania, in the Mooney. We had just flown past Puerto Rico and were cruising north of the island of Hispaniola. I recalculated my fuel reserve and began to feel uncomfortable. We had sufficient fuel to fly to Grand Turk, but not with the amount of reserve that I like to have when flying over water. The island of Hispaniola is divided into two countries. The Dominican Republic is a Spanish-speaking country. Its citizens are light skinned. Haiti, on the other hand, is a country made up from the descendents of African slaves, where French is the official language. I decided to refuel in Port-au-Prince, Haiti, rather than Grand Turk and turned southwestward. I had considerable experience flying around the Caribbean, and I had never been refused permission to land anywhere. Just like in America, if you are flying using visual flight rules, you must call the tower at least five miles out for permission and instructions to land.

More than five miles out, I called Port-au-Prince and requested landing instructions. To my utter amazement they responded, "Landing permission denied."

Whoa, now we were in trouble! I had just flown 30 minutes out of my direct route, I would have to fly 30 minutes back, and this would add one hour to my time to Grand Turk. I got back on the radio to Port-au-Prince and said I had to land to refuel as I did not have fuel to go elsewhere. Again they said it was not possible to land here, but I insisted and said it was an emergency. The tower operator was not sympathetic to me. He asked me to hold. I put the Mooney in a holding pattern at minimum fuel consumption and waited. Ten minutes later they called me. They asked many questions: all the details of the flight plan we had filed, the names and nationalities of everybody on board, the type of the airplane, and what cargo we were carrying. They then ordered us to continue holding. Another ten minutes—no calls from Port-au-Prince. I called again. I pleaded that I just wanted to refuel and depart. Again they said that they did not know if I would be granted permission to land and if it did occur it would take some time and they were consulting with the authorities.

After well over a half hour in the holding pattern, we were given orders to land. Upon rolling to a stop, we were surrounded by soldiers armed with automatic weapons.

We exited the plane and were escorted to the airport office, where an officer in uniform repeated most of the questions. His demeanor was official but not particularly unfriendly, and after the questioning session he smiled, the armed soldiers departed, and he ordered the plane refueled. We filed a flight plan for Nassau and departed.

The experience stirred up my curiosity about Haiti; that, and the fact that I became friends with a young man at my hospital who was married to a Haitian girl. He told stories about Haiti. Haiti is the poorest country in the western hemisphere. The population is 95% black. For years it was a dictatorship under the

Duvalier family. Francois Duvalier (Papa Doc) was dictator from 1957 to his death in 1971. His son Jean Claude Duvalier (Baby Doc) was dictator during my visits to the country. Jean Claude was exiled in 1987.

In spite of the enormous poverty, there are a few rare areas of extreme luxury. *Playboy* magazine had an article about Le Habitat, a tiny hotel which they called the most exotic place to stay in the world, which was in Haiti, and they reported that the price was extremely reasonable. I became determined to return to Haiti and stay at Le Habitat.

End of March 1975 Pat, John Timo, and I returned to Haiti in the Mooney. There are only twenty rooms in Le Habitat. It is surrounded by jungle and each guest room is high above the ground supported by a combination of trees and high stakes stuck in the ground. Each room is separate from the others and connected together by swinging rope bridges between the trees. The small dining room is unique in that each guest is given his own linen napkin. No other person ever uses your napkin. There is a wall of drawers with bronze name tags of famous people who had visited there with their napkins inside their drawer. Jacqueline Kennedy Onasis, Marilyn Monroe, and John Wayne were among the many celebrities who had their napkins saved for them to use again if they returned.

John Timo was not impressed by the luxury; he would have preferred to have been camping out, but Pat and I welcomed it. After a gourmet meal, we retired to our rooms. The jungle is full of strange noises at night. We heard animal and bird noises and screams, many of which we could not identify. There was one noise which aroused John's curiosity. Somewhere deep in the jungle, a drum was beating. The drumbeat continued with no letup for hours. At about ten or eleven o'clock, John suggested we should investigate the source of the drumbeat. Pat said there was no way she was going to explore the jungle at night. We had a single flashlight with weak batteries, so John and I left Pat in her room and left to determine the source of the drumming.

Our flashlight was quite dim, but we could make out an overgrown path in the direction of the steady drumming. It became progressively louder as we pushed our way through the thick jungle. It was difficult to follow the path, and we often lost our direction. Eventually we saw a dim light ahead. A few feet further and through the thick leaves we saw a small clearing. We were able to distinguish a ramshackle building. Through the window we could see a single, very low wattage light bulb hanging in the center and some torches burning. There was no glass in the windows, only open window holes. John and I had been walking softly, occasionally whispering to each other. Upon seeing this scene we both stood perfectly still, barely breathing. It was pitch-black in the jungle with our flashlight turned off. The drumbeat, which had never stopped for hours, came from the old cabin. It appeared that we had come upon a voodoo temple. John and I wanted to creep closer to see the scene inside the building. We recognized that there was a voodoo ceremony going on inside. People were dancing and appeared to be in a trance. Although the drumbeat was loud and John and I were very quiet, somebody inside detected us. Suddenly the drumbeat, which had been completely unbroken for hours, stopped, and John and I were immediately surrounded by half-naked black men. They nodded and bid us to enter the cabin. We were not prone to argue with them. Inside there were perhaps 20 to 30 people, men and women, sitting facing the center of the room. We were the only white people. We were ushered into the inner circle. I got the impression that we were being given seats of honor. The voodoo priest made a great fuss over us. With each of us in turn, he grasped both of our hands in his and performed chants. He inhaled smoke from a pipe and blew it into our faces. He splattered liquid from a bottle onto our bodies. The drum began to beat again—first softly, then gradually louder and faster till it was beating the same tempo that it had for hours before. The dancing once again began, and within a short time the dancers appeared to be in a trance. Various people would get up and dance, sometimes shake, and occasionally fall on the hard earth floor and writhe. Throughout the night, the worshipers were singing and chanting. Someone might shout out at the top of their lungs, then scream and dance or roll on the floor. At the same time, another might be mumbling to himself or herself very quietly and continuously. Once I thought a heavy black woman had an epileptic seizure because with her eyes rolled to the back of her head, she shook violently and rolled on the floor as saliva drooled from her mouth.

John and I hardly moved for hours. We didn't even turn our heads very much. We only followed the scene by moving our eyes, which I'm sure were wide open. From time to time the priest would come with a bottle from which every person in the room would drink. When presented to me, refusal was no option; I would put my tongue over the opening and tip the bottle up, allowing none of the fluid to get into my mouth. I'm sure John did the same. We did not try to talk to each other. Every now and then the priest would fill his mouth from the bottle which was presented, or from another bottle, and spray it from his mouth onto someone. He did this to John and me. I got the impression that this was considered an honor and a blessing. He also occasionally would blow smoke from a pipe he was smoking into someone's face, then take another drag on the pipe and blow the smoke, spreading it back and forth and up and down over their body. This appeared to be a cleansing routine. He also did this to John and me. Two or three times during the night, a cup was passed for a donation. Most people put a coin in when they were presented with the cup. Fortunately I had some money with me, and the first time I put in a one dollar bill. I'm sure this pleased the priest, and as a result he blessed us profusely. I wonder how we might have been received if we had departed the hotel with no cash in our pockets.

Hour after hour the drummer continued the incessant beat. He also appeared to be in a trance. After about two and a half hours of this, the priest motioned for John and me to rise. From his body language, we got the impression that we were to follow him. We both hesitated, but as we slowly turned to look behind us there were several huge glaring Negroes who did not appear pleased. We slowly followed him through a low doorway, where we had to stoop and bend nearly to our knees to pass through. We were inside a small chamber with a low ceiling and an altar. Candles were burning on the altar and in front of the altar. The altar was covered with various strange objects, and there were weird, crude drawings on the walls. Clearly we were in the holiest of places. Only the priest, John, and I were in the little chamber. Our heads would strike the ceiling unless we kept our heads bowed. The priest kneeled in front of the altar, and it seemed appropriate that we do the same. The priest began an elaborate ceremony with chanting, singing, spitting, blowing smoke, and drinking liquid, which we were also to partake of. We were being inducted into the voodoo religion. The ritual lasted about ten minutes, then we all departed the chamber and returned to our previous sites. Nobody in the room acknowledged our return. Everybody was engrossed in their own world.

Then the most fearful event occurred. One huge black man, deep in a trance, began swinging his machete in wide arcs. The room was small and there were about 20 or 30 people in the room. His eyes were glazed and sometimes appeared to be shut. John and I leaned back and ducked, but most of the worshipers paid no attention to this dangerous new development. The first light of day was showing in the sky and I whispered to John, do you think we could get away? He made a slight nod of his head, and we began very slowly to slide backward toward the door. Away from the center of the room we slowly stood up. Keeping our faces toward the crowd, we slowly backed toward the doorway. We kept our heads bowed and a reverent countenance on our faces. Nobody appeared to notice our departure. When we had backed to the doorway, we bowed a few times more and backed out. We had been away five hours. It was light enough to find the path back to the hotel without a flashlight. When we got in Pat shouted, "Where have you been? I was scared to death here by myself."

Amsterdam – 2002

BEWARE OF PICKPOCKETS – This warning was in the brochure issued by the Amsterdam Tourist Office as well as posted on the wall in the main railroad station. I enjoy visiting Holland because, having spent five years in Belgium studying medicine in the Flemish language, which is simply a dialect of Dutch, I like to converse with the Netherlanders in their native language. Everybody in The Netherlands speaks English, but it is always a surprise to them to hear a native-born American speaking Dutch.

I was reading the menu outside of a restaurant in an elegant section of Amsterdam. My black leather backpack was slung over my right shoulder. I felt a slight tug on the backpack. I turned and saw a young man with my wallet in his hand. He was slick; he had unzipped the outside pocket and removed the wallet and I had barely felt it.

He took off running down the street with my wallet in his hand, and I took off about ten yards behind him yelling at the top of my voice, "PICKPOCKET! ROBBER! THIEF!" He was running as though he were trying to qualify for the Olympic 100-meter finals. And I was right behind him. The blocks in Amsterdam are small; he reached the end of the first block, and the distance between us had neither increased nor decreased. He ran on. He hit the second and the third corner and his pace had not slowed. He was about 19 and I was 69. He turned a corner and I turned right behind him. I'm sure he had paced himself for a 100-yard dash, thinking this would be enough to get away from that old man. I'm sure that he couldn't believe that I was still with him after six 100-yard dashes. After about five or six blocks at an anaerobic pace, he collapsed. He threw the wallet to the ground and attempted to get away. But I wanted the wallet and him too. I grabbed him by the blue baseball jacket which he was wearing. His jacket was unzipped, and he slipped out of it and ran away. Now I had the wallet and his jacket. I didn't know his passport and identification papers were in the pocket.

The credit cards had been scattered out of the wallet when he threw it, and I got down and was gathering up the contents of the wallet. As I was down on my knees, he came back and attempted to retrieve his jacket. I held fast to the jacket, and for a brief time we had a tug of war. Then he swung his foot back and kicked me full force in the face. This was not enough to release my grip.

By this time we had attracted an audience. Our theatrics were taking place within a circle of about six or seven people. He had enough and sped away, leaving me with his jacket.

In America people don't like to become involved. This was not true here. I had a large number of sympathetic people who wanted to help me. They said that the police station was about two and a half blocks away, and three or four insisted that they would accompany me to the station and give testimony as witnesses.

We walked in a group of about five to the police station. There was no delay in seeing me, but the whole affair there required more than one hour. Each of the witnesses gave a signed statement. When the police saw his passport, they said they knew him well. He was from Algeria, and they would have no trouble picking him up. Then, against my objections, they insisted that I must be transported to the hospital for examination.

At the hospital, my face was X-rayed and the wounds cleansed.

Two days later I was back in my office in Torrance, California, doing hair transplant surgery. Everywhere I went people asked, how did I get that black eye? I took great pride in answering, "I was mugged in Amsterdam. But I took the wallet back and the robber is now in jail."

The Tiger Moth, Anna Marie in front.

Learning to Fly

"As soon as you get signed off to fly solo, you can fly all of the airplanes." That's what the guys from the flying club told me. I was ecstatic. The only problem was I didn't have any money.

The flying club at the University of Louvain in Belgium had a number of planes. I don't know where they came from, but I strongly suspect that various people gave them to us because they felt they were junk and no longer able to fly.

The cheapest thing I could do was fly the gliders. We had a Tiger Moth to tow the gliders to about 3,000 feet. A Tiger Moth is an open cabin bi-wing contraption that has dozens of wires and projections for streamlining. The British gave Spitfire pilots their training and first solos in Tiger Moths. If they survived that, they were perfectly capable of fighting the Battle of Britain in the sky above London. It had no starter or brakes. We put chocks under the wheels when spinning the prop. When the pilot was ready to taxi, the sign to remove the chocks was both thumbs pointing out-ward. We would tie a rope to the tail wheel of the Tiger Moth and to the nose of what we called a training glider. The Tiger Moth would tow us to about 3,000 feet altitude, where I would pull a cord on the floor. The rope would come loose from the training glider, and I and the other person who was in the glider would glide down to the ground. The other person was another student who wanted to fly. He had taken a number of glider flights before me; therefore, he acted as the instructor. We would try to find a thermal to climb or maintain altitude with the old gliders, but we never did it. It was kind of like trying to glide a brick with a couple of boards attached for wings.

This was great fun, but I longed to be the guy who flew airplanes which had motors. It cost fifty cents an hour to fly the Aeronca. The airplane had been donated to the University, the gas was donated, the instructor (this one actually had a pilot's license but not an instructor's rating) donated his time, and the fifty cents went for insurance.

But fifty cents was a lot of money. I often collected empty bottles and turned them in for deposit to get something to eat.

But this was important—a chance to fly. So I collected a few more bottles and found some money to fly.

After a few hours my mentor said you are ready to solo, but I can't let you do that; you have to go to a real instructor to do this.

So I went to Madam DeVleminck. She operated a flying school at Vilvoorde airport, another little airport near Brussels. Madam DeVleminck was quite a character. Belgium is an artificially formed country consisting of Flanders, where Flemish is spoken, and Walloon, where the language is French. The Flemish and the Walloons hate each other. Madam DeVleminck, in spite of the fact that her name means "from Flanders" would speak nothing but French. Therefore, my instruction was given totally in French. I think I understood most of it, but I may have misunderstood some things.

The airplane which we flew was a J-2 cub. William Piper made history when he mass-produced the J-3 Piper Cub, the yellow plane which for years most people associated with private aviation and thousands of people learned to fly in after W.W. II.

Well, this airplane came before that. The J-3 Piper Cub had a tail wheel. The J-2 had a skid where the tail wheel should be. Like all of our planes, you spun the prop to start the engine. And it had no brakes. But this was not much of a problem since you landed on grass, not a paved runway. The grass eventually stopped you, and the longer time it was since mowing, the faster you stopped.

Madam DeVleminck was quite a stickler. My log book shows that she made me fly three hours and 56 minutes before letting me solo. Then I went around the pattern three times by myself. Three takeoffs and landings—the last landing I landed on the tail-skid and broke it. Madam DeVleminck bolted another skid on with two bolts. It was a little piece of steel which cost perhaps 25 cents. She kept a stock of them because her students broke them often. I didn't have to pay for it, but Madam DeVleminck was mad. She let go a barrage of swear words in French. That was the last time I ever saw Madam DeVleminck. But this was what I wanted—now I could fly the club's airplanes by myself.

The very next weekend I was back in Tiehnan. I could now fly the Tipsy Nipper. The Tipsy Nipper was a tiny airplane, painted blue and white, seating only the pilot, with a modified Volkswagen automobile engine. From wingtip to wingtip, it was nine feet. Of course, it didn't have a starter or brakes, so you spun the wooden propeller by hand to start it and, unlike other aviation engines, it had only one sparkplug and ignition system. The fuel tank was located in front of the instrument panel and had a very simple gas gauge—a cork floated in the tank and a wire extended upwards from the cork through a hole in the gas cap. The upper end of the wire was bent. The pilot estimated how much fuel was left by how far the wire stuck out of the tank. To me the Tipsy Nipper was the prettiest thing that I ever saw.

Now I was a member of the club whom many of the other members of the club could look up to. I had soloed in a motorized plane. I was no longer confined to flying only the wooden gliders. I could fly the airplanes with motors.

One of the other members who flew the Tipsy Nipper gave me a check out. Since this was a one-person airplane, this means he showed me where the stick was, he told me to pull back on it when the plane reached flying speed, and he probably told me a few other things. Then he called, "Switch off!" I repeated, "Switch off!" and he spun the prop a couple of times to prime the engine. He then called, "Contact!" I turned on the magneto switch and called back, "Contact!" He spun the prop and got away fast. Since the plane has no brakes, if you rev up the engine it starts to roll. Another member of our club was holding the tail. When he let loose, I was off.

I taxied downwind to the end of the field. None of our planes had radios, and we had no runways. You always took off and landed in the grass field into the wind. That was nice; you never had to worry about crosswinds. I gunned the engine to about 4,000 rpms (remember this is an automobile engine), and the little plane took off.

The Tipsy Nipper was really the plane that taught me how to fly. It was classified as semi-acrobatic. I had watched some of the other guys do acrobatics, and I wanted to do them too. They would explain them to me on the ground, and I would go up in the air and try them. My log book shows that after 4 hours and 15 minutes in the Tipsy Nipper, I did loops. I remember having trouble getting up the nerve to do rolls. The guys said it's not hard, just push the stick over and keep it over. When you are upside down, push the stick a bit forward so the nose doesn't drop and continue on around. I would push it over, but when the plane got into a 90-degree bank, I would get scared and shove the stick back to turn the plane upright again. It took me a good many tries before I left the stick in place and rolled the whole way around. This was two hours and 40 minutes of flying time after I first did loops. Now I was an experienced pilot, having logged 6 hours and 30 minutes of duel and 13 hours and 30 minutes of solo.

You learn an awful lot about flying by taking an acrobatic

plane to a high altitude and putting it through the paces. I used to see how long I could fly it upside down before the engine quit. It had no inverted fuel system, and the fuel would pour out of the gas tank around the wire, which served as a gas gauge. It would cover the windshield. Once I counted to 17 seconds before it quit. The engine quitting was no problem; you just put the nose down in a dive and it would start again. I used to do a series of rolls—four, five, or six in a row. This was great fun. The Tipsy Nipper was underpowered. To do most acrobatics, you had to dive to get up enough speed for a loop or even to start a roll, but you could continue a series of rolls by keeping the nose down. I would dive to pick up speed, then head vertically until it lost all of its airspeed and slid backwards. I never knew which way it would fall—forwards, backwards, or to either side. You had to center the controls during a back slide and make no movements until the nose went down and the backslide was finished, because the air going backwards over the control surfaces might tear the surfaces away from the aircraft. All of this gives a lot of confidence about recovery from unusual attitudes. I have been in just about every unusual attitude that you can imagine.

Later when I got my licenses, I continued my self-study. Most airmen take courses to pass the written tests. I simply studied books and passed the private pilot written test with no ground school. I did the same thing for the commercial and instrument written tests.

My First Automobile — 1949

The car had a starter but the battery was always dead, so I always used the crank which hung out front. The crank handle could be removed, kept in the trunk, and just used for emergencies, but I just left it where it was ready for immediate use.

The Second World War had ended, and factories were churning out new cars for car hungry Americans. People were getting rid of the old junkers that they had nursed through the war years. My father still had his 1936 Chrysler Airflow, which he had bought new for $800. I was working as a busboy at Howard Johnson's Restaurant on the Pennsylvania Turnpike earning twenty-five cents per hour, which is $2 per day. Standard work week at that time was six days. You had one day off per week. My total pay was $14 per week because I worked more than eight hours per day. Two dollars were deducted for income tax so my check was for $12. I was rich. I saved $10 per week and was allowed to spend the other $2. I was sixteen years old and I wanted to buy a car. Surprisingly enough, my parents did not protest too much when I suggested this. Earlier, when I wanted to buy a camera for six dollars because I had an intense interest in photography, using money which I had earned, my mother had protested violently that this was a frivolous expenditure.

But they felt that I could use the car to get to work. I was now sharing a taxi with four or five other employees.

Shaulis's garage was across the street from our house. Shaulis was a Nash dealer. He had a 1933 Oldsmobile four-door sedan, which he said was a good buy. It was a six-wheeler. That is, it had six wheels, four on the ground and one in each of the front fenders as spares in case you got two flat tires at the same time. He wanted $110 for it. I was determined to buy it for $100 but he wouldn't budge, so I paid the full amount and I was a car owner.

I started the car once or twice with the battery, and then the battery went dead. From that time on I used the crank. The car was black; the upholstery, faded velour. After a few months, I took it to the auto shop at our high school to be painted.

Clyde Saylor was the auto shop teacher. He lived on a farm and kept an old airplane on his farm. Years later, when I came back from Belgium and wanted an American pilot license, Clyde gave me a few hours of the required instruction. There was an electric line at each end of the field which he used for a runway. We used to land under the electric line and take off (hopefully) above the line. When I was on approach under the light wires in his Cessna 172, Clyde would begin to tell me a story. "Did I ever tell you what a farmer is? That's a man who is out standing in his field." Perhaps this was designed to relax me when I was white knuckled; if so, it worked. We never overran the runway or hit the light wires.

His 172 had an AD (that's an aircraft directive). The carburetor float should be changed because it might stick and cause the engine to stop. He bought a new part and set out to change it. He put the old part and the new part together, and my friend swears that he picked up the old part and put it back in the airplane. My friend says he told him that he was putting the same part back, but Clyde wouldn't believe him.

One day when I was at Clyde's farm I said to Clyde, "Your fly's open."

"Oh," he said, "I leave it down. If I pull it up it just falls down again."

"Well," Clyde said, "we'll have the students paint your car. You will only have to pay for the paint. The work is free." If you looked at the quality of the work, you would understand why it was free. I chose an unusual design. The bottom was painted light grey and the top, dark blue. The blue continued in a curve over the hood to meet at a point near the hood ornament. The whole car was supposed to look like a motorboat.

If you were a car owner in high school in Somerset, Pennsylvania, in 1949, you had plenty of friends who wanted to ride to school in your car. We lived in the east end of Somerset, two doors from the railroad tracks. This was the poorer section of town. It was one mile from our house to school. The car was built to accommodate six—we usually carried ten or twelve to school. There was a routine getting the car ready to go to school. First I would get out the hand pump and pump up one or two tires which were flat, and then I would fill the radiator with water from a bucket. Then I would pull out the choke and crank the engine a few times to prime it, then push in the choke, crank it again and the engine would start. We would all pile in and be off. About halfway to the school, the radiator would start boiling and steam would pour out from under the hood. We would continue to school. Three hours later at lunch time, we would repeat the routine. I carried a pot with me to put water in the radiator, pumped up the tires, and we drove home with 10 or 12 kids for lunch. Sometimes we didn't need to add air to the tires to return to school a half hour later, but we always needed water. At four o'clock we did the same to go home.

Since I was always trying to save money on gas, I usually put it in neutral to coast downhill. One time when we were returning on Route 30 from swimming in Ligonier, it got a little away from me. On this road is a three-mile steep hill sloping toward Jennerstown. Automobile companies from Detroit use this hill to test brakes. Well, I put her in neutral at the top of the hill and she kept picking up speed. The steering wasn't too good and the front wheels wobbled. A 1933 Oldsmobile had mechanical brakes, not the hydraulic which are on all cars now. She hit 90 miles per hour, the front wheels wobbling so fast I could hardly hold the steering wheel on the downgrade. That's probably the fastest that the old buggy had ever run. At the bottom of the hill there was an upgrade which slowed her down. At about twenty miles per hour, we heard a loud bang. One of the front tires had blown out.

The diamond in Somerset is the main intersection in the center of town. One day in heavy traffic, I let out the clutch too fast just as I was crossing the diamond and stalled the car. I was by myself so I had to get out of the car and crank the engine. All four lanes were blocked. If you have another person in the car, they can push in the choke just as the engine starts and it will continue running. If one person is doing it, he must rapidly jump in the car and push in the choke or the engine will fire a couple of times, then stop again. I repeated this procedure five or six times, but I was always a second too late pushing in the choke, and the engine had stopped by the time I could get back in the car. Meantime no traffic could move on all four of the main streets of the town. Small town drivers have a lot of patience, but eventually the horns started to blow. Finally I was fast enough jumping into the driver's seat to keep the car running. It was flooded and backfired every few seconds, but I was able to creep out of the main intersection and sheepishly drive away.

I had gotten my permit, practiced my driving, and taken my driving test on snowy, icy roads, so slippery roads were nothing new to me. But one day, on icy roads when I tried to make a left turn at the railroad tracks two doors below our house, she refused to turn and slid into the railroad tracks. The front axle was bent. From that time on, the bottom of the right front wheel was bent inward and the top of the wheel extended outside of the fenders. It was really hard to steer, so I bought a knob to attach to the steering wheel to give me more leverage to turn the wheel. This eventually was the demise of the old buggy. It took a really strong man to turn the steering wheel. We had to tow her to the junkyard. I used to drive by occasionally and see her from a distance sitting, brightly painted, among the other rusting, junked vehicles and remember the good times we'd had.

Diving

"I built this homemade scuba apparatus out of some plans in *Popular Mechanics* magazine but I'm afraid to test it. You have some experience underwater. Would you make the first dive with it?" We were on the beach in Monterey, California. It was the summer of 1955, and my friends and I were in the army and students at the Armed Forces Language School at the Presidio one mile away.

"Well," I hesitantly answered, "I suppose I could give it a try. I'll take it very shallow in the beginning; if it doesn't work I'll ditch the heavy gear and swim to the surface."

The device was a piece of plywood with four holes drilled into it. Two leather belts passed through the holes, forming two straps which I was to put my arms through to hold the plywood on my back. Onto the plywood was tacked an assembly of homemade valves, copper tubes, and a tank which held compressed air. It was a primitive demand valve, which theoretically would provide me with air underwater when I sucked on the mouthpiece. A short length of garden hose led from the back of the plywood to a wooden mouthpiece, which I was supposed to hold in my teeth.

My friend opened the tank and I put the mouthpiece in my mouth. Sure enough, if I sucked real hard some air came out. Two of my classmates held up the plywood, and I slipped my arms in the straps. There was a considerable amount of hilarity among my friends. I don't think they appreciated the seriousness of our experiment. By this time we had attracted a couple of dozen curious onlookers with our circus on the beach. I felt at this point I could not disappoint this large audience by chickening out. So I began to wade into the calm water from the beach. First my waist, then my chest, and finally my neck was covered with water. Only my head was out of water. But when I tried to wade further, I began to float. The plywood and the tank were lighter than water, and they were acting like a giant life preserver on my back. I paddled back to shore.

Next time I picked up a gigantic rock in both arms and again walked back into the water. This time I didn't float. I had put the mouthpiece in my mouth and I was strenuously sucking and getting air. I continued walking. The water covered my head. The straps at my shoulders tugged strongly to try to pull me upward. Step by step I continued carrying the rock. I wore a pair of swimming goggles, and I could see underwater. Mostly I saw the dirt, which I was stirring up from the bottom. But the test was working. I was breathing underwater with no connection to the surface. I rather enjoyed the experience, but the heavy pull upward on my shoulders and downward on my arms by the weight of the rock, and the fact that I had to suck so hard to get air, eventually was too much for me, and I let go of the rock. I promptly shot to the surface. My audience cheered and applauded, and I paddled back to the shore and declared the test a success.

Jacques Cousteau developed the "aqualung" during the war, and it was used to mine enemy ships in harbors and surreptitiously land on enemy shores. In 1955, the sport of scuba diving had not yet taken hold and you couldn't buy self-contained underwater breathing apparatus (scuba) at the store. Two years earlier, when I aspired to spend time below the water surface, I had built a hard hat diving apparatus.

I was lucky to get a cushy job as an analytical chemist at the U.S. Steel Research Laboratory when I was an undergraduate at the University of Pittsburgh. They only hired me because they couldn't get anybody who was qualified to take the job. My position usually required me to analyze canned tomatoes for steel or the components of steel, which might have gotten into the product after it was left in the cans for a period of time. Each afternoon from Monday through Friday, I would arrive at the laboratory at 3 PM and leave at 11 PM. I could usually finish the work which was assigned to me in four or five hours, leaving me three or four hours to study or goof off. The security guard had nothing to do, and he liked to work in the machine shop. Together in our spare time, we built a hard hat diving outfit.

I found an old hot-water tank, and we cut the end off in a manner that it fit over my shoulders and extended lower in front and back. We slit a garden hose and wired it around the opening for padding. We cut a large window in front and bent a piece of clear plastic to cover the opening and riveted it on with a waterproof gasket. We cast lead weights, which we bolted to the breastplate and to the back plate. We welded handles on the top to lift it because the helmet now weighed 72 lbs. We welded a pipe fitting on top to attach a garden hose. I painted the helmet yellow.

For an air supply I again went to the junkyard, where I found a refrigerator compressor. I "borrowed" the Briggs and Stratton gas engine from my father's garden tractor to power it. Fifty feet of green garden hose was connected from the compressor to the helmet. I used a rubber noise maker from a joke store inside the helmet as a safety valve. This is a short section of a flat rubber tube. If you blow in the one end, it would make a disgusting noise called a Bronx cheer. Because the walls collapsed, the air would only pass one way. I attached this to the end of the pipe inside the helmet. I reasoned that if the compressor at the surface should fail, the air would not all rush out of the helmet. Fortunately, the flow of air into the helmet was insufficient to incite the Bronx cheer.

This kind of a helmet is called a shallow water diving helmet because the air flows out the bottom. I did a lot of diving with this outfit. Later I found a rubber survival suit at the surplus store, which had boots and gloves built into the suit. If I could have kept the neck above the water level in the helmet, I could remain dry. But I could never do that, so the water got in the suit but it still was warmer than being in cold water with no protection. Also, the suit was already rotting when I bought it and had holes in it.

I spent many hours underwater in this helmet. I recovered an outboard motor that had fallen overboard for a boater at Deep Creek Lake, Maryland. I recovered numerous things underwater for people. But mostly I just walked around on the bottom and tried to see something in the muddy waters of the lakes and rivers of western Pennsylvania. I discovered that the myth that it was more than one hundred feet deep at the bridge at Deep Creek was not true. It is about fifty-seven feet deep because I was able to walk from one side to the other. In the middle, my fifty-foot hose just reached to the top of the helmet, which was about seven feet from my feet. The compressor was pumping oily air into the helmet, so I filled the compressor crankcase with castor oil. I had the mistaken idea that this would not harm my lungs. I made a definite effort to aim the exhaust from the engine in the other direction from the input of the air compressor, and usually this worked; but if the wind shifted, it smelled like it was pumping exhaust fumes below the surface. In the beginning, I always had a person acting as a tender on the surface, but later I would dive with nobody tending the compressor on the dock or in the boat. I walked all over the bottom of the local lakes pulling a rowboat with only the compressor in it; I went to the local golf courses and got permission to retrieve golf balls from the ponds. When I first went in I couldn't believe it. The mud bottom was completely covered with golf balls. When I sat down, I sat on golf balls. I gathered them in with both arms and put them in a cloth sack. I filled several bushel baskets. Many of the balls had been underwater for a long time and were black and rotted and were worthless, but some appeared brand new and others had lost their gloss from being underwater. These I sprayed with white paint and sold to the driving range. I went back several times till it became difficult to find more balls. I continued to dive occasionally with my homemade outfit until we began to dive with tanks. Years later I was in the Bahamas where there was a diving museum. I was tempted to donate my old apparatus but I never did.

About 1964 the YMCA in Johnstown, Pennsylvania, offered a scuba diving course. Wally Mundell was the instructor. A group of us took it together and became friends for life. When the course was over we formed a club. I was elected the first president, and I named the club the Flood City Divers. We were very active; we had dives in all of the local quarries, lakes, dams, and rivers. In winter we chopped holes in the ice and dove under the ice. I can say with authority that if a diver ever became separated from the line leading to the hole in the ice, he would drown. It is impossible to find the hole by looking for light. It is all a universal dim haze under the ice. And the diver could not chop a hole from below through the ice with his diving knife—I tried it.

We flew in my Mooney to Hatteras, where there are hundreds of shipwrecks off the North Carolina shore. We landed at First Flight Airport, where the Wright brothers made their famous flight in 1903. Along the shore are metal markers every couple hundred of yards or so, marking a shipwreck. It is only necessary to wade in from the shore at these markers with your diving gear to come upon the wrecks. I had purchased a book describing the wrecks and the treasures that they carried as cargo. We had illusions that we were going to find some gold bars but, of course, we never found any.

I have a tile from the steps of the Argentine ship *Rio De Le Plata* sunk in 1944 in 110 feet of water in the harbor of Acapulco,

Mexico. She was 600 feet long and carried a cargo of automobiles. The top deck was fifty feet under water. I recovered the tile September 22, 1973.

The deepest dive which I ever made was with my wife, Toni, whom I had certified to dive. It was in the Bahamas to 144 feet. At that depth we saw giant crabs at least six feet in diameter crawling on a sandy bottom.

Each spring we rode the rapids in the Youghiogheny River below the waterfall at Ohio Pyle, Pennsylvania. You put on your wet suit, and then you covered it with old blue jeans and an old sweat shirt. You wore a rubber hood and rubber diving gloves. You wore your mask, fins, and snorkel but you had a cord tied to each of them and to your belt because they were going to be torn off of you. You also must tie a cord to each fin and around your ankle because they will most likely also be torn off. Then you removed the valve stem from an automobile inner tube, blew it up with your mouth, then replaced the cap. This was so you could blow more air into the tube if it got punctured. You now folded the inner tube, stuffed it into several layers of burlap bags, and wrapped ropes around it as if you were securely tying a package. Sometimes we would put our lunch in a clean paint can with a lid, then put the can inside the inner tube. At the end of the ride, the can would be mangled. Now you were ready to go.

You lay on the folded inner tube with the ends under your armpits and held onto the ropes tightly with your hands. If you were about to hit a rock, theoretically you were to put the inner tube between you and the rock. You push out from the shore and the first fifty feet of water are calm. Gently paddle with your fins toward the current. When the fellow ten feet ahead of you hits the current, he is swept away in one second. In a moment it's your turn. When the current takes you, you can hardly believe what happens. Within seconds you are thrown into the cataract and summersault down the first section. My fins, mask, and snorkel were torn off. I got bounced from one rock to another, and within ten seconds I was spit out below in slightly calmer water. Laughing hilariously, we try to regroup a bit and put our masks, fins, and snorkels back on. The current tugs at us as we hang onto a rock and try to reinstall our equipment. When we release our grip, we're off again. The trip is about six miles, and almost all of it is fast rapids. Some have names such as The Two Sisters, etc.

When you get to the pick-up point at the end, the covering over your wet suit is shredded, you are black and blue, and, if you had a paint can protected by the inner tube, it is crushed. Each of the riders rolls out exhausted and laughing.

This was an annual event for us until the state stopped it because of a death. The victim, not part of our group, was not a scuba driver. He was a parachutist. He had run a set of rapids and pulled up on a flat rock to rest. He was hanging with his chest on the rock and his feet in the river. There was a strong current that tugged on his legs and pulled him into a crevice between two rocks. He couldn't get out. His buddies reported that as they were swept past him, they saw his fins up in the air and his head under water. After that, inner tube riders were prohibited.

Once two kayak riders drowned. They had put their life vests in the bottom of the kayak with the idea that they would don the vests if they got into trouble. The Flood City Divers were called out to search for the bodies. We tied ropes at points at the sides of the river and hung on the ends of the ropes as we searched the fast-moving stream for them. We didn't recover these bodies, but it was a thrill searching for them.

We also used to scuba dive under the falls. If you got very low on the bottom, which was smooth rock from the years of erosion from the rapidly moving water, you could progress very slowly against the current up under the falls. When you got directly under the falls, the deluge of water had carved a deep rounded trench in the rock. Once you had pulled yourself up the other side of the trench, you were under the falls and there was a small area where you could pull yourself out of the water and you were totally isolated by the roaring water.

One of my students, whom I had certified as a scuba diver, performed a dramatic rescue at the falls after I left for California. A father and a young boy were canoeing above the falls. They got swept over the falls. The father swam to safety, but the boy was not found. He was assumed drowned. Our club was called to search for the body. They searched for hours. It was after dark. The fire trucks were illuminating the area with their floodlights. Don Schaffer dove up behind the falls and found the boy alive, shivering and scared. He had to make a decision; he had only one scuba tank and one mouthpiece. Should he give the boy the air or should he take it. The boy was too frightened to be left there to bring in a second tank. He decided that he should have the air to be able to swim. He told the boy to hold his breath, and Don swam with all his might with the boy in his arms out from under the falls. As soon as they were out, Don thrust the boy upwards into the air. Everybody was searching for a body, and into the lights appeared a living boy. Don was declared a hero and the miracle was written up in *Reader's Digest*.

We were often called out to search for bodies. We had a search routine using a motorboat or a rowboat. We would hang a water ski rope behind the boat, and one diver would be towed in a regular search pattern back and forth. Or we would put on a longer bar on the water ski rope and put two divers down, one on each end of the bar with his arm extended wide. This covered a wider area. Most of the places where we were asked to search had very poor visibility, and the search was mostly by feel. One time Rich White and I were searching on a double bar and Rich found the body. It is strange to feel a body under water where you can see nothing. Sometimes we dove in water so black, I couldn't tell any difference if my eyes were open or shut.

After a short time, the YMCA held an instructor's course. It occurred on two weekends and I became an instructor. To become a YMCA instructor now would require a longer training period. Rich White also went and became an instructor. We had to swim two lengths of an Olympic pool in a certain time as one of the qualifiers to be accepted to take the course. We swam in several groups. The leader of the course said if anybody beats James (a champion swimmer), they will get extra points. The race was on; James took off so fast all Rich saw was foam as he sped away. The rest of the group swam and Rich got further and further behind. At the end Rich pulled up and saw that there was one other man a few feet behind him. He said to himself at least I wasn't the last person to finish. When the last swimmer pulled himself out of the pool, Rich saw that he had only one leg.

We started to give certification courses at the Johnstown YMCA. At the first courses, Rich and I were assistants to Wally Mundell. Later Wally quit teaching and Rich and I were the instructors. Rich White was a full-time employee of the YMCA, and after a few years he quit his job to do other things. I was then the only active certified instructor. Fortunately I had many assistants from the club, many of whom dove more often and knew more about diving than me. Our course met once a week for ten weeks. In later years I would teach the physics lesson one evening, and the rest of the course was taught by my assistants. I was the only one who could sign the cards, so there are a lot of divers running around with my name on their cards.

One of my former students, Jim Epstein, opened a dive shop and would provide the equipment that we would include in the course for each of the new students.

Some of the guys that I dove with are still going on dive trips like we did in the sixties. The Flood City Divers continued to be active for decades, and as far as I know, still is.

The riders cover their wetsuits with old clothes. The inner tubes can be seen wrapped in burlap.

The riders start in calm water. The Ohio Pyle Falls can be seen in the distance.

The riders reach the fast water.

The first rider has been swept away by the fast water the second is about to go.

After six miles the exhausted riders exit the rapids.

Skiing – 1973

"Here's my business card. Give me a call. I'm from *Skiing Magazine* and we want to do a story about you." It was a Sunday afternoon at Seven Springs, the largest ski resort in Western Pennsylvania. I was dressed in a skintight, one-piece blue and white spandex jumpsuit. I looked like Spiderman in blue and white. I had on a white pilots helmet—the soft one, not the hard one—and pilots goggles and skis. In the middle of my back, I had a gasoline engine and a propeller. I didn't look like any other skier at the resort.

I had just finished skiing with my backpack engine. While all the other skiers were making carved S-turns down the steep bowl, I was doing the same thing uphill. The ski area is laid out such that you can see most of the slopes from the lodge. My propulsion system was not exactly quiet. The owner of the resort, a friend of mine, said he heard a noise and looked out. He said there were 10,000 skiers on the slopes, and not a one of them was moving. Every one of them was standing still, watching me zigzag up the steep slope.

Seven Springs Ski resort was owned by two friends of mine, Herman and Philip Dupree. It was started by their father Adolph.

Philip liked to fly. A few years later Philip asked me where I got my instrument ticket. I referred him to Sowell Aviation in Panama City, Florida. Unfortunately he got into bad weather on the way down, crashed, and was killed. If he had entered into the same weather on the way back, he would have had the skill to fly through it.

I had bought the backpack engine to convert my hang glider into a powered aircraft. In those days, we felt that if you attached a motor to a hang glider you had to get a license for an airplane. But if the motor was on my back and I sat on the hang glider, we were not subject to all of these rules. In recent years these regulations have been relaxed, and such a machine is called an ultra light.

I had one of the earliest hang gliders built. It was called a Rogalo wing. It was canvas stretched over two poles, and it looked like a big kite. I had the poles made in sections so I could put them together like a fishing pole, and the glider and backpack engine were small enough to put inside my Mooney. This way I had an airplane inside of an airplane. I could fly somewhere, get out my hang glider and engine, and fly some more. I liked to be independent of ground transportation and, in addition to the motor glider which I could carry in the Mooney, I also had an inflatable boat with an outboard motor, a motor scooter, and a motorcycle, which I could take apart in pieces and carry in the plane. The motorcycle was a 180 cc Suzuki and was legal for two people on the freeway. I could fly somewhere; put my camping gear, rubber boat, and outboard motor on the motorcycle. If I wanted to cross a river or get to an island, I would put the motorcycle in the rubber boat and use the outboard motor to cross the water. On the other side I would deflate the boat, load it on the motorcycle, and continue.

Under the glider wing was a swing which served as a seat. I would start sliding down the ski slope on skis, and when I had enough speed, ease my butt back on the seat, pull back on the bar and begin to fly. The problem was I never got too good at it. At Seven Springs they had poles everywhere for snow machines and lights. I could just fit the glider between the poles. A sudden change in the wind and I would crash into the poles. And I couldn't fly on a windless day because I needed a headwind to take off. This was not a good place to learn. I flew out to Sun Valley, Idaho, and took a one-week course. On these open slopes I did OK, but not to the point where I wanted to add the engine. I flew to Hatteras, North Carolina, to fly on the same sand dunes that Wilbur and Orville Wright had learned on. As I was preparing to fly there, a pretty girl about 15 years old climbed the dune and said, "My daddy invented that glider." She said her name was Rogalo, and Professor Rogalo was her father.

The Rogalo wing hang glider at Hatteras, North Carolina

I brought the hang glider with me to California, thinking I would glide from my house down to the shore by the ocean; however, after a few years in the garage I was able to put my fingers through the rotten fabric, and I thought I better put this thing in the garbage or I'm going to kill myself.

The backpack engine, on the other hand, gave me a lot of fun. It was quite powerful. It had a four-cycle gasoline engine and a wooden shrouded propeller. I converted the throttle to a twist grip with a stiff cable that you could adjust from the front. Unless you were holding onto something, it would blow you over if you fully opened the throttle. On skis on the level, you couldn't leave it fully open. You would go too fast. Uphill you could give it full gas. It was the same on a bicycle. I couldn't control the bicycle on the level at full throttle, but it would climb hills well. I lived in a hilly country area, and since the engine was rather noisy, my neighbors often looked out their windows to see that strange Dr. Straub riding his bicycle with a propeller on his back.

I lived in a mobile home deep in the woods near a lake. One day the doorbell rang and the boys who lived in the next farmhouse asked, "Dr. Straub, won't you sell us that motor that you wear on your back?" I answered that I enjoyed the engine and wanted to keep it. Some months later when I looked for it, it was not to be found in my garage.

Parachuting – 1964

The sign said "Learn to Parachute." Wow, that's for me! I was driving from Pittsburgh to Johnstown. I braked and pulled the car to the side of the road. When I was a young boy, I had written a list of things that I wanted to do in my lifetime. Among other things, I wanted to run one marathon, learn to fly an airplane, then pilot the airplane over the ocean, write a book, and make one parachute jump. Here was a chance to fulfill one of my goals.

I backed up the car a hundred feet and turned up the dirt road by the sign. Five hundred yards up the hill was a shanty. Two men—one appeared to be in his twenties and the other in his forties—were just getting in their car to leave. There was no airport or airplanes to be seen. They explained that this was only the drop zone where you hopefully landed, and parachuting took place every weekend on Saturday and Sunday. I could come here, take a lesson, and parachute the same day.

I was an intern at Conemaugh Valley Memorial Hospital in Johnstown, Pennsylvania, and I usually was on duty seven days a week, but I knew I could get away from the hospital a few hours on Sunday.

The next Saturday I called to make sure that parachuting was going on, and Sunday, after I made my rounds, I headed for the drop zone. The first jump was fifty dollars, and each jump after that was thirty-five dollars. The instructor had me stand on the seat of a kitchen chair and jump off. I was supposed to keep my feet together, bend my knees, and roll either to the right or left and fall on my hip. He said this was a PLF, or parachute landing fall. He said the rip cord would be attached to the airplane; I would not have to pull it, and after it pulled the parachute out of the backpack, the cord string would break, the parachute would open, and I would float down to the ground. He also said in case the parachute did not open, I was to pull this handle and the reserve parachute would pop out and I would float down to the ground.

The parachutes that we used were not the highly controllable flying wings that are now in use for sport parachuting. Instead these were surplus military chutes that the paratroopers had used during the war. I hoped that the military had not sold the poor ones and kept the best for themselves. These chutes were modified by cutting two panels out of the back of the canopy. This made the chute travel a bit in the forward direction, but it also made it descend faster, meaning you hit the ground harder. A length of clothesline was attached to the bottom of each of the triangular cutouts. If you pulled one, it was supposed to make the chute rotate so that you could direct the chute where you wanted to go.

After I had my instruction and while I was waiting for a car to take me to the airport, a few experienced parachutists landed. It was a pleasure to see them fly in, land exactly on the X in the middle of the landing zone, and land standing up. None of the experienced jumpers rolled on the ground like he had taught me.

The pickup truck took me out to the airport. The jump plane was an old 182 Cessna with the back door off and no back seat. My instructor had me sit on the floor facing backwards beside the open door. The instructor also sat on the floor facing backwards, but he had me between him and the open door. Of course there was a seat belt and, even though I had quite a bit of flying experience, it is quite a thrill to sit six inches away from an open door in an airplane,

After a while, we had climbed to altitude and were over the drop zone. The instructor snapped the static line to my ripcord. He leaned over me to check our position over the ground. After a while he yelled in my ear, "Put your legs out." Now I was sitting with my legs out of the plane and my left foot on the step. He had told me during ground instruction that when he tapped me on the shoulder, I was to push myself as far as possible away from the plane and spread my arms and legs. That way I would float through the air with my stomach down and my back upward until the chute opened.

When the tap came you couldn't miss it. It was a hard one. I pushed off and I didn't fly like a bird; it was more like a sack of potatoes falling, but it was only a few seconds until the parachute opened, Wow, the chute opened and I was floating. I was ecstatic! Nothing could go wrong now.

I tried to steer the chute but it wasn't too responsive; the parachute had a mind of its own and wanted to go where it wanted to go. But it did land within the several acres that were designated for parachute landings. Well I had seen the experts land, and I wanted my first jump to be top quality—I would land just like them—do a stand up landing—no rolling on the ground for me.

As I approached the ground, did I keep my feet together as the instructor had said? No, I put them wide apart so I could land without falling to the ground.

As I hit the ground, I heard a crack and felt a pain in my right ankle. Of course, the ankle was broken. The guys drove me back to Conemaugh Valley Memorial Hospital, where I had made rounds a few hours earlier. Monday morning Dr. Griffith put a screw in the outside ankle, and that screw is still there.

Within two days I was back performing my duties as an intern on crutches. There was nothing that I couldn't do on crutches. I worked ten or twelve hours a day, even fourteen or sixteen hours on some days. I actually went up and down the halls faster on crutches than I could have without them. I delivered a large number of babies. I would use the crutches to go to the scrub sink, hop on one foot into the delivery room, and deliver the baby by forceps if necessary. I would sit on a stool to suture an episiotomy, whether I was on crutches or not. I worked in the emergency room many nights all night long as the only physician. Fortunately, this was not the time of my rotation on surgery or I would have had to stand at the operating table for hours on one foot. I drove my car with the left foot on the gas and brakes and the right leg on the seat. There was no duty from which I was excused or that I couldn't do during the six to eight weeks that I was on crutches.

A few years later, I had to redeem myself for the dumb thing which I had done on my first parachute jump. Indian Lake had a parachute club, and I could fly there in my Tripacer and later in my Mooney. I took a course with some other people and made fourteen more jumps for a total of fifteen. I never became proficient because there was too much time between the jumps. Most of my jumps were static line, but I made a few free falls where I pulled the rip cord. I never got stable like the experienced jumpers and sort of tumbled through the air. One time I was falling with my back to the ground and my arms and legs waving behind in the breeze. It was a five-second free fall but I wasn't stable. When I pulled the cord while falling backwards, the instructor said he was afraid that the parachute would wrap around my body but it didn't. Once, just as I was stepping out of the plane, my parachute came open. This is a very dangerous situation because the parachute will catch the wind and perhaps damage the plane or pull me out through the side of the plane. The instructor said he couldn't decide whether to push me out of the plane or pull me back in. He elected to pull me back in.

One of the fellows who took the course with me broke his hip when he landed in the cellar of a house which had been torn down.

Later when I got my own plane, the Tripacer, we would take the back door off and I would take two of my friends up to higher altitudes, perhaps 9,000 or 10,000 feet, and treat them to a long freefall.

A small girl who took the same course became a better parachutist than me because she continued and took more jumps. One day she jumped and her parachute didn't open. She tried to pull the reserve chute but she wasn't strong enough. She pulled and pulled, and finally, a few seconds before she would have hit the ground, she gave one last strong pull and it opened and billowed out enough so that she could land without being hurt. She had a lot of guts. The other club members said the thing to do was to get back in the plane right away and jump again. Within hours she did that and went on to become an accomplished parachutist.

Orizaba

There are three volcanoes near Mexico City: Iztacchuati, 17,343 ft.; Popocatepetl, 17,930 ft.; and Orizaba, 18,700 ft. Orizaba is the third highest mountain in North America after McKinley in Alaska and Logan in Canada. My good friend John Timo called me in Johnstown from Pittsburgh, Pennsylvania. He wanted me to meet him in Mexico City in February 1975 and climb Orizaba. Unfortunately, on the date that he wanted to go I had already scheduled surgery, and it was impossible for me to go with him. John made arrangements with David Heckert, an 18-year-old college student, to meet him at a cabin at 14,000 ft. on the mountain. Traveling from Pittsburgh, John unfortunately arrived one day late. When John did not arrive at the arranged time, David decided to climb by himself. Sadly, he died on the mountain. Nobody is certain what happened but his crampons were found at the top. It is speculated that he climbed to the top and for some unknown reason removed his crampons and fell from the top.

The following year, John called me and said he wanted to climb Orizaba and mount a bronze plaque at the summit to honor the student. I agreed to go. John Timo, George Bogel, and I flew to Mexico City in the Mooney. In 1971 the three of us had flown to Venezuela in the Mooney to make the first ascent of the face of Angel Falls. Both John and George were excellent, experienced climbers. I considered myself fortunate to be climbing with such experts.

We arrived at our base camp at 14,000 ft. after dark. It was a stone cabin with a few wooden double-deck bunks and little more. The cabin was filled with jubilant climbers. All of them had reached the summit that day; they reported excellent weather and perfect climbing conditions.

John, George, and I departed about 3 AM in the dark, roped together, and properly outfitted for climbing. We made reasonable progress for hours ascending the face, first in the dark and later in daylight. As the morning progressed, it became obvious that we were not going to have the excellent weather that the people had experienced the day before. Visibility was poor. We were climbing in the clouds. About 11 or 12 o'clock, the snow began. When it started, it became fierce in a very short time. And the wind became torrential. Gusts would come that certainly would sweep you off the mountain unless you huddled down against the face of the cliff. I couldn't see my fellow climbers on the same rope forty feet away. We were in trouble. It was nearly impossible to shout to the others in the face of the gale, but we pulled on the ropes and eventually got together. John questioned whether we should give up and go down, but George, always the aggressive one, didn't want to quit. He said maybe it would blow over in a short time. We continued upward for another short stretch in the face of an intensive gale. George was leading. I was in the middle and John was bringing up the rear. Suddenly, over the gale, I heard a scream and saw the line running down to John rapidly running out. I turned around, sat on the slope, planted my crampons as firmly as I could, and put my ice ax in as firmly as I could. I was preparing for a strong shock, which could pull me and later George off the face. I took the last bit of slack and wrapped it around my waist so I could stop his fall gradually rather than with a sudden jolt, which might pull me down as well.

I was lucky enough to stop John's fall without being pulled down myself. John crawled back up the rope to me. He was obviously shook up. "Thanks, Paul," he said. Some days later he said to me, "I've climbed many mountains and been in many dangerous situations, but that was the day I thought I was going to die."

We elected to quit after that. Everybody had to get back and there was no time for another attempt. John decided to mount the bronze plaque on the wood walls inside the cabin. The plaque read:

David Daniel Heckert
Pittsburgh, Pennsylvania, E.U.A.
Julio 13, 1953 – Febrero 15, 1975
THIS EARTH WE ALL INHERIT. IT IS
OURS TO LOVE AND LIVE UPON
AND USE WISELY FOR ALL THE
GENERATIONS OF THE FUTURE.

Placed Here
DICIEMBRE 1975

John Timo is a very persistent fellow. He could not long tolerate the fact that we had not been able to reach the summit of Orezaba. By the spring of 1979, he was organizing another trip to Mexico to finish the task which we had begun in 1975. On June 15, 1979, I again left Johnstown in the Mooney for Mexico City. This time I conned Toni into accompanying us on the trip and the climb. We got as far as Brownsville, Texas, when we had electrical failure in the airplane.

Toni and I left the plane to be repaired and continued by Mexican bus to Mexico City. This was not too bad except that the chickens cackling prevented us from sleeping. In Mexico City we met John and Dennis Cybert, one of the scuba divers from Johnstown who wanted to climb with us. Timo had driven his

Camero from Pittsburgh, but the previous trip up the mountain had torn the transmission out of it. We tried to rent a Jeep in Mexico City but none was available, so we rented a four-door Chevrolet sedan with higher clearance. The Hertz Company had no idea what rigors its vehicle would be subject to when they turned it over to us.

Orezaba is about one hundred and fifty miles southeast of Mexico City. On the drive there you can see Popocatepetl, which from some angles appears like a reclining female figure. Most of the drive is on good roads, but when you start up the volcano the situation changes. We planned to spend the night at the stone cabin at 14,000 ft. and climb the mountain the next day. The cabin is about the altitude of the summit of Mount Whitney. We had the illusion that we could drive our car to the cabin, and then drive it down after climbing the mountain. In reality, John said we would drive the car as far as it would go, then hike the rest of the way to the cabin. A very short distance up the mountain, the one-lane potholed road became a rutted single lane dirt road. For a while, every half mile or so, there was a shanty with a tin roof and a half dozen dirty children sharing the yard with the chickens and a dog. We wound our way upward in the lowest gear, the bottom of the car scraping the dirt every couple of seconds. Then it got worse. We forded streams without drowning out the engine. Then we came to a gully with only one log for a bridge. Our Hertz sedan couldn't get past this. We stopped the car and hunted for another log. After a brief search, Dennis came up with a fallen tree trunk which might be suitable. Unfortunately, it was not per-fectly straight but had a slight bend in it. With our ice axes, we trimmed the limbs from the trunk and cut it to size. After laying this in place, all we had to do was drive the car about eight feet over the two logs without falling off and we could continue our journey. Dennis was delegated the driver. I lined the logs up as near as I could to match the width of the wheels. Very slowly, we eased the front wheels onto the logs. They didn't want to mount the logs and the rear wheels spun in the sandy dirt, so everybody got behind the car and pushed until the front wheels were on the logs. Inch by inch we continued over the logs, with me giving hand motions to indicate the slightest movement of the steering wheel to the right or left. Miraculously, the front wheels stayed on the logs until the car had just about crossed the ravine and the rear wheels were ready to mount the logs. A bit of a push from the passengers and the rear wheels were crossing our makeshift bridge. We were within one foot of celebrating a victory of ingenuity over nature when the rear wheels slid off the logs. Now the car was sitting on the frame with the rear wheels, which are the drive wheels, hanging in the ravine. The ravine was about 18 inches deep where the wheels hung over, so we gathered rocks to fill it up enough to put the jack under it and jack up the rear of the car. When we had jacked the wheels up such that they were above the ravine edge, I told Denny to get in the car and gun the engine. Then we all got in the ravine behind the car and on a signal, gave one big shove. The car was pushed off the jack and the wheels spun as Denny jumped up the trail. A little bit further and things got worse.

The steep trail was composed of sandy soil. I got the impression that four-wheel drive vehicles had passed through here, but not too many of them and not too easily. We began to get stuck on the steep slopes. The rear wheels would spin in the sand and dig us in until we were sitting on the frame. The best way to progress was for everybody to push while one person drove. We tried to avoid digging in with the wheels, but when this happened I would jack up the car and we would put some stones under the drive wheels and try to drive out. Sometimes we would have to do it in steps. Jack it up, put some rocks under the wheels, take out the jack and put some rocks under the jack to move the wheels even higher, and then add more rocks under the wheel followed by driving it off. Sometimes we would just jack up the car and push it off the jack out of the hole. Now our progress was slowing until we could measure it by the yard rather than by the mile. It was time to abandon our Hertz car, which had started out shiny and now was covered with dust.

We proceeded up the trail on foot. Surprisingly, we had gotten rather far up the volcano. Carrying our packs on our backs, we passed the tree line after about one mile and had only two or three miles more till we reached the cabin that was to be our base camp. Of course we were flatlanders, and walking up a steep slope at 14,000 feet is not the same as three miles at our home altitude.

Night had just fallen when we opened the cabin door. About half a dozen other climbers were bivouacked there; most had already turned in in preparation for an early morning attack on the mountain. The last few were cleaning up after their evening meal. Immediately, John looked for the bronze plaque which he had nailed to the wall inside of the cabin. It was gone. Bronze is too valuable as scrap material for these poor people to leave nailed to a wall. That plaque may have brought enough money at the scrap yard for a man to feed his family for a day.

We prepared our dinner, ate it, and crawled into our sleeping bags. The alarm went off at 1 AM. We wanted to be climbing by two. Some of the other climbers left before we did. It is recommended that climbers spend a day or two at a medium altitude to acclimate before ascending to avoid altitude sickness. In altitude sickness, your lungs fill with water and your brain swells. The only treatment is to descend immediately to a lower altitude. Unfortunately, we did not have the luxury of time to allow for acclimation.

It was well below freezing when we stepped out into the crisp, clear, starry night. There was about a quarter moon on the horizon. It would be a small help until it set in an hour or two. We each wore several layers with heavy parkas and hoods, face masks, ski mittens, waterproof trousers, and hiking boots. We put on our crampons at the cabin and roped ourselves together because we would be starting immediately up a steep snow- and ice-covered slope in the darkness. John had instructed Toni and Dennis on how to stop a slide with an ice ax. Each of us carried a flashlight and a small backpack. We left our sleeping bags and unnecessary equipment at the base camp, hoping it would be there when we got back.

John was in the lead, and he followed the footprints in the snow of the climbers ahead of us. Occasionally we could see their flashlights ahead of us. Our team of four seemed pretty well matched for speed in the early hours, and indeed throughout the entire climb nobody held up the group of any consequence. We plodded upward in the darkness, one step at a time, roped in a line, planting each foot carefully with the spikes of our crampons. Our ice axes functioned as canes. The frozen snow held our boots well, and there rarely was a tendency for the foot to slip backwards. John led, followed by me, then Toni, then Dennis. If there was any concern that Toni might slow our progress, this proved not to be true. John and I had skied enough with Toni to know that she could climb as fast as any of us.

Eventually it became light enough to stow our flashlights. We paused now and then to drink water and eat a high energy snack. John encouraged us to drink plenty of water, as the high altitude can rapidly dehydrate you.

When the full light of day dawned, you could see we were on a forty-five degree snow- and ice-covered slope with very little features. On the previous trip, we were enveloped in clouds. Today the visibility was unlimited. We could spot several climbing parties ahead of us, and later we could see groups behind us. It was a beautiful day for climbing.

This was essentially an endurance task, not the life-threatening event of the last trip. When I start out at 14,000 feet, I generally take one breath per step. As the altitude increases, I switch to two deep breaths per step. Still higher, three breaths per step, and near the summit I would step, pause, then count four deep breaths before moving the other foot forward.

We made the summit at about 2 PM. The crater was snow filled. Orizaba is a dormant volcano, whereas Popocatepetl is an active volcano and emits smoke, steam, and fumes constantly, and occasionally lava. I saw no exposed rocks at the summit—only snow and ice. There would have been no place for John to bolt the bronze plaque.

We descended in about four hours; our sleeping bags and possessions were intact. After a warm meal, nobody had any trouble falling asleep.

The next day we walked to the car, which also had not been disturbed. Turning the car on that narrow steep trail proved to be a challenge. There was no place to turn the car where we had stopped. Since a steep slope was on our left and a high ridge on our right, there was no other choice than to back it down until we could find a place to turn; I functioned as the driver. With the driver's door open and my head turned backwards, I began the long trip home. Nobody tried to ride in the car, as walking was much faster and not too difficult downhill. Besides, I don't think they felt too comfortable when they looked down the slope that the car would roll if I veered slightly to the left.

Eventually I got dizzy with my head turned that far backwards for so long a time, but fortunately there was no shortage of critics of my driving technique. More to the left; more to the right—sometimes two people would yell out conflicting instructions at the same time.

I was lucky enough to get down to a point where Dennis said, "I think we can turn here." I got out of the car to look and was very skeptical, but all of us knew that if we passed up this spot, it would be a great distance before we had another chance to turn. So I tried.

The car immediately became stuck up to the frame in the sand. If I spun the wheels, the car slid further downhill. I got out the jack, dug out the sand under the car to accept the jack, and tried to jack it up. The jack would bore itself into the sand rather than lift the car. We gathered rocks. We pushed with the wheels spinning. We weren't getting very far. We dug the sand out from in front of the wheels and everybody pushed. We moved three inches. We repeated this sequence and we gained another three inches. I dug the sand out enough to put rocks in the hole before I put in the jack. This raised both back wheels off the ground. We pushed it forward off the jack. This way we gained about six or eight inches. We had to dig the sand away from both the front and rear wheels to make a place for the car to move before pushing it off the jack. We had been busy for two and a half to three hours and had moved two or three feet. We had six to ten feet to go.

Dennis began to argue that we should abandon the car and walk down to civilization. He reasoned that the insurance would pay for the car. The downhill walk would have been relatively easy, but I can't imagine walking into Hertz and telling them that we lost your car. I continued to dig out the sand, jack up the car, and push it off the jack, gaining a few inches. Dennis became more insistent that it was impossible to save this car and that we should begin to walk.

Another hour or so went by and eventually the car reached firmer ground, and with the wheels spinning and three people pushing it, turned back on the path. Now we had the front end headed downhill.

The rest of the trip was relatively uneventful. We crossed over our improvised log bridge without falling off. It was easier to keep the car moving downhill than uphill.

That evening in Mexico City, John, Toni, and I had an excellent gourmet dinner, our first decent meal in days. Toni had severe facial sunburn because she had refused my pleadings to apply sunscreen. Dennis had to leave earlier to catch a flight back.

Toni and Paul at the cabin at 14,000 ft and after the successful climb of Orizaba. Paul has gathered some mountain flowers for Toni. Orizaba towers above.

Growing Up in the Depression

People who lived through the Great Depression of the 1930s are different from people who didn't. The depression must have made permanent changes in their brains. And these changes stayed the rest of their lives.

At the time that I was born in 1932, we lived in a company house in Boswell. Boswell is a small coal mining town in western Pennsylvania. The mining company owned most of the houses in town, which they rented to the miners for high rents compared to the quality of the houses. Our house had indoor plumbing, but it also had an outhouse in the back yard, which was the facility before a toilet was put inside the house. We continued to use both the outhouse and the inside toilet. My father, who had been a school teacher, was now a clerk in the company store. He was on the Boswell school board, and that is how he met my mother who was a teacher in Boswell for ten years.

The miners who lived in Boswell seldom worked. During the depression there was little demand for coal. In the year 1936, when I was four, we moved to Somerset about twelve miles away. My uncle Theodore, who was a dentist in Somerset, was also the president of the local bank. He gave a job to my father as a clerk in his bank. My dad bought a house, two doors from the railroad tracks, which the bank had foreclosed. He paid $3,000 cash. My father never bought anything in his life on payments.

We had a coal stove in the kitchen and a coal furnace in the basement. A coal bucket sat beside the kitchen stove with a pile of kindling wood. Saturday night was weekly bath time, so we would be clean to go to Sunday school and church on Sunday. We had a galvanized wash tub which my mother would fill with water and put on top of the coal stove. When the water was warm, the tub would be put on the kitchen floor. My mother kept a kettle of water on the stove to occasionally heat up the water in the tub. Each child would be bathed in turn, then pulled out to dry in front of the coal stove. After the bath, we either went to bed or put on our weekly change of clean underwear and socks. The last child in, frequently me, bathed in the dirty water from one week's dirt of the two previous children. We had electric lights and kerosene lamps to use when the electricity failed. There was no radio, television, telephone, or record player. Nobody had very much money during the depression. We all learned to live frugally. We learned never to leave any food on our plates, a habit which has remained with me. We learned that when you wore a hole in the bottom of your shoe, you cut a piece of cardboard to put into the shoe. When the cardboard wore through, you put another piece of cardboard in the shoe. You learned that the littlest child—that was me—could survive on clothing handed down from the older children.

Later, at the time of the Second World War, victory gardens were encouraged. We were well ahead of this. We always had a garden, which was spaded by hand with a shovel. This provided the vegetables for the family; corn, tomatoes, peppers, red beets, pumpkins, lettuce, cabbage, cauliflower, rhubarb, and many other things were provided from the fruits of our labor in the back yard. We also had fruit trees for our real fruit. In December my father went hunting and shot a deer, which provided us meat for the winter. Autumn was canning season when all of the vegetables, fruit, and even meat were preserved for eating during the winter.

In spite of the apparent poverty, we were quite happy because nobody else had any money, and my father and mother were experts in making a small amount of money go a long way. We had a car, and many people didn't have one. The earliest price of gasoline I can remember was fifteen cents a gallon. It was the custom to buy gasoline by gallons rather than dollars. My father would buy five gallons or two gallons and pay in change. Of course we never ate at a restaurant; however, I can remember going to Johnstown, a major trip of 30 miles. My father took the family to eat at the lunch counter in McCory's five and dime store. We were told to choose something less than a dollar. My mother advised a hot roast beef sandwich with gravy over it. She said this was the best buy.

The Second World War brought our country out of the depression, but the lessons which the depression taught stayed with me. These were: you can be happy with very little money; with ingenuity and hard work you can take care of yourself; and each person is responsible for himself, nobody else is responsible for him.

My First Job

"You say I can just go out there and get a job the same day?" I was elated. I was eleven years old; it was August 1943. Another boy had just told me that he had gone out to the country club and been put to work as a caddy on the golf course.

The next morning I crossed the railroad tracks below our house and crossed the creek which ran parallel to it. The only name I ever knew for it was "Shit Creek," apparently because it had garbage and sewerage in it. Walking three more miles up a dirt road brought me to the back entrance of the Somerset Country Club. There the wealthier citizens of our town played golf. The Straubs were not members. I found my way to the caddy shack avoiding the club building. The caddy master looked sternly down from a window in the back of the shack; he didn't ask any questions. He knew what I was there for. He barked at me, "Go sit on the bench and wait."

There were eight to ten boys sitting on a long bench behind the caddy shack. All of them were bigger than me. They didn't welcome me. They all seemed to know each other. They were laughing and talking. I quietly eased myself on to the end of the bench. For a short while nobody paid any attention to me. They talked about the players and how much they tipped and stories about kicking a player's ball out of the rough and getting a good tip for that. Then one of the most boisterous of the group addressed me. "Did you ever caddy here before?"

"No, I never caddied anywhere before." With that answer the whole group turned their attention to me, laughing and deriding me. I'm glad I didn't say that I had never been on a golf course before, and I had never seen anybody play golf before except from a long distance away. One shouted, "How are you going to know what club to give your player?"

Eventually the caddy master began sticking his head out of the window and calling one or two of the boys by name. Each of these would then get up and go to the front of the shack. Sometimes the caddy master would call a boy's name and say a specific player had asked for him.

It began to appear that he would call the boys in the order that they had arrived unless a player requested a special caddy. New boys arrived and sat on the bench. I began to think that my turn might soon be coming up. But the later arrivals were called ahead of me. Hour after hour I sat there while the others came and went. I had been told that the caddies were never to go anywhere except behind the shack until they were called.

Late in the day I was the only one remaining on the bench. The caddy master stuck his head out the window. "Come 'mere. You never caddied here before, have you? I have a have a bag for you."

I went to the front of the caddy shack. The caddy master had one of the largest, heaviest golf bags that I had seen all day in front of him. He pushed it over to me. "You take Mr. Barkman."

I put the strap over my shoulder and stood up. Man, that was heavy. But I didn't want to show it. I tried to walk straight but I staggered out the door.

I walked up to the first tee, set down the bag, and waited. About five minutes later Mr. Barkman came out. He was playing a twosome and the other player was carrying his own bag. This was in the day before golf carts or pull carts. They came later.

Mr. Barkman looked at me. "Are you my caddy?"

"Yes Sir," I answered. He took a golf ball and a tee out of the huge side pocket and a driver out of the bag. He put the tee in the ground and the ball on the tee. He took two or three practice swings, then addressed the ball. He swung the club and the ball flew down the fairway.

His friend now took his turn, repeated the motions of Mr. Barkman, and hit his ball a nice shot down the fairway. His friend picked up his small white cloth bag, and the two of them started down the middle of the fairway talking animatedly. I put the strap of the big bag on my shoulder and struggled behind them.

About one hundred yards down the fairway, the players paused in their talking and Mr. Barkman turned back to me and said, "Where's my ball?"

I looked astounded and mumbled something like, "I don't know."

"What! You don't know where my ball is?! You're supposed to know where it is."

With that the three of us began to look for Mr. Barkman's ball. I had not known that it was my job to follow the ball and mark it with my eyes and arrive at the ball ahead of the player. We looked around the fairway and Mr. Barkman found it. I moved as fast as I could over to Mr. Barkman after he found his ball, but he had to wait too long to get his club. His second shot once again flew down the center of the fairway, and I made my best effort to follow the ball in its flight. However, there was a dip in the fairway, and the final location of the ball was out of my sight. This time I tried to hurry ahead of the players but couldn't keep ahead of them with the heavy bag for more than a few yards. I huffed and I puffed and tried to get to the ball ahead of Mr. Barkman, but to my dismay when I got to the top of the knoll where I thought I would see the ball ahead,

I saw no ball. One more time the three of us had to walk back and forth from one side of the fairway to the other looking for Mr. Barkman's ball. Once again Mr. Barkman found it on the other side of the fairway from where I was looking, and he had to wait for me to bring the bag to him. Eventually we got to the first green. Mr. Barkman took his putter. He told me, "Hold the flag."

I laid the heavy bag down on its side on the green and ran toward the flag. Mr. Barkman went ballistic. "Never lay a bag on a green!" he shouted. Mr. Barkman was not having a good day. I was seriously affecting his golf game.

The two players putted in. Mr. Barkman was about ten feet from the hole. He three putted. He swore loudly and called for me. "Get out of here. I'll take the bag." He gave me a dime.

In spite of the discouraging first day, I was back early on the bench the next day. I was happy to learn that Mr. Barkman had not taken the time to complain about me or I might never have been given another bag. The other caddies gradually warmed up to me, but it took a long time. They would give me occasional advice on how to do my job better. Usually there were four caddies for a foursome, and I would watch what the other caddies did. Eventually I became an excellent caddy, and most golf bags were much lighter than Mr. Barkman's. In later years I often carried two bags. There were only three weeks remaining until school started the summer that I was eleven. The next two summers, when I was twelve and thirteen, I reported for duty the day after school was out and rarely missed a day unless it was raining,

Somerset Country Club is a nine-hole course. To play 18 holes, you went around twice. We got fifty cents for nine holes and one dollar for eighteen holes. A caddy gave five cents to the caddy master for each nine holes. Thus you usually took home forty-five cents or ninety cents a day. The days that I carried two bags, I might take home $1.80. Most players gave a dime or a quarter tip in addition.

The caddies could play golf on Monday mornings free. My uncle Theodore had an old set of clubs which he let me use. I really enjoyed it. The people who played golf had more money than we had. I always thought that I would like to be a golfer some day, but I always had something else like running that I felt I should do. I think I'll take up the game when I get older.

Putting Myself through School

I put myself through college and medical school and graduated with no debts. And I had a good time doing it. At age eleven I started working and I never got around to quitting. The first three summers, when I was eleven, twelve, and thirteen, I hiked around the local golf course with a bag of clubs on my back to make the game easy for the players. After school and on weekends, I found other employment. One of the first jobs I secured was scrubbing the floors at the Rural Electric Company on Saturdays. Later, once a week, I washed the show windows and scrubbed the floors at Mary Jane's, a women's clothing store. For a long time I worked at McCory's five and ten cent store every day after school and Saturdays. My daily duties included sweeping the floor and laboring in the stockroom. Whatever money I made, my parents advised me from the beginning to save for college. They felt that it was OK to spend ten cents out of every dollar that I made, and that I should save ninety cents. They didn't force me; however, I usually I followed their recommendations.

For three years I spent my summers outdoors carrying golf bags; for the next three years, I carried dishes and garbage. At the age of fourteen, fifteen, and sixteen I was a busboy and dishwasher at Howard

Johnson restaurant on the Pennsylvania Turnpike in Somerset. My job included moving several 55-gallon cans of wet garbage, each weighing about 300 pounds, about 500 feet from the kitchen to the garbage storage area. I would tilt the can on one edge and pivot it 180 degrees, then tilt it on the other side, and then turn the can again. In this manner I would walk the garbage can about one tenth of a mile to the dump. The busboys also had to carry the bins of dirty dishes to the kitchen, run them through the dishwasher, and carry the clean dishes back to the restaurant. I washed more dishes than any housewife will ever wash in her lifetime.

My remuneration was the princely sum of twenty-five cents per hour. In those days a work week was six days, and you got a day off once a week. I earned $12 per week; $2 was taken off my check for income tax, and my weekly check was for $10. I think my employer studied business by reading Charles Dickens's *A Christmas Carol*. My parents thought I should save $8, and theoretically $2 should have been mine to spend as I pleased. However, my mother objected to me spending $6 of my own money for a camera, although I did it anyway. I was able to save enough money to buy a car for $110 at age 16. The only time I took off from work was during football season in my sophomore, junior, and senior years of high school.

I was born during the depression. People who lived through the depression have a different feeling about work and money than those that did not. My father was one of thirteen children of Gottlieb and Mammy Straub, who had a farm at Stoystown, Pennsylvania. My father, Ralph Rand Straub, was born in 1882. He was 21 years old when the Wright brothers made the first airplane flight at Kitty Hawk, North Carolina. Gottlieb Straub, my grandfather, was brought to America by his parents shortly after his birth and before he could walk. The German work ethic and love of life was imparted to the family, and all thirteen of Gottlieb's and Mammy's children advanced further in life. One of my father's brothers was a surgeon, one was a dentist and president of the bank where my father worked, and one had a store in Scalp Level, Pennsylvania, and was a notary public. Two others built apartment buildings and did well in real estate. All of the girls married well.

My father advised me never to spend more than I earned and to save a portion of everything that I earned. He said never to buy anything except real estate or something which would make you money on credit. He approved of taking a loan to buy a home because this would save you the rent, which you would otherwise have to pay. He also felt that it was proper to buy a car on credit if it was necessary for work, but not if it was only for pleasure. Even though he worked in a bank where the business was to lend money, he never bought anything on credit. Our home was bought for cash in 1936 for $3,000. Someone had lost it to the bank. He also paid for all of his cars in cash. The car that we drove through most of my childhood was a 1936 airflow Chrysler, which he purchased new for $800. When my uncle died in 1952, he bought his 1951 Pontiac from the estate and drove it until Dad died in 1962. Thus he drove only two cars in the last 26 years of his life. Maintain things well and keep them for a long time, Dad advised. Following his recommendations, I drove a Corvette for 19 years, a Rolls Royce for 23 years, flew my Mooney for 20 years, and I still have the same wife after 28 years.

Adhering to his guidance, I bought nothing except real estate for credit. I paid $110 for my first car, a 1933 Oldsmobile, $950 for my second car, a 1950 Ford that had been used by the FBI. I longed for a convertible, and about 1953 I bought a light green 1951 Chrysler convertible with a white top and white sidewall tires for $1,050. Boy, was I on top of the world with that car! This was my transportation until I left with the army for Europe. I have never bought a car, a boat, or an airplane on credit. The only things that I ever bought on credit are my house and apartment buildings, which buy themselves from the rental income. My father said if you didn't have the money, you couldn't buy it. If you wanted something, save for it, and then buy it.

For a short time Jim Saylor, a neighbor boy my age who lived across the street, and I had a better paying job. We were hired to weed the red beet field of the agriculture department of the high school. The field was to be an elegant display of modern agriculture and should be weed free. This paid 40 cents per hour. Considerably more than the 25 cents I was making at Howard Johnston's. The red beet field was huge. God knows how many acres it was, but I could barely see the other edge in the distance. Jim Saylor's and my job was to pull all of the weeds from between the red beets and between the rows. We set diligently to work. Working very hard, we were able to clear about 25 feet of a row of red beets per hour. There is no question that the area that we cleared of weeds looked better than the other approximately 50 acres of the field. We continued to weed the field the first day. There was nobody there to supervise or tell us if we were doing a good job. In the evening we went home and returned the next morning. Without any supervision we continued to weed, but not quite at the same pace as the first day. We were making little progress in this huge field. About once a day, someone would come out to the field to see what we were doing and gave us a bit of advice, but not much. The second night it rained. The next day the field was muddy and we sloshed around in the mud. By this time Jim Saylor had lost most of his enthusiasm for this job, in spite of the enormous amount of money that we were to be paid. By the fourth day, the weeds had grown back in the area that we had weeded the first day, such that you could barely see that we had done anything. Now Jim got the idea that we really didn't have to do anything since you couldn't see that anything was done. He sat on his butt and pulled about one weed a minute. I continued to weed, but at a slower pace than I did the first day. One evening my father drove out to the field to pick us up after work. He said we were two tiny figures sitting in the middle of about fifty acres, and that he couldn't find us for a while. After about a week, someone from the agriculture department came out to the field and said we could quit weeding. The field looked the same as before we started, except the red beets and the weeds had grown higher. All of the areas that we'd weeded were re-grown with weeds three to four days after we left them.

Earlier, I had a similar experience pulling dandelions out of our yard. My father said he would pay my brother, Rand, and me ten cents per bushel of dandelion that we extracted. The method was to insert a screwdriver deep into the ground and loosen up the earth, then ease out the long deep root. If you just broke off the stalk which was above the ground, the plant would immediately grow back. Rand was two and a half years older than me. We both sweated for three or four hours, and Rand was able to fill one bushel basket with dandelion stalks. I, being smaller, didn't get my basket completely filled. When it became dark, it was filled to about four inches below the top. I explained that I would complete the filling in the morning, and Dad said then I would get my dime. During the night the leaves settled, and when I went out in the morning to complete my task, the basket was only about one quarter full. I tried to fluff it up a bit but it didn't work. After a few more hours, the bushel basket was nearly, but not completely, full. That evening my father took pity on me and paid me my dime. He had seen that it was nearly full the day before.

In November 1949, the football season had just ended. I was 16 years old and in my senior year in high school. As was my custom, I looked for work to do after school and on weekends. A men's clothing store named Talleywoods had recently opened on West Main Street in Somerset. I went in and explained I was looking for work. Joe Weimer, the store's owner, hired me. He taught me how to stock the shelves, clean the store, and be a salesclerk. I enjoyed the work, and Mr. Weimer treated me like an adult. I continued to work at Talleywoods the summer after graduating from high school and before entering college. That summer, I built new shelves for the storeroom. Mr. Weimer decided to put new florescent lights in the store. This job consisted of completely rewiring a moderate-sized store with armored cable, which I accomplished completely by myself. When the electrical inspector inspected my work and found no defects, he told me, "If you are ever looking for a job, come and see me."

When it came time to go to college I was offered an academic scholarship at the University of Pittsburgh, which paid part of my tuition. The remainder of the tuition was paid from my savings. My father and mother were constantly offering me money. They would have sacrificed relentlessly to send me to college, but they were old and at this time I felt it would be more appropriate for me to be providing for my parents rather than taking from them. I did, however, accept small sums, often twenty dollar bills, which in those days was a significant amount of money and went a long way toward helping me.

I chose to attend the Johnstown campus of the University of Pittsburgh, lived at home, and traveled the 30 miles from Somerset to Johnstown with a group of other students including my brother, Rand. After my first year in Johnstown, Rand got admitted to dental school at Pittsburgh after only three years of college, and I followed him to the main campus.

I became a member of the Pitt football team as a walk on. I was much smaller than most of the college players, and I was assigned to the suicide squad. This group learned the plays of the next week's opponents and scrimmaged against the first team. We were forbidden to tackle the first team's runners because the coach didn't want any of his stars to be injured, but the blocking was full contact. I, in spite of my small size, was a guard. In those days we lined up in what was called a single wing formation, with one guard on each side of the center and two tackles on the "strong side." The weak side guard often pulled out and ran interference in front of the ball carrier. That was my job. I was to throw a full-size block against one of the monsters who made up the first team line and stop him from getting to the ball carrier.

In high school, the coaches commented several times that I had "guts." This is another way of saying I was crazy. Tom Rodgers, our line coach, was a huge fellow who played professional football as a lineman for the Philadelphia Eagles. He did something that nobody would ever do now because it could make a quadriplegic. He told each of the linemen to run at him and hit him head on. We were not to move our head to either side, but charge him at full speed and hit him with our helmet. He said I was the only one who hit him full blast with my head without ducking. The others ducked to the side such that their shoulder struck him. At that time we had soft leather football helmets. In my senior year, our team got fifteen modern plastic helmets. When a player came off the field, he handed his helmet to the player who was replacing him. To toughen our stomachs and neck, Tom Rodgers would also have us lie on our backs on the ground, then rise up from the ground until only our feet and head were supporting our entire weight. No hands were used. Coach Rodgers said this built a strong neck, and he said nothing looked worse than a skinny neck. Then, while I was supported only by my neck, Tom, who must have weighed 250 pounds, would stand on my stomach wearing football cleats. I was able to support him, but many of the others collapsed under his weight.

Before the football season at the University of Pittsburgh came to an end, I heard of a fantastic opportunity at the United States Steel Research Laboratory. They were looking for an analytical chemist to work evening shifts. The job was supposed to be filled by a college graduate with a degree in chemistry, but they couldn't fill it and would consider an undergraduate. I applied and was accepted. I cut the football season short by about four weeks. I didn't think anybody noticed me among all the scholarship players. But about a month after I quit coming to practice, I was walking down the street when one of the coaches passed me. He stopped, came back, and said, "Straub, what happened to you? We were just talking about you when you disappeared. We were saying that you had a lot of guts." I hated to leave football, but now I was installed in my new position and this was the wisest thing for me to do.

I worked at the research laboratory for United States Steel for the next three years, and at the same time took a full time schedule of 16 credits with a major in physics. I was competing against a lot of brilliant students who were not working an outside job forty hours a week. My grades reflected that. They were satisfactory but not excellent. I went to work at 3 PM and left at 11 PM, Monday through Friday. But I earned good money and had no problem to pay my tuition as well as my apartment and buy the Chrysler convertible.

The Korean War gradually came to an end. Our government said in mid-December that the official end of the war would be December 31, 1954. After that the draft would continue, but all soldiers entering after that date would not get the G. I. bill. I had always planned to use the G.I. bill to go to graduate school after I graduated with a Bachelor of Science in physics. In 1954, vast numbers of college students enlisted between Christmas and New Year's. The day that I went to the enlistment office, the candidates were lined up around the block. It was the headline news, and there was a large photo on the front page of the Pittsburgh Press showing all the students lined up to join the military. So many wanted to join the army that they stopped enlistments two days after I signed up. If I had waited two more days, I would not have been accepted. On the recommendation of the enlistment officer, I signed up for the Army Security Agency, abbreviated A.S.A. Later when I took an aptitude test, I was informed that I was qualified for any school that the military had. I chose the Armed Forces Language School in Monterey, California, because this appeared to be the most useful after I would be discharged. In retrospect, this was a wise choice.

After basic training at Fort Knox and an introductory course in military intelligence at Fort Devins in Lowell, Massachusetts, I reported to the Presidio of Monterey in California. The A.S.A. had assigned me to study German.

The army, the navy, and the air force were at the Armed Forces Language School, but I don't remember seeing any marines; however, there might have been some there. It was an intensive, total immersion six-month course. There was one native-born instructor for every six students. The instructors could not be too long away from their native country. After a period of time, it was felt that these instructors may not know the slight new variations which occur in any language over time. We had three hours of class in the morning and three hours in the afternoon. After a brief introduction, only German was spoken. You were given an assignment each evening, which consisted of memorizing the lines of a short skit and phonograph with records and a headphone to give you correct pronunciation. The next day, each student played each part in the skit. Friday afternoon was singing time. We learned all the German drinking songs. When I got to Germany, my German friends said I knew more songs than they did. Near the end of the course, our six-member class took a trip to a department store. If we saw anything which we did not know in German, we were to ask the instructor.

The six-month total immersion course gave us a good basis in German. One instructor advised this: "If you really want to learn the language, find a German girlfriend who can't speak English." I followed his advice. Most of the people, girls or men, wanted to practice their English with the Americans. I rejected several attractive girls because they insisted on speaking English and eventually found a German girlfriend with the rare American name of Doris, who didn't speak English. Eventually I became so proficient that when I told the Germans that I was an American G.I., they would think I was a crazy German with delusions. When I tell my German friends how I learned German, they say, "Ach, du sprechts Schlafzimmer Deutch." (Oh, you speak bedroom German.)

My two years in Germany were fantastic. This was ten years after the end of the Second World War, and Americans were regarded as heroes. The dollar was strong. Even our soldier's salary was plenty to live well in Europe. The United States was rebuilding war-ravished Europe, and everybody was thankful to us.

I worked for the Army Security Agency in Frankfurt am Main. I lived in the Gutleut Kasserne behind the Hauptbahnhof. That is a small military barracks behind the main train station. Each morning I would ride the German Strassenbaun (street car) from the Hauptbahnhof to the I.G. Farben building, which is a large, well-known office building in Frankfurt. Sometimes I would wear a uniform, and sometimes I would wear civilian clothes. When we were discharged from the Army Security Agency, they told us we were forever forbidden to reveal what we did. However, a recent issue of *Time* magazine was devoted to espionage and it explained virtually our entire Top Secret mission. It said that during the cold war there were 3,000 spies in Berlin. I made many trips to Berlin on the train through the Russian sector. It said a tunnel was dug under the border to tap the phone lines of the communists. This was before the construction of the Berlin wall. I was never in the tunnel, but I was given tapes from there to translate. I found myself in a very unique position because I had a scientific background and knew German. The military had many translators and inter-preters, but most of them had a literary arts background. Some of the material was highly technical, and in order to translate it you had to understand what you were translating. Soon all the technical material was passed on to me, and there was a good bit of it—too much for one person. They asked me to find some other personnel and form a scientific department. I did this, and the agency was delighted with the results. One of my discoveries resulted in the establishment of a new listening post, thus a new small military base in Germany. The lieutenant in charge was so pleased with my results he told me, "If I had my way I would just tell you to do whatever you feel like doing." This was because most of the other people didn't understand what was going on, but they were pleased with the results. Unfortunately, much of the military didn't have the same opinion of me as the officer who supervised our office. The rest of the military had no idea what went on in our office and saw me as a poor soldier. I didn't keep my hair cut; I didn't keep my bed made. I paid little attention to any of the military rules. This was very aggravating to the Military Police, who had a barracks nearby and were pure spit and polish—Yes, Sir, No, Sir, stand tall soldiers. When I was ready to leave after two years in Germany, the lieutenant at my office said the Army Security Agency was going to give me a commendation for my work there. A day or two after this, I was in the Hauptbahnhof about one AM changing some military script to German marks. I wore a leather jacket and my hair had grown over my collar. I was speaking German, and naturally everybody assumed that I was German. It was illegal for Germans to possess military script, so the money changer alerted the German police. When the police asked for my identification I showed my military I.D., and they then called the Military Police. The M.P.'s asked for my pass and, of course, I didn't have one. I had been coming and going for years when I wanted to and nobody had ever asked me for a pass. In theory when we left the barracks, we were to stop by the duty office and pick up a pass. I hadn't done that for years, and I don't think anybody else in my outfit bothered with it either. So I was hauled before the captain who was the company commander and who didn't know anything about our work, and officially I was A.W.O.L. He turned out to be a strict officer, and apparently he was going to court marshal me. The next day when I went to the office, the lieutenant there said, "Don't worry; I'll take care of it." However, after talking to the captain, he told me he doesn't want to bend. He is determined to court marshal me. Now I was in the unique position of being awarded a commendation and a court marshal at the same time. A day or two later, the lieutenant said the captain was willing to forget about the court marshal if he would give up the commendation. He said, "I'll try to get it authorized after you are discharged and get it awarded to you then."

I said, "Don't bother. I don't care about commendations." The lieutenant appeared quite surprised that I had said that. In retrospect, I'm sorry I said that. I would have liked to have gotten a commendation for the work that I did when I was in the Army Security Agency and that we were never supposed to talk about.

I had one more semester to complete to get my degree at the University of Pittsburgh. I loved living in Europe. I loved living in a foreign country so much that when I came back to Pittsburgh, I searched for a room in the African-American section of town because I would be living among a different culture. However, I couldn't find suitable housing there so I got a room near the university and applied myself for six months and graduated.

I wanted to get a PhD in physics, and I had applied and been accepted after an interview to the University of Gottingen in Germany, which was Oppenheimer's university. The person who interviewed me said that they accept very few foreign students because of language problems but would accept me.

After graduating from the University of Pittsburgh, I set out to return to Europe with the intention of beginning studies in November. My mother was very distraught that I wanted to return to Europe. She used every tactic possible in an attempt to persuade me not to leave. She cried and told me that it would kill her if I left. It was not easy for me to leave because, of course, I wanted to please my mother, but I reasoned that if I don't leave now I would be perpetually tied to her apron strings. When I walked down the street with my pack on my back, she followed me, crying, and said I would never see her again.

Always being conservative with the little money that I had, I hitchhiked to New Jersey, where I hoped to be able to find a ship that I could work on to pay my passage. I carried a backpack with a pup tent and sleeping bag. All of my clothes were wash and wear, requiring no pressing. I also had a tiny stove and eating utensils. I hitchhiked up and down the east coast but eventually realized that I was not going to be able to work for my passage to Europe. So I bought a passage on a freighter to Bremerhaven. Freighters often took up to twelve passengers. The accommodations and food were good and the cost was less than an ocean liner. I paid $160 for my passage.

Upon getting to Germany, the first thing I did was hitchhike to Frankfurt to see my old girlfriend, Doris. I found that she had taken up with another American soldier, and my love was lost. One night in a German beer garden and I had forgotten about her. Life must go on.

It is difficult to work in Germany if you are not a citizen. You must have a work permit. The year was 1958, and the World's Fair was being held in Brussels. Often, work permits are not required for international events. I decided to hitchhike to Brussels and see if I could get a job. I had pitched my pup tent at a campground on the bank of the Main River in Frankfurt, and I packed it up and was on my way.

Brussels was bristling with activity because of the World's Fair. I found a campground within sight of the Atomium, which was the architectural landmark of the exposition and was a building designed to look like an atom. I pitched my pup tent. I would sleep on the ground there for the next three months. I paid a day's admission to the fair and went directly to the American Pavilion, where I applied for a job as a waiter. One of the waiters, a Belgium, who was working there, asked me as I was filling out the application, "Are you a waiter?"

"Yes," I answered.

"Where's your white coat?" was his caustic response. He was a trained waiter, in a proud profession that he had spent years perfecting, and didn't fancy a non-professional working beside him. Apparently, professional waiters provide their own white coats in Belgium. Anyway, the American pavilion provided the white coats and dark trousers for their waiters.

Working as a waiter at the '58 World's Fair was interesting every day. Within a short time I knew the menu in French, German,

English, Dutch, and Spanish. I also could direct people to the restrooms and answer a few basic questions in these languages. I would address one table in German, move to another table and take an order in French, then the next table might be English. More than once I was asked, "How many languages do you speak?" In reality, I knew only a few phrases in French and Spanish.

I also learned to be a good waiter, but I still was not as fine as some of the professionals. I was what they called a tray waiter. I carried things to and from the table on a tray. True professionals lined the food and dirty dishes up on their arm and served without trays. In general I was fairly efficient, but I made some serious goofs. Once I was carrying six steaks, the most expensive meals that the restaurant served, on a tray, holding it about ear height above my right shoulder. As I entered the dining room, there were two carpeted steps downward. My foot caught in the carpet of the top step and the tray and the six steak dinners flew ahead of me, making a trail of food for 15 or 20 feet down the aisle between the dining tables. The entire restaurant laughed hilariously-----except me. The servers paid for the food then collected from the diners. This would cost me more than I would earn on this day. The restaurant manager, of course, saw this and told me to go back and get six more steaks. That was nice of him.

Many famous people came in. Red Adair, the famous oil well firefighter was at my table once. He ordered rare steak and whisky. He didn't want anything else on the plate, just steak and nothing else.

I earned good money there, $400 per month for three months. This was a lot of money for me at that time. I had almost no living expenses, living in a tent and getting one free meal at the American pavilion each day.

These were exciting times. The Russian pavilion was close to the American pavilion. Russia had just orbited Sputnik. It sailed across the sky at night, and just at dusk you could occasionally see it. It transmitted a signal that could be heard on the radio, which sounded like "ping….ping….ping…." In 1958 the United States had no satellites, but they were quick to catch up in the next few years.

I went to all of the pavilions and studied the other cultures. My job got me into the expo and I took advantage of the opportunity.

I also met Monica, a Belgium girl. Actually, she met me. She came right up to me when I was working as a waiter and said she and her family were so fascinated by America and Americans. She invited me to her home. She was an absolutely gorgeous 18-year-old girl with a perfect figure. Both her mother and her father were good looking. She was an only child. They invited me lo their home several times and we all went out a few evenings together, but they never left Monica out of their sight. The following summer, I rode my Vespa from Belgium the whole way through France to visit Monica and her family on the Rivera. Both Monica and her mother looked like dynamite in their tiny bikinis; both had small waists and large breasts. I never spent any time with Monica alone, but her parents were likeable, personable people.

Francis Connor was one of the supervisors of the waiters at the American pavilion. He was from New Jersey and going to medical school at the University of Louvain, which is 23 kilometers from Brussels. He began to encourage me to study medicine in Belgium. I did not know that an American could go to a foreign medical school and practice in the United States. I had never considered any career other than a scientist, and I had my acceptance into the Ph.D. Program at the University of Gottingen. Yet there were some negatives. The atomic energy program was being scaled back at this time. Many physicists were out of work. There were programs to convert physicists with a PhD to medical doctors in two years. Also, I remember a professor whom I idolized and would have loved to imitate say once in the laboratory, "If I had it to do over again, I would have been a physician." That astounded me. I knew I could never afford to attend medical school in the United States, and I knew how hard they were to get into.

One day Francis said, "I'm going to be driving to Louvain tomorrow and I want you to go with me. Just look around and see what you think of it." I agreed to go. Louvain is the second oldest Catholic University after Rome. It was started in the 13th century. Francis was a friend of the rector. This is an almost impossible situation. It is like being a personal friend of the pope or the president of the United States. Nobody even talks to the rector. It is rare to be able to talk to any of the professors. Francis's friendship with the rector came about because he was the president of the Belgo-American Club. And the Americans were very generous to the University of Louvain after the war. They donated a beautiful marble library to the university and filled it with books. We went directly to the rector's office and were immediately directed in. The rector greeted us with, "Hello Francis," and the two talked like friends and equals.

After they had finished their business about the Belgo-American Club, Francis said, "This is Paul Straub. He would like to study medicine at the University of Louvain." The rector asked me about what I had studied, and after I said that I had a B.S. from the University of Pittsburgh, he took a notepad which said at the top **From the Desk of the Rector** and wrote, "Please admit Paul Straub to the School of Medicine," and signed it. Now I had an admission to medical school, something many worthy students were longing to get. I hadn't decided to study medicine. Francis was trying to persuade me to do that.

The University of Gottingen started classes in November. The University of Louvain started classes in October. Classes would start and registration would go on for the first two weeks of classes. It was possible to attend classes for two weeks, decide that this was not for me, and go to Gottingen. I decided that this was what I would do. The University of Louvain, like the country of Belgium, has two languages, French and Flemish, and medicine is taught in both of these languages. All of the Americans studied in the French facility. I would guess that there were 40 to 50 Americans studying in Louvain. I went to some lectures in French. I listened. I watched some of the other Americans taking notes. Clearly they understood what the professor was saying. I was not. After two or three days of sitting in the classes, understanding very little, I decided that I would try to go to medical school. I was walking down the street to register, about one block from the registration area, when Mark, a black American student, approached from the other direction. We greeted and I volunteered that I was going to register, but I was worried about the language. He advised, "You know German. Why don't you attend some of the Flemish classes and see if you don't understand more." I turned around and did not register that day.

The next day I attended some lectures in Flemish. I got the impression I understood much more than I had during the French lectures. I decided to chart a new trail and become the first American student in the Flemish faculty of medicine. Later I found that I was not the first American student. An American had graduated from the Flemish division some years ago. Also, much to my surprise, there was another American in my class, Jerry Schumsky. He had married a Dutch girl. Dutch and Flemish are two dialects of the same language, as are American and English.

An extraordinary chain of incidents had occurred. I wonder what would have happened to me if I had not met Mark that day and if he had not suggested that I try to learn in Flemish. I probably would not have gotten through medical school in the French faculty. I wonder what would have happened to me if Francis Connor had not taken me with him to see the rector that day.

The Flemish-speaking Belgiums and the French-speaking Belgiums are always competing. Since most Americans study in the French facility, the Flemish were proud to have Americans in their classes. The students were very helpful and kind. I always felt very welcome.

For Americans, medicine is a five-year course in Louvain, and a one year internship which can be taken in the United States. In

Belgium, it is easy to be admitted to study medicine but hard to graduate. Each year they fail students, and you don't know if you are going to make it until the end. In America, the most difficult thing is to be accepted to medical school, and 97% of the students that are accepted graduate. We had over 500 in my class the first year and 180 graduated.

The studies are divided into three candidature years and four doctorate years. The first candidature year is excused for students with a bachelor's degree. I began in second candidature year. Examinations are oral and only given once a year at the end. You must pass all subjects; if you fail one, you may repeat the examinations at the end of the summer. You must repeat all examinations even if you failed only one.

The medical school of the University of Louvain is excellent. As a result of my education there, I have never failed an examination. I passed E.C.F.M.G. (Educational Council for Foreign Medical Graduates), National Boards, Pennsylvania Medical License Examination, Otolaryngology—Head and Neck Surgery Board all the first time. Many of these have a high failure rate. When I applied for a license in Nevada, I was told that if I was out of medical school for more than eight years, I would have to take National Boards over. In my present specialty, I am divorced from general medicine. I studied one summer, evenings and weekends. I sat out under a tree in our back yard and studied; I loved it. I felt like a student again. When I took the test, most of the applicants were in general practice or internists who use this information every day. One was a tenured professor of internal medicine at Harvard. At lunchtime, everybody compared their answers. I felt sick. I felt I had so many wrong, and I had to guess on so many. When they called me to tell me I had passed I said, "If I passed, I guess everybody passed."

"No," the secretary answered. "About 50% of your group passed." I tell this to explain the quality of education that I got at the University of Louvain.

I paid the highest rate of tuition because I was a foreign student. I paid $96 per year tuition. That is two semesters. I paid $16 per month for my room, and if you could have seen it, you would have said I paid too much. The first three years I lived on Parijsstraat (Paris Street). The building was 300 years old and had a steel winding staircase like a fire escape in the back. My room was on the third floor. If I wanted to use the toilet, I would walk down the two flights of fire escape to a French toilet, which means a hole in the floor and two footprints that you stand on. To flush it, you pulled the chain and water gushed over the floor and theoretically washed your droppings down the hole. I learned early to get out of the stall before pulling the cord. If you didn't, your shoes and feet would get wet with your excrement. I kept a pot with a lid in the room in case I wanted to urinate at night. In the morning, I had to carry it down the stairs and empty it down the hole.

My quarters were actually two rooms, each with a tiny coal stove in the middle of the room and a single dim light bulb with no shade hanging from the center of the ceiling of each room. I would go to the store; a little mom-and-pop shop a few doors away, and buy a bag of coal to fuel my stoves. With a fire burning in the stove, I would put one leg on each side of the stove and study by the light of the single bulb.

I was extremely happy there. It looked like I was accomplishing what I had set out to do. I was picking up Flemish rapidly. Geographically, Holland lies between England and Germany. Flemish is a separate language, but where it differs from German it moves toward English. If you know German and English, you can rapidly learn Flemish.

I had very little money. Occasionally I would gather bottles to take in for deposit to get something to eat. At home my mother used to say, "Don't waste food; think of all the starving people in Europe." Now I was one of them. The G.I. bill would pay for four years of school. My school would be five years. I would not request payment several months of each year to extend it to the final year.

Attending medical school is the most thing that I have ever done in my life. Since the only examinations are at the end of the year, there is a tendency to take it easy in the beginning of the year. As it gets closer to examination time, the pressure gets greater. There are about two weeks between the last class and the beginning of examinations. This is called the block period, when every student is studying day and night.

The first year was the most stressful because I didn't know what to expect, and I didn't know how to study on my own. Each year became a bit less stressful as I learned the system. My final year there, I almost gained distinction. I just missed it by a few points.

After the first set of exams, I had completed second candidature. Most of the American students fly home in the summer, but this was too expensive for me. I bought a used Vespa motor scooter for $200. This machine lasted throughout my next four years in Belgium and took me to the south of France the first summer as well as Italy and later to Denmark and a good bit of Europe. I strapped the backpack with the pup tent and sleeping bag that I had brought with me to Europe on the carrier on the Vespa. I made countless trips to Amsterdam, a distance of about 120 miles. I remember once riding the Vespa to Amsterdam at Christmastime. The roads were mostly glare ice, and I had another American student on the back. He was a big, overweight rugby player. Much of the trip I made with my feet dragging on the icy road to prevent us from becoming a part of it. A Vespa—the name of which means "bee" in Italian, presumably because of the sound that it makes—is a very sturdy machine.

At the beginning of my second year, I met Anna Marie at a Belgo-American Club meeting. She was a pretty blond who was always smiling and laughing. She taught me Flemish. We were together for the next four years, and I attribute much of my happy memories to Anna Marie.

After passing my third year of examinations, I began to think it was possible that I would complete the full program. I felt braver about spending a bit more money, and I moved from the hovel on Parijsstrat to a much nicer place. It was a studio apartment in a newer building. It had a tiny elevator which two people could get into. It had central heating. I was living in luxury.

Upon completing two years, I returned home the summer of 1960. I arrived home after dark one evening and, even though I had not seen my family for nearly two years, set out early the next morning to find summer work. There was a recession at this time, and work was scarce. I visited a half a dozen places at random, then, as I was going down the street, noticed a sign on a building identifying the office of the Pennsylvania Department of Labor. You could go in there and they would find a job for you. I had never done anything like that before, but I went in and registered. Then I continued to check other places of business for work and, at the end of the day, had found three places who would hire me. I took the job at Johnstown Memorial Hospital transcribing medical records because it was in the medical field. I was allowed to live at the hospital, and I could follow the interns around at night. I learned a vast amount about the practical side of medicine. Two weeks after my first foray to look for work, the State Department of Labor called and announced they had found me a job. I replied I had found three jobs on the day that I was in their office, and I had been working ever since. They observed, "If everyone was like you we wouldn't have any work to do."

Two years later when I returned home, I worked at the hospital as an extern. Basically I did everything that the interns did, but I didn't have any patients assigned specifically to me. Once again I lived at the hospital and spent most of the summer, day and night, treating patients and learning about medicine.

The next time I returned home, it was to complete my fourth year of medical school. In Belgium, you are not given your degree until after internship. Pennsylvania required me to also do an internship after receiving my M.D. Thus I had two internships. The American students had more practical experience, for example, more time in the operating room, but in some aspects, I was ahead of them. I could read EKG's better than them.

After I became a licensed M.D., I knew I wanted to become a specialist in some surgical field, but I wanted to earn some money prior to starting a residency. I took a job as an emergency room physician at Lee Hospital in Johnstown. This was before emergency medicine became a specialty. I worked five days in one week, 19 hours a day, and had two days off. The next week I worked two days, 19 hours a day, and had five days off. I earned $14,000 the first year. The second year I earned $16,000. I calculated that I worked 4,000 hours per year. The normal working person working 40 hours per week for 50 weeks with two weeks vacation works 2,000 hours per year.

The Tripacer

For years, my dream was to have my own airplane. As soon as I began to earn money as a licensed doctor, I set out to fulfill this dream. My lifetime policy has been to only buy what I have the money to pay for, thus new airplanes were out of the question. I decided a Piper Tripacer would suit me perfectly.

The Tripacer

William Piper had done for the small airplane after the Second World War what Henry Ford had done for the automobile. Henry Ford began mass-producing the model T, an inexpensive automobile. He said the people could have any color they wanted as long as it was black. William Piper began mass producing the Piper Cub and made all of them yellow. Eventually Ford had to improve his vehicle and produced the model A. Piper eventually improved his airplane and produced the Pacer. Then came the improvement of a tricycle landing gear rather than tail wheel. This, in theory, made airplanes easier to land, particularly in a crosswind. The Pacer was a metal frame covered with fabric, the same construction as the Piper Cub. Other companies were making all metal airplanes, but the Piper Company was used to making fabric-covered aircraft, so they modified the Pacer by adding tricycle landing gear. The result was not the prettiest plane on the airport, but a reliable and inexpensive plane which was easy to fly. Inexpensive and easy to fly sounded good to me because I didn't have a pilot's license yet. The stubby plane sitting high on three legs was nicknamed the flying milk stool.

I found a 1960 model, green in color, one of the last ones produced with a 160 hp engine (most of the earlier had smaller engines) for $4,500. This was to become my pride and joy. In the five years that I owned this slow but reliable airplane, I completed my private pilot's license, flew several times to the Bahamas, flew to California, landed at Washington National many times, landed at LaGuardia many times, and took my instrument rating in it.

Originally it was fabric covered. The fabric was in fair shape, but later it started coming loose above the windscreen. I had been warned that there was a danger that the fabric could come loose there and the slipstream could tear the fabric rearwards, in which case it could wrap around the tail, making it impossible to control the plane and causing a crash. For this reason I developed the habit, as part of my preflight, to put a fresh strip of four-inch adhesive tape from the hospital above the windshield to make this less likely. One day I was flying from Somerset to Deep Creek, Maryland, a flight of about half of an hour, when I heard a flapping noise above me. I was concerned that the top of my airplane was coming off, so I decided to make an emergency landing. I landed in a farmer's field, parallel to a fence row, and got out to check. As luck would have it, it was only a bit of the adhesive tape that was loose and not the fabric tearing, so I put on a bit more adhesive tape and continued my journey. Later I had the airplane covered with aluminum and painted red and white. She looked prettier and was safer.

I hangared my plane at the Somerset airport, for the princely sum of $15/month. One time, when I had only a student's permit, I landed at Somerset when they had a 45-knot wind. I had to keep full power on until I had her on the ground. She rocked terribly when I tried taxi. When I got to the tiny terminal at this village airport, several more experienced aviators came running out and grabbed the wings to prevent her from being blown over. It turned out nobody else was flying because of the high winds, and they had bigger and heavier airplanes than I was flying.

The communications and navigations equipment in my Tripacer consisted of one radio, which was known as a coffee grinder radio because it had a handle like a coffee grinder which you turned to tune the communications receiver. The receiver tuned with a variable condenser like an old-fashioned vacuum tube radio. In fact, the receiver did have vacuum tubes. I could only transmit on six frequencies, but I could receive an infinite number of frequencies. I could receive VOR frequencies and I had a VOR indicator, but I could not navigate and communicate at the same time. While I talked to someone on the ground, the navigation was shut down. Most other aircraft were using crystal controlled radios. You can imagine the trouble I caused the controllers at Washington National or LaGuardia landing there. They would assign me a communications frequency and I would answer "unable." They would command another and I would say the same. Eventually disgusted, they would ask just what frequencies can you transmit on, and I would read them my only six frequencies. They would have liked to tell me to go away, but at that time they couldn't do it because the airports were tax supported and supposed to be open to all tax payers. You couldn't do that now. They have changed the rules.

One day a patient who was also a friend said, "Paul, we want you to go bear hunting with us. The reason is that you have a plane and we will use the plane to locate the bears for the hunters on the ground." They planned to hunt on a Saturday from a cabin deep in the woods, high in the mountains of western Pennsylvania. My friend said there was a strip next to the cabin where a few planes had landed, and I could come in there. The problem was that the group was driving up on Friday, and I had office hours until late Friday. He said, "That's OK, fly up in the night and we will light up the strip with our car lights."

By the time I could make the takeoff it was 8:30 in the evening, which was nighttime in the autumn hunting season. My friend said fly to a VOR station on a mountaintop which I knew, then fly outbound on the 132-degree radial for eight miles. I calculated this to be four minutes and fifty seconds.

The terrain over the VOR station had no lights, but my coffee grinder radio indicated station passage and I turned outbound on the designated radial. The entire area under me had only rare dim lights, which I assumed to be isolated cabins or houses, usually one half mile or a mile apart. I saw no automobile lights driving on any roads in the region. The terrain was rolling hills or mountains totally covered by forest.

I continued at what I assumed to be about 1,000 foot above the terrain, and then, as I approached the four minutes and 50 second time, I dropped down to what I assumed to be about 500 feet over the woods. I saw a dim light ahead, which I thought might be the cabin. I switched on the landing lights. I had no DME (distance mea-suring equipment), no radio contact with the people on the ground or anyone else. This was before the age of cell phones. If I used the radio to communicate, I could not use it to navigate at the same time. Sure enough, in about 30 seconds the ground lit up in the middle of miles and miles of black space. They had told me that they would place two cars at the corners of the runway threshold with their head-lights pointing down the strip, not in my eyes as I approached, and they said the cars would be to the side, not in my approach path. One other car was placed halfway up the strip with the headlights aimed in the direction of my landing roll. I made a low pass and a 180-degree turn to downwind, then turned base and final. They had said the approach was clear, but I didn't feel safe making a shallow approach over dark woods. I had about a quarter moon, so that helped a bit. I had checked the sectional maps for power lines and towers, but the sectionals don't show high trees. But my friends did exactly what they said they would, and the landing and roll out on the unlighted 2,000 feet strip, which was unfamiliar to me in the middle of dense woods, preceded uneventfully.

The following morning, I took off with two spotters with binoculars to look for bears. One person scanned the starboard side and one checked the port side. The leaves had fallen from the trees, and the ground between the trees could easily be seen. The men explained that the bears were preparing to hibernate and would be foraging for food to last them through the winter sleep. Now the men had a walkie-talkie and could communicate with their pals on the ground; the only problem was that we never spotted any bears.

The day that I married Marjorie, we flew out of Somerset to Washington National for the start of our honeymoon. The following day we flew to Atlanta with plans to fly the next day to the Bahamas. When we returned to the Atlanta airport the next morning, we were told that an airliner had spun up its jet engines and overturned the Tripacer. The airline gave us tickets to the Bahamas and repaired our plane, but we were without our plane for a period of time.

Marjorie and I loaded the Tripacer with a motor scooter, camping gear and mask, fins and snorkel, and flew out to California. We flew low. The field borders are all north-south or east-west, and we simply followed the hedge rows until we got to Denver when we climbed up to go through the mountain passes below the mountain tops in the mornings before turbulence began. We were flying across Utah when we noted a straight black streak on the ground. I knew what it was; we were flying over the Bonneville

Salt Flats. We dropped down and landed, had a picnic lunch, then continued on. There was no taxiing; we just took off straight ahead in the same direction that we landed from the point where we stopped. In those days nobody cared if you flew below the walls in the Grand Canyon; now this is prohibited. We camped at the Canyon and flew below the walls. We got to California but we didn't stop; we just overflew it and landed at Catalina, where we camped.

The Tripacer was the beginning of 41 unbroken years that I was an airplane owner. When Marjorie died, I sold the Tripacer and bought the Mooney.

Starting out in California. The back seat was removed to accommodate all of our gear. In addition to sleeping bags, air mattresses, tent and clothes, we packed the Centaur motor scooter (110 lbs) seen just in front of the plane's main wheel, and a four man rubber life raft powered by a 3 ½ H.P. outboard motor which can be seen to Marjorie's right. Scuba gear was limited to masks, fins, snorkels, spear gun and knife. The tanks could not be taken because these would exceed the maximum allowable weight. With full fuel tanks we weighed a few pounds less than 2,000 lbs. maximum takeoff weight.

Grand Canyon Airport. We have packed our camping gear on the scooter and will follow mountain trails into the woods where we will set up the tent and spend the night.

At the Bonneville Salt Flats.

We stop for lunch. No airport necessary.

Marjorie

Another call to the emergency room just like hundreds before; an intern, within a few weeks of becoming a licensed doctor, was always rushing. But this was one call that will always be remembered. As I hurried past the new receptionist, I was met with a warm smile from an attractive schoolgirl. This dark-haired lass followed me in the emergency room ostensibly to deliver a chart, but she lingered beside me longer than that task required. Soon eye contact was made for a second time, and we both smiled.

What followed was a courtship for about a year and a half, and one evening, in a fever of emotion, I asked her to marry me. I must confess that I questioned my judgment for a short time before the wedding. Could a free spirit like me ever settle down? But afterwards, I never doubted that that was the best thing that had ever happened to me up until that time.

Marjorie was an amazing, intelligent, beautiful girl, 14 years younger than me. We courted when she was 18 and married when she was 19. She excelled in everything that she attempted, and she took part in a myriad of activities. She played the flute—and became so proficient that she was a soloist with an orchestra concert at the Atlantic City boardwalk. She took a course in modeling—and was named model of the month at her school in Pittsburgh, Miss Seven Springs at the local ski resort, and runner-up in Pennsylvania state competition. Later she studied acting and showed promise in dramatics. I taught her to fly and eventually she exceeded me in that field. She went on to become a flight instructor, something that I never did.

One day when I was working at my residency at the New York Eye and Ear Infirmary, a uniformed policeman asked to see me. He said there had been an accident and Marjorie was dead. She had been instructing a student, and both had been killed during stall practice. One week before she had written in a book flap, *"Life is not a brief candle to me. It is a blazing torch which I want to experience and pass on to future generations."*

Following this I sold the Tripacer, put all of my savings together, and bought the Mooney from Tom Mitchell, who was her employer at the time of the accident. On the first flight, which was to Venezuela to climb Angels Falls, the engine was found to be using massive amounts of oil and the avionics failed. When attempting to have this rectified, I wrote the following to Tom's mother: *"I have lost the two things which meant the most to me; Marjorie and my airplane. I dreamed of taking long-distance flights by myself but imagining that Marjorie was at my side as she always had been."*

Angel Falls

This story begins in a bar room in Cuidad Bolivar in 1921. Jimmy Angel was having a few drinks in this prospecting town at the edge of the jungle in Venezuela when he was approached by an old prospector named J. R. McCracken. McCracken said he wanted to hire Jimmy's plane. Jimmy Angel was a bush pilot who had a reputation of being able to land and take off in places where other pilots couldn't. Jimmy wanted to be paid in advance because McCracken didn't look like he had enough money to pay for it. McCracken then opened a cloth bag and poured out a pile of gold nuggets.

McCracken and Angel agreed to a price, and they flew south a few days later. Everything south of Cuidad Bolivar in those days was jungle, essentially unexplored, and inhabited only by native Indian tribes. Little has changed to this day. About 100 miles south of Cuidad Bolivar, the thick green rain forest is interrupted by multiple flattop mountains similar to what we might call mesa in Arizona or Utah. The mesas in Venezuela were formed by different forces than the mesas in the western United States. In the western states, most mesas were formed by water erosion. In the South American jungle, they were formed by forces within the earth pushing the areas skyward. This led Sir Arthur Conan Doyle to write his classic book *The Lost World*. In it he imagined that dinosaurs and pterodactyls survived on top.

Angel Falls. Our climbing route was on the right side of the falls.

McCracken told Jimmy to fly this way and that way until he had Angel lost. This was not easy as Jimmy Angel was familiar with the terrain from the air. Eventually, McCracken pointed to a small clearing and asked Angel if he could land there. Jimmy successfully landed in the clearing and McCracken left while Angel stayed with the plane. Several hours later, the prospector returned with as much gold as the little plane could carry. They flew back to Cuidad Bolivar and the old prospector died within six months from overindulgence in alcohol and women. Jimmy Angel spent the rest of his life searching for the clearing where he had landed. Clearly, McCracken had found a major gold vein within walking distance of the landing area.

One day, while Jimmy was searching, he came upon what he described as water flowing out of the clouds above and into the clouds below. He flew to the top and the bottom and measured the altitude. He had discovered the world's highest waterfall flowing from a flat tableland called the Auyan-Tepui. In the language of the Indians, Auyan-Tepui means Devil Mountain. So it is a bit of irony that Angel Falls descends from Devil Mountain.

Angel Falls, 3,282 feet in the unbroken first drop, is three times the height of the Empire State Building, twenty times as high as Niagara Falls, and three quarters of a mile in its total drop. The water takes 14 seconds, nearly one quarter of a minute to fall from the top to the bottom.

In 1937, Jimmy Angel attempted to land on the top of the Auyan-Tepui near the origin of the falls. His high-winged plane became mired in a marsh and was unable to take off. Jimmy and his two passengers were able to get off of the mesa in two weeks by descending in the back where the cliff is not vertical.

In 1968, the Explorers Club of Pittsburgh organized a major expedition to Angel Falls. It was supported by National Geographic and a large number of corporate and individual sponsors. Approximately fifty people were involved and flown to Venezuela in a large transport plane. The Venezuelan government provided a helicopter. There were eight goals. They wanted to parachute and land on top of the Auyan-Tepui near Jimmy Angel's plane, which remained where he had landed in 1937. Incidentally, the plane was later removed by a Venezuelan military helicopter and now is enshrined on a pedestal in a park in Cuidad Bolivar. Another goal was reaching the brink of the falls. Others had reached Angel's plane by ascending the gradually sloping south side, but nobody had ever been to the brink of the falls. They planned to study the flora and the fauna on top of the mesa. They found unique species of plants on the top, but there are no animals and no dinosaurs. They exploded dynamite in the river on top to determine if any fish lived there. There are no fish on top. Any fish would have had to evolve there because there was no way they could climb to the top. They wanted to determine from where all the water comes. It became obvious that the rivers drained 100 square miles of rain forest on top. And also, they planned to climb the face of the cliff by the falls. All of these goals were accomplished except climbing the face. The vertical face of the Auyan-Tepui, from which the highest waterfall in the world descended, had never been scaled. The climbing group expected to climb it in one day but only got a short distance up the cliff. They were in the rainy season and the rock was slimy and slippery. John Timo had suggested adding the climb to the goals in the planning stage and was in the first attempt. One year later, in 1969, he organized a second trip to Angel Falls with only one goal, to ascend the vertical cliff. This time they attempted to climb during the dry season, when the rock was not so slippery. During the wet season, they had no problem obtaining water from the many springs on the wall. But this time the springs had gone dry. They ran out of water and were stopped by a major overhang about 400 feet from the summit. In late 1970, Timo called me in New York and asked me to go on the third attempt. He wanted me to fly the team to Angel Falls in my airplane. After collecting donations to support the previous two unsuccessful attempts, the money sources had dried up like the springs on the Auyan-Tepui. This was to be a frugal trip, self-financed by the impoverished climbers themselves.

Marjorie had just died about four months previously, and I was entitled to two weeks of vacation from my Otolaryngology—Head and Neck Surgery residency in New York. I decided to go, but on one condition. John had in mind that I would fly the plane to South America and deep into the jungle, then wait at the bottom while the climbers ascended the mountain. I would fly them down, but only if I could climb with them.

I picked up my new purchase, the 1965 Mooney airplane, at Linden airport in New Jersey. Tom Mitchell left it there with a note. This was to be my first flight as the airplane's owner. I then flew to Pittsburgh to pick up my two passengers, John and George. We loaded some climbing gear—most of it had been shipped ahead—and began our two thousand eight hundred mile trip to Caracas.

John Timo, age 28 and from Pittsburgh, was the organizer and leader of the trip. I had met him at Seven Springs, a Pennsylvania Ski Resort, where for one winter I was the doctor caring for ski injuries and John was the X-ray technician. John was younger than me but a serious and dedicated person. He had devoted virtually all of his spare time in the past two years planning, practicing climbing, and arranging this trip. He had the incontestable notion that this time, failure was not an option.

George Bogel, age 26 and also from Pittsburgh, was an experienced climber. He lived to climb. He wore a down-curving Mexican moustache and shaved his head to hide his premature balding. He died a year or two later in an avalanche while climbing Nanga Parbat in Pakistan. His body was never recovered.

We flew south to Fort Lauderdale, stopping for fuel in Charleston. From Fort Lauderdale we followed the windward and leeward island chain, stopping for fuel in Great Inagua and Grenada. At night we rolled out our sleeping bags and slept under the wing. Next stop was Caracas, where we met for the first time the fourth member of our team.

David Nott is an Englishman who lived in Caracas, Venezuela. He was an experienced climber and had taught in a mountain climbing school. He earned his living as a foreign correspondent for a London newspaper. Thirty years later, after he retired, I visited him where he now lives in Guatemala. At that time he said, "Now that I am retired I can tell you that I was employed by the British Intelligence Service." He said he was similar to James Bond and even had a code number with the number seven as part of it. Dave was 42 at the time of the climb and I was 38. In 1972 he wrote the story of our adventure in a book, *Angels Four*, published by Prentice-Hall

Joseph Jesensky, age 65, had flown commercial from Akron, Ohio, to accompany us. He would not be on the climb, but he was a major contributor to the expedition. Mr. Jesensky was an illustrator and had made a study of waterfalls. He liked all waterfalls but Angel Falls, being the world's highest, was his favorite. He corresponded with every explorer who had ventured into the area. He kept records, and from the information which he obtained from others, drew the most accurate maps of the region. He became the world's expert on Angel Falls. At the 1968 World's Fair in New York, the Venezuelan government hired Joseph Jesensky to prepare the exhibit on Angel Falls. But Joseph had never traveled. He was what is known as an armchair traveler. He had never been to South America and, of course, had not seen Angel Falls. I flew him in the Mooney to see the falls, and he said this was the highest point in his life. For the rest of his life we exchanged Christmas cards, and Joseph Jesensky died in 2008 at the age of 103.

I left for Camarata with George Bogel and Joseph and some of our gear. The round trip was 1,000 miles. I refueled halfway there in Cuidad Bolivar because there would be no fuel south of there and I would have to fly there and return. In Camarata, there was a mission where George and Joseph could stay while I flew back to Caracas to pick up John and David. Camarata was also to be the location where we would begin our river trip to the base of Angel Falls.

John had been having a terrible time because our dry powdered rations had not yet arrived from New York. They arrived almost at the same time that I got back to Caracas, and we got immediately in the Mooney and departed again for Camarata. We landed in Cuidad Bolivar after dark with rockets exploding around us. It was New Year's Eve. Upon departing the plane, I saw the oil streaks along the fuselage from the cowling to the tail. I refrained from telling the others for a while, but at dinner I had to tell them. We had to find a sober mechanic to look at the plane on New Year's Day, which was not easy, and he had to manufacture a wrench of the proper size to tighten the gasket bolts. After a day of problems, we felt we had the plane in safe enough condition to continue the flight. We released brakes for takeoff at 4:40 PM. We had 175 miles of trackless jungle to cross and had to arrive before dark, as there were no lights at any air strip south of Cuidad Bolivar—nothing but black jungle. We followed the Caroni River to the much smaller falls at Canaima. Then we had to cross or go around the Auyan-Tepui before it was dark. Soon the mountain loomed up in the gathering darkness. I pushed the throttle forward and climbed above it. Now we were in shifting clouds with only occasional holes to see the ground below. We passed over Angel Falls but gave it no thought. Our concern was with the rapidly approaching darkness. We were only eight degrees above the equator, and near the equator the time of twilight is short. There is a sudden shift from light to darkness. There was minimum light even though we were flying at a higher altitude. A small hole appeared with a river in it. John said he thought it was the Acanan. I put the nose of the plane nearly straight down and dove into the small hole between the cliffs and the clouds. Under the clouds, John guessed we should try turning right. Fortunately, he guessed correct because a short distance up the river we spotted a building, the mission. I knew the dirt strip was on the right, and I went straight in as the last light faded from the sky. I couldn't even see to the end of the strip. It was total blackness.

The next morning I replenished the oil and took Jesensky, Timo, and Bogel to see Angel Falls. This was not a pleasure sightseeing trip. John wanted to study and photograph the upper third of the climb. Two years ago, they had been stopped on the last 500 feet by overhung rock and lack of water. He was searching for a route around the overhang, but the danger was that we might end up on a pinnacle instead of the main body of the mountain. The clouds hung around the summit and we only got occasional glances at the rim, where we wanted to further define our route, but Joseph got good views of the majority of the falls. He would remember this day for the rest of his life.

We dropped Joseph off at Canaima. A small hotel is located there with several rooms that have a view of the Canaima falls, which have a drop of about thirty feet. There also is an airstrip. David, being a newspaper reporter, had made arrangements with Radio Caracas Television to film our climb from a small plane, which would be stationed at Canaima. We had a small radio to contact the plane when it came by. Jesensky would be our front man in Canaima. I then topped the engine with oil and flew back to Camarata.

We left on our sixty-mile river trip to the falls at 2 PM Saturday and arrived Monday morning. We had hired four Indians with a dugout canoe and a nine-and-a-half horsepower motor. We traveled on four rivers both downstream and upstream. Some of it was smooth water and some of it was rapids. All of us, the four Indians and the four climbers, got out and pushed the boat upstream in the rapids. There are anacondas, the world's largest snakes, which lie at river's edge just under water, and there are schools of piranha, which can devour a man in a few minutes, in these rivers, but we didn't see any of them. There also are reports of native tribes who have never had contact with civilization and who may or may not practice cannibalism.

Two days and sixty miles on the river each way. We had to pull our boat, dug out of a single tree, upstream some of the way. I am the second man on the rope. The Indians all wear hats. Bogel is second on the boat and Timo is third. Knott took the photo.

After two days, we unloaded our gear and walked a three-mile trail following the Angel River to the base of the falls. We had to cross the river. David Nott, in his book, uses four words: "We crossed the river." I will elaborate. There was rushing water waist deep. John began to cross dragging a rope. He was swept off his feet several times but saved by the rope. Eventually, he made it to the other side and tied the rope to a tree. The rope was also tied on the starting side. We now could make multiple crossings moving the gear to the other side. The person in the middle of the stream was likely to have his feet dragged out from under him halfway through. When we were done, each of us was totally soaked with ice cold water that had just come over the falls.

We expected to spend four to five days climbing and descending the falls. It took us nine and a half days to reach the top, and a day and a half to come down. Part of the delay was because of me. I was an inexperienced climber, whereas the others were expert climbers. After a cold rainy night at the base, we began the climb with our day's goal, a ledge 300 feet above. We planned to carry 90 pounds of water in two containers. We needed this for drinking and preparing our dry food. Before starting up, John found that one of the water containers had been perforated during the trip. We had only eight gallons of water remaining. Now we would have no choice but to catch some water on the climb. After an entire day of climbing, we had only climbed 150 feet—a poor start for a 3,000-foot climb. Much of the slow progress this first day can be attributed to me. The first night on the wall, we had the worst location of the trip. During dinner preparation, our lantern tumbled over the edge. We would have no further light at night. A tiny tree grew on a small foothold, and David and I drove in some pitons and roped ourselves between this tree and the wall. John slept in a hammock hung from a single piton over the drop-off. All of us were roped to the spindly tree. In the morning, John led and George followed upwards over an overhang; difficult climbing with pitons and etriers. Pitons are spikes which are driven into cracks, and etriers are five-foot ladders of nylon cord and aluminum strips for steps. It was five hours before David and I left our perch. On the second day, I lost my pack over the edge. It was totally my fault, as I had secured it to a rope with which it would be pulled upwards, but my knot failed. From then on I continued with only what I wore, a tee shirt and jeans—no sleeping bag, ground cloth, or contact lens case.

We had to climb at night on the second day because we found ourselves under an overhang. Bogel had climbed it and installed a fixed rope. With a fixed rope and a belay, we felt safe to climb at night after sixteen hours of daylight climbing. We finally reached a two-foot-wide cave where we built a fire, ate supper, and slept.

Much of the climb was vegetation covered. Slimy, slippery green stuff grew on every square inch of soil that would support growth. Some of these soil patches were only one half inch thick. A climber could put his weight on it, and you could feel it slowly tearing away from the rock below it. It was necessary to move your feet to another position or the foothold would give way, leaving nothing but slippery mud. The first man had the best chance that his foot and handholds would stay in place. Each of the following climbers would tear out more of the vegetation. I was often the last climber, and was left a rare unstable foothold between areas of slick wet mud.

Timo and Bogel, who usually did the leading, did some spectacular mountain climbing tricks. John, on one occasion, jumped from a tiny ridge across a gap ten feet wide over a drop 2,600 feet to the jungle below. He landed on a nearly perpendicular slope of mud and grass, digging in his fingers and toes to control his slide. We then set up a Tyrolean on the rope, which he carried across, and pulled our packs and the other climbers across. A Tyrolean can be compared to a homemade cable car. The packs and other climbers could be clipped to the rope and pulled across the ten-foot, 2,600-foot deep gap.

I am the last person off this ledge where we spent the night to begin the seventh day of climbing.

We came into a huge break in the rock where the sides were covered with vegetation, a small palm tree grew, and a pretty waterfall flowed from the rock. The floor was covered with moss, and I was struck by the beauty of the scene. I then realized that we were the first people in the history of the world ever to view this miniature valley. Nobody had ever climbed this high, and the Indians couldn't get up here.

We had been worried that our route would lead us to the top of a pinnacle rather than the main surface on top of the Auyan-

Tepui, and just as we had feared, this occurred. However, there was a chockstone, a stone that had been wedged in the gap perhaps thousands of years ago, which formed a bridge 25 feet long, 10 feet wide between the pinnacle and the main body of the Auyan-Tepui, which we crossed above a drop of 2,700 feet.

Arriving on the main body of the mountain, we found ourselves in a strange terrain which we named the labyrinth. Channels 60 feet deep had been cut in the edge from years of erosion. It was like being in city streets with tall buildings built to the edge of the sidewalks. We wandered through the maze searching for an opportunity to climb the smooth walls. Eventually John identified a finger hold about twelve feet up the wall. He stepped on my knee, then on my shoulder followed by my head, and finally onto my hand, which I raised straight up. To gain another inch, I raised myself up on my toes while leaning against the wall, at which time he was able to get his fingertips in the crack and pull himself up to a better position, enabling him to scale the remaining elevation. He leaned over the brink and announced, "Gentlemen, this is the top."

On the top, the clouds obstructed our view. We put a camera on a rock and with a self timer took our picture. On the left is George Bogel with the Explorers Club of Pittsburgh's flag, next, David Knott with the Union Jack, then, John Timo holds the Venezuelan flag and I have an American flag.

Nine and a half days since starting the climb, the last day with only a minimum of food and having overcome appalling odds, we were the first people to climb the face of Angel Falls. And we couldn't see more than 20 yards. We put a camera with a self-timer on a rock and took our picture; four filthy vagabonds grinning into the camera holding four banners. Timo had brought tiny American, Venezuelan, and British flags and a larger standard from the Pittsburgh Explorer's Society.

We stayed on top for only about twenty minutes because we could see very little, and we had to get back down the mountain because David and I had to be back to work and we had no more food. Before leaving, we put a note in a metal film container and buried it inside an 18-inch pile of rocks, which we erected on a boulder. The note said that we were the first people to scale the face of Angel Falls and named all four of us. It then gave the date as January 13, 1970. This was incorrect—it was 1971. This was the first time this year we had written the date, and everybody writes the wrong year for a while after New Year. We now had a day and a half of rappelling down the cliff, with no food, ahead of us, most of the time in rain and chilling wind.

I am about to step backwards over the edge in a rappel on the descent. The jungle and the Churun River are 2,600 feet below. George Bogel is to the right.

We set up our rappel ropes and began our descent. We had no safety ropes, which are called, in climbing parlance, belays. We couldn't spare the rope. Everybody was on their own 3,000 feet above the jungle. The hope when we started down a rope was that we would reach a ledge where we could stand before the rope came to an end or the person rappelling might be left hanging in space with no way of getting back on the rock. Or, even worse, he might rappel off the end of the rope. To prevent this, we put a knot at the end of the rope.

When night fell, we huddled in the pounding rain on a sloping ledge covered with mud. In the middle of the night, the entire mass of mud began to slide toward the edge with all of us riding on it. Nobody was sleeping. We were sitting huddled together in an attempt to be warm. We grasped the rock to prevent the four of us sliding together over the edge. When daylight appeared we continued our descent. The very last pitch, Timo fell the last 30 feet. Imagine climbing down 3,000 feet and falling the last 30 feet. His shoulder was painfully injured but not broken. I fashioned a sling for his arm. We worked our way down over the rocks, which had over centuries fallen from the top, crossed the Angel River, and found the path down to where the Indians were to wait for us. They were gone. They left a note that said they had run out of food and would go back to the mission, then return for us. Fortunately they came motoring up the river shortly after we arrived on the bank.

A two-day trip in the dugout canoe followed. A bit revived, we got in the plane and flew from Camarata past Angel Falls to Canaima. Joseph Jesensky had caught a small plane to Caracas and an airliner to Akron. Helicopters were stationed at Canaima by oil companies who used them to prospect for oil. I had used too much gasoline going back and forth around the falls to fly back to Caracas. I begged the pilot to sell me some of their gasoline, which they kept in drums at the strip. At first he didn't want to do it, but later they succumbed to my pleading. We filled my tanks from the 55 gallon drums while filtering it through a chamois. He would take no money. No money could pay the value of aviation fuel in the middle of the jungle. I filled the engine with oil and we flew to Caracas, 500 miles over the jungle at night.

Caracas – 1971

It was a black night with no stars or moon. The airplane engine, which had sputtered a few times before, suddenly stopped. I had been flying in the clouds for hours but had just come into small break between the clouds. I headed the nose down in a spiral, trying to stay clear of the clouds.

This was the third time I had tried to fly my Mooney from Caracas, Venezuela, back to New York. John Timo, George Bogel, and I had flown deep into the Venezuelan jungle to make the first ascent of the cliff beside Angel Falls, the world's highest waterfall. It was as we were flying into the jungle that I discovered the plane's engine was using too much oil. After the climb, we flew back to Caracas and I left it at the Maiquetia Airport, where we had been told the best mechanics were, for repair. John, George, and I flew back on the commercial jet, and about two weeks later the shop called me and reported the plane had been repaired and was ready to fly. I took the red-eye on a Friday night from New York to Caracas, intending to fly my plane back and be in time to be at the hospital for work Monday morning.

The Saturday morning in mid-January was clear. The weather forecast was for excellent flying weather and tailwinds on my way home. The shop said they had replaced some gaskets and the engine was now fine. I paid the bill, which I felt was an overcharge, but if I could get home it was worth it. The shop recommended a test flight before leaving to measure the oil consumption. We filled the oil level to eight quarts, and I took off for a one-hour test flight. When I landed, oil streaks ran from the engine to the tail of the plane, and the dipstick showed barely any oil remaining in the engine.

Back in New York after returning in the airliner, I got to work on time, but I fumed about the expense and time lost by repeated trips to South America. Tom Mitchell, the man from whom I had bought the plane in Poughkeepsie, New York, kept telling me that he would repair the airplane under warrantee if I would bring it back to him. Another two weeks went by and another phone call was received saying this time the plane was certainly fixed. I took the red-eye again to Caracas on a Friday night. Another test flight the next day produced the same result—oil consumption much too high.

This time we decided to jury-rig the system to add oil in flight. We removed the oil dipstick and put a rubber hose in the oil filler port. We ran the hose through the firewall into the cabin and stuck a funnel in the other end. Now, if I held the funnel high enough, I could pour a quart of oil into the funnel and it would drain into the engine.

It was fairly late on Saturday, but still light when I took off. I had a case of airplane oil on the copilot's seat; a cord string hanging from the sun visor held the hose with the funnel high enough that the oil would drain from the funnel to the engine. It is 600 miles over water from Caracas to San Juan, Puerto Rico. In theory I had enough fuel to fly direct, but there is no place to go if I should decide that I wanted to abort the flight. I elected to follow the island chain around, which is much longer. The mechanic said I should be all right adding a quart of oil per hour. But that proved to be much too little.

The first hour was OK—I added one quart by pouring from the bottle into the funnel near the ceiling in the cabin. Long before the second hour was up, the oil pressure was dropping and flicking to zero for a moment, then back up. This indicated the oil in the engine was almost gone. I had started with eight quarts in the engine, I had added one quart, and before two hours were up most of the nine quarts were gone! It was a little more than 400 miles to Grenada, all over water, but if I had to, I could turn right and reach the northern coast of South America in about half an hour.

It was still light when I landed in Grenada, and I filled up with fuel and bought more oil. I then took off for Puerto Rico. I intended to follow the Lesser Antilles. These islands, including Saint Lucia, Martinique, Guadeloupe, Saint Kitts, and Saint Martin, are about fifty miles apart and would provide a measure of safety in case of emergency.

Shortly after takeoff from Grenada, it turned dark, and the weather, much to my surprise, turned nasty. Light turbulence turned into heavy turbulence, visibility was reduced to zero; then the lightning followed. There were lightning strikes both to starboard and port. Thus there was no chance of turning away from the weather. Pouring oil in the funnel in heavy turbulence meant that half of the quart ended on the cockpit floor.

Grenada to San Juan via the island chain is about 750 miles, but I couldn't see the islands; I couldn't see the water; all I could see was the rain dashing on the windscreen. I decided to head direct to San Juan. I don't think I was ever in the true center of a thunderstorm—that would have torn the Mooney apart—but the thunderstorms were everywhere. All I could do was plough ahead and hope I didn't hit the center of one. Modern navigation is by GPS, but I navigated by ADF (automatic direction finder) over water and VOR when I got within about 100 miles of the transmitter. Thunderstorms are notorious for making the ADF inaccurate.

After about 500 miles of open water, pitch black darkness, thunderstorms in all quadrants, and watching the oil pressure drop to zero if I failed to feed it more than a few minutes, I began to pick up the VOR at San Juan. I was within 100 miles of landing. It was about 1 AM when I shot the instrument approach at San Juan.

The next day was Sunday, and it dawned as a beautiful day—cloudless sky, light winds, and endless visibility. I refueled, cleared customs, bought another full case of oil, and filled a flight plan for Nassau. You couldn't have asked for better weather than I had for that leg of the trip. Except for the constant pouring of oil, the flight was very pleasant. Because of the extreme visibility, an island was almost always in sight and navigation was no problem.

From Nassau, I flew to Fort Lauderdale to clear U.S. customs. Each time I landed, I took on fuel and oil. The weather north to New York promised to be different from the sunny day which I had just experienced. I flew north to Savannah, dodging clouds to remain legally in visual flight conditions. In Savannah I refueled and bought more oil.

I departed Savannah about 10 PM, and shortly afterwards found myself in worse weather. I was no longer able to stay clear of clouds and flew most of the time in the clouds. Here my problem was not thunderstorms, but icing. With my flashlight, I inspected the wings and the windshield and found that I'd picked up considerable ice in the clouds. The only options were to fly higher or lower in another temperature zone. I opted for higher because there were mountains in the region. Hour after hour I flew on, instruments in the clouds pouring oil into the funnel, watching the oil pressure gauge quiver. Then the engine started running rough. I played with the mixture, checked the gas gauge, and checked for engine air inlet icing. The engine would run OK for a few minutes, then run rough again. I checked both magnetos. I was completely in the clouds most of the time.

When the engine suddenly quit, I had just come out of a cloud and passed over an airport. I kept the airport in sight and glided to a landing. The propeller was turning, but the engine had no power. It felt like the engine was idling. I don't know what airport it was, and I don't know to this day. There was nobody there. The place was quiet. There was no sign which would identify it. I was somewhere in West Virginia, I assumed. The engine was idling on the ground, and I ran the engine very lean on both magnetos. This appeared to clear the plugs. I am under the impression that the excessive oil fouled the sparkplugs, and running the engine on a very lean fuel mixture cleaned the sparkplugs. I took off, flew to Linden, New Jersey, put the plane in the hangar, and drove into New York. I arrived on time to start my day's duties at 8:00 AM Monday at New York Eye and Ear Infirmary. I never told any of my colleagues I had gone to South America over the weekend or how I returned.

Prison Riot

"Thank God you came," yelled the warden. "Maybe you can calm them. They're screaming for their medication." The entrance to the prison, the infamous "Tombs" in New York City, was bathed in the floodlights from the police cars and the television news cameras because this was front page news for all of the major newspapers and TV stations in the country. My personal goal was to sneak into the prison without being photographed or interviewed.

Perhaps I better start in the beginning. After finishing internship and passing the medical license test, I was finally a licensed doctor. I worked for two years in the Lee hospital emergency room in Johnstown during which time I got married and bought the Tripacer. I then took a one-year residency in general surgery at Conemaugh Valley Memorial Hospital under the mentorship of Dr. Richard Zimmerman. Dr. Zimmerman, a man who I grew to idolize, was a hard taskmaster but a superb teacher. He gave me an excellent foundation in surgery and instilled in me the true ethics of good medicine. He worked hard, and he expected the same from me. I was on call every other night, often after working 12 or 14 hours a day. And if he or his partner, Dr. Glenn Griffith, were called into the hospital after hours, I was expected to come in also even if I was not on call.

After the year of general surgery training, I had been accepted for a three-year residency in otolaryngology and head and neck surgery at New York Eye and Ear Infirmary. This was a prestigious position because this is the oldest specialty hospital in the United States.

The New York residency began on July first 1968, and the Pennsylvania residency ended on June 30. I asked Dr. Zimmerman for permission to leave a few hours early to arrive on time for my new position. He said no. The residency ended at five PM and I should work to that time. At five, I ran from the hospital and jumped into the driver's seat of a rented moving van, which we had packed in the preceding days, and raced at top speed, ignoring speed limits and fortunately not being stopped by the police, for New York. I arrived at the infirmary just in time for the eight AM start of new residency. I leaped out of the truck and ran into the hospital, leaving Marjorie in bumper to bumper traffic driving a huge truck with tears running down her face. She had only been to the city once before and had no idea where she was going. Horns were honking all the time. I had told her to find a parking lot to store the van until I could unload it in the evening. No parking lot would accept the large truck, and there were no cell phones at that time to communicate.

But we survived that ordeal, and I settled into the daily routine of my residency training. After a few months, I heard via the grapevine that some of the students were moonlighting as prison doctors. Moonlighting means working at night to earn extra money because the residents were paid a small amount, but barely enough to survive in New York. Moonlighting was prohibited because the residents were supposed to use their time away from the hospital to study. When I heard that one of the residents was leaving his nighttime job, I applied for his position and was accepted.

At first I was assigned to various prisons around the city and had no regular schedule, but I slowly worked my way up higher in the seniority ranking. Eventually I was working exclusively at the Tombs. The prison got this nickname because of the somber appearance outside from the street. Inside the gloomy atmosphere was worse. There were two shifts for doctors, 4 PM to 12 and 12 to 8 AM. Our hours at the infirmary ended at 4 PM and it took about half an hour to get to the prison, so we always arrived late, but the prison was used to that and had adapted to it. Our duties consisted of doing a brief medical examination for new inmates being admitted, and caring for the inmates who were housed there. New admissions could number from a few to well over one hundred every night. I listened to the heart and lungs of every admission, noted any obvious variations from normal, and took a history. Most inmates were addicts. All of them lied. I wrote what they said even though I knew it was not true. Some said they didn't use drugs because they wanted to use this as evidence in court. Some exaggerated their drug usage because they wanted to receive medication to ease withdrawal symptoms. In addition to that, I would take care of any emergencies which occurred at night and make my rounds and administer the daily medication to the inmates that had been ordered by the daytime physicians, whom I never saw. By the time the medications were passed, all of the prisoners were locked in their cells. I would go through the entire prison, which was four stories and housed hundreds of prisoners with one guard, and dispense their medications. I carried my pills in a plastic tray divided into sections. The inmates were constantly trying to con me into giving them something from my pill box which contained Valium, Methadone, and a myriad of other substances. More than once I heard a man demand me to give him pills, and when I refused, say, "I am a convicted murderer, in here for life, if I kill you it will make no difference because they can't give me any more." This was in the time when the death sentence was suspended in New York. Many people would complain of pain or other medical symptoms. I listened to them, evaluated each complaint, occasionally had the guard open the cell to examine the patient, and made a medical judgment. Anybody I felt might be truly ill, I would treat appropriately, but the majority were malingerers. Most of the other doctors ignored them and could have missed a true problem, but I listened to every complaint. I soon was regarded differently than the other doctors because if they were truly sick, they could count on me to care for them properly.

The prison authorities liked me. They were getting fewer complaints from the inmates about medical care. Occasionally, one of the doctors would not be able to come in, and I would work double shifts at the prison. When one of the doctors left, I volunteered to work 16 hours a day in the prison every weekday. The day doctors were delighted because I did a lot of their work for them. Other doctors would simply tell the guard to put complaining inmates on the sick call list for the morning. I would handle most of the simple problems and only schedule seriously ill patients requiring further evaluation for sick call. So, for the last approximately a year and a half, I worked 24 hours a day during the week. On Monday morning, I went to the infirmary for eight hours of surgical training. At four in the afternoon I left for the prison job. I arrived about half an hour after my scheduled time, then worked two eight-hour shifts, then left a half hour early to arrive at the hospital by 8 AM. I continued this routine until Friday evening. I didn't work at the prison Friday night, Saturday, or Sunday. I wanted to provide a good life for Marjorie in New York, and I succeeded. Of course, I got to sleep at the prison. I like to tell people I have more prison time than many of the prisoners.

One weekend when I was away from the prison, there was breaking news on the television. The prisoners had taken over the Tombs. They had taken guards hostage and had total control of the building. For three days they held out. The police could not storm the facility because they would kill the hostages. After three days of negotiations, the prisoners had not eaten, and they released the hostages in return for food. THAT'S WHEN I ARRIVED.

I was successful in ducking in the front door with my face away from the cameras and without talking with anybody. Any publicity could have cost me my residency and my future as a board certified otolaryngologist and head and neck surgeon. The warden immediately grabbed my arm and asked me to make medication rounds. During my normal rounds the prisoners were locked in their cells, and bars separated me from them. Now there were four stories of violent prisoners milling around the building. I grabbed my tray of medicines and with one guard to protect me, entered the fray. The inside of the prison was shambles. They had destroyed everything a vicious crowd could in three days. They had burned any areas on all four floors that had anything flammable. This was like walking through a severe earthquake area combined with a fire storm. Hundreds of addicted men crowded around me, demanding medication from my box. I maintained the same professional manner that I had before when I made my rounds, but I must confess I was a bit more lenient in handing out medication in questionable cases. But the majority of the malingerers, who would take anything I would hand them, were denied. Occasionally I was threatened, but never manhandled. Several times when an inmate would try to accost me, another inmate would defend me. Such was the respect which I had earned from treating the prisoners as citizens for about one year. The guard was of help, but we both knew that he could not control the mob by himself. I got to the deepest depths of all four floors of the prison, many times climbing over debris, and returned safely. A short time later, they began rioting again. I was able to travel the entire length of the prison. Just imagine if they would have taken me hostage. Having the doctor as a hostage would have given the rioters great leverage, and me great unwanted nationwide publicity.

The guards were given a certain number of sick days. They, of course, used these as extra vacation days. They required a doctor's note that they were healthy enough to return to work after taking a sick day off. I would sign these notes every day. I had no problem doing that, as I was not certifying that they had been ill, only that they were healthy enough to work on that day. I never took a sick day working at the prison and, to the best of my memory, in my entire working life. I scheduled myself off work occasionally, but was never too ill to report to work. I remember one occasion, when I was seeing sick patients in the prison, one malingerer after another appeared before me but I didn't feel well. I put the thermometer under my tongue and found I had a fever of 103. When I was within one month of graduating at the New York Eye and Ear Infirmary and would also be quitting at the prison, the guards came to me and said you have never taken a sick day, you can take the last month off as sick leave. But I refused to do it. I said I will be glad to do this if you want to give it to me, but not if I have to declare myself sick. So I worked the last month when I could have been paid for not working by doing what the others did. They always had regarded me as an oddball, and when I did this, they were sure that I was nuts.

Across the Atlantic in the Mooney

In the 1970s, the newspapers were full of the exploits of Max Conrad. He was a ferry pilot for Piper Aircraft Company and had set many long-distance records. I had flown many hours over water, and after reading the exploits of Max and after hearing him speak at the Flying Physicians meetings, I began to think, "Heck, I've flown over a lot of water. Why can't I fly over the Atlantic?"

(written in 1977) Often people ask why fly the ocean? The answer is that only living is not enough; a person must challenge themselves. More than anything else, the satisfaction comes from the feeling that you did it yourself. But actually I didn't do this trip by myself. The preparation of the plane was done by others and the invaluable advice was gleaned from the experienced pilots.

The first day I called Phil Waldman of Globe Aero, my pulse pounded twenty beats a minute faster. I was searching for someone to install the ferry tanks for the first Atlantic crossing. I imagined that the easiest method was to cross from Canada to Greenland to Iceland and then to Scotland. He casually commented, it would be easier to fly nonstop Gander to Shannon, remarking that that was the way his men flew almost all the time. Here at last I was speaking to someone with experience. For the first time in my life, I was dealing with someone who did not look on my plans with ridicule or at least suspicion. He didn't think of me as a foolhardy, irresponsible nut. Instead he spoke clearly and precisely of the undertaking as a normal matter. He made no effort to dissuade me, but approached it in a serious tone of voice. Later, when I was planning my around-the-world trip, it was Phil who advised me to go eastbound rather than westbound, informing me that on a world average I could probably count on about plus ten knots around the world eastbound compared to minus ten knots average if I travel westbound, making a difference of 20 knots. That was good advice.

I was impressed with the professionalism with which Phil approached the idea of transoceanic flying. His company had been in business seventeen years and had averaged 270 overseas deliveries per year, some years delivering as many as 400 aircraft. They had never lost a pilot and they had never lost an airplane. True, every ferry pilot could entertain you for days with tales of experiences, but in the long run they always delivered. When I had my plane first tanked by Globe Aero, Phil had prepared a flight plan (plan of action). He had written on tablet paper exactly how I was to cross the Atlantic. Begin fuel conservation immediately with takeoff, cut power back as soon as you clear the ground. Perhaps don't even use full power on takeoff. Climb 50 or 100 feet per minute at greatly reduced power to altitude, taking as long as necessary to get there. Use enough power to indicate 110 knots. As you lose weight by burning fuel, reduce your power to continue to indicate 110 knots. He instilled me with a lot of confidence. He also said when I get to Gander, ask if there are any other Globe Aero pilots around. They will give me good advice. He said, if the other Globe Aero pilots go, it was O.K. for me to go. If they didn't go I shouldn't go. That is where I met George Reed again.

As soon as I lumbered into Gander, I was impressed. It was no ordinary airport, its massive terminal almost empty now. The long runways were laid out during the Second World War for use as a refueling station for thousands of war-related missions. After the war, the huge terminal building was built and the Newfies, as the people from Newfoundland are known, expected a bountiful economy since this was a necessary stopping point for the expected boom in civilian American-European air traffic. Unfortunately the terminal was barely completed before the introduction of the first generation of jet airplanes with sufficient range to fly from New York to London and Paris nonstop. Now these planes report overhead to Gander oceanic F.I.R. (flight information region) and continue eastbound to Europe and west to New York. Only a small percentage of the planes, including some of the larger propeller-driven aircraft and, of course, the tiny ferry aircraft such as the Cherokees, and the small singles and the light twins, consistently stop for filling their ferry tanks and the excellent weather briefings which are available.

In response to my question whether any Globe Aero pilots were here, the amiable briefer in the control room replied, "George Reed is here. Everybody in Gander knows George, he usually stays at the Albatross, but if he's not there, I'll give you the name of a second hotel." A call to the Albatross confirmed that indeed they did know George, and sure enough, he was in his room sleeping at noontime. A sleepy voice answered the phone. George was getting some shut-eye as he was planning a 4 PM takeoff. He had one of the just introduced Aero Commander 200's, which he was ferrying for display at the Paris air show. He would meet me in the coffee shop at 2 PM.

When George Reed showed up I had charts and calculators spread out over the entire table, and he had no problem identifying me as a new and somewhat apprehensive transatlantic pilot. As soon as he walked in the restaurant door, the waitresses all got a big smile and stopped what they were doing to call out a hello to George. He greeted them all by name and asked each something specific like how the kids were or how the other was getting along with her boyfriend. It was obvious that George was not only well-known but also well liked in Gander. Even his disapproving glance at the mess I had on the table did not last long, but it was enough to know that George Reed would have folded the charts in order rather than crumple them and scatter them randomly as I had done. It was apparent I was a raw novice at flying and, if I would scatter things in this manner on a restaurant table, Lord knows what the cockpit would look like as I tried to read maps and chart a course.

George did not have the physical appearance of a movie idea of a ferry pilot. He was short of stature but long on personality. He had fifty transatlantic crossings and ten Pacific crossings to his credit at that time. In experience he was the most senior of the present Globe Aero pilots next to Phil Waldman. But George was a different type personality from Phil. After a short questioning as to whether I really wanted to do this, he ascertained that my desire could not be shaken, and he apparently resigned himself to making my trip as safe as possible. One thing, however, he said he would not do. He would not fly in formation and nursemaid any new pilot over the Atlantic. The reason for this was that he felt he would be obligated to the other pilot, and if the other plane should go down, he would be obligated to circle and remain there as long as possible so search and rescue parties could find him. Because one should stay as long as possible, this would be dangerous to him. This was the last thing which I would have wanted, to have someone fly in formation and "nursemaid me" over the Atlantic. If I had done that, I never would have felt I did it by myself.

We went up to the weather office and the briefer gave a bad report. There was a low lying in the middle of our route. It usually moved northeasterly in six to twelve hours, but this particular low had remained in place for the past twenty-four hours

(written later) In the summer of 1975 I flew to Lakeland, Florida. Philip Waldman, the owner of Globe Aero in Lakeland, had a contract to deliver New Piper airplanes all over the world. In the mid-1970s the American aircraft industry was booming and exporting many aircraft. Almost daily, several single-engine airplanes left the Piper factory in Vero Beach, Florida, for Europe, South Africa, the Middle East, Australia, and Asia. Many were tanked and prepared by Globe Aero.

In my airplane, the rear seat was removed and a 55-gallon drum was installed in its place. The copilot's was also removed and a 45-gallon tank installed. Theoretically, there was enough fuel to fly nonstop from Gander, Newfoundland, to Prestwick, Scotland.

The radios which we use to communicate over land are very high frequency (VHF) and are limited to line of sight. Because of the earth's curvature, these would not work over the ocean. We installed a high frequency radio (HF) which, in theory, would allow me to communicate with ATC (aircraft traffic control) when the Mooney was in the middle of the ocean. A hole was bored in the floor just below my feet, and a reel with a wire was mounted nearby. The antenna wire passed through the hole in the floor. We punched a hole in the bottom of a Styrofoam coffee cup, ran a wire through it, and tied a knot in the wire. The idea was, when I was in the middle of the Atlantic Ocean and wanted to talk to ATC, I was to release the brake on the reel between my feet, the slipstream would pull on the coffee cup, the coffee cup would pull on the wire, and the wire would trail as much as 100 feet behind the airplane. If I was successful in contacting ATC, reception could be improved by lengthening or shortening the antenna. Should the pilot fail to reel in the antenna prior to landing, it is possible he might experience an aircraft carrier type of tail hook landing. Should I be unable to contact ATC, I was to call on 121.5 (the emergency VHF frequency), and any airliner who could hear me would relay my position reports to ATC.

Just as valuable as the tanking service was the fact that I could sit in the lounge and hear the stories and get advice from the ferry pilots who flew all over the world in single engine airplanes as part of their routine work. The pilots were all helpful, but George Reed took me under his wing and gave me the most advice. He had over 50 trans-Atlantic flights and many trans-Pacific flights. The trans-Atlantic flights leave from Goose Bay, Labrador, or Gander in Newfoundland. Monckton is a required stop to get a permit to depart from Canada. The short written test which pilots must pass is about communication and emergency procedures. The aircraft is inspected for required equipment. Navigation over the ocean at that time was by ADF (automatic direction finding). Two ADFs were required because if one of these radios failed in the middle of the ocean, there would be no way to navigate. If I wanted to fly from Canada to England, for example, I was supposed to fly by dead reckoning to about the middle of the ocean. Dead reckoning, I hoped, had nothing to do with death; instead it meant that you calculate your estimated position from the time and speed and the forecast winds. You don't know your exact position, but that is where you would be if the forecasts were actually correct. Now we have GPS (global positioning system), and aircraft know their positions within a few meters at all times. But in those days we relied on ADF, which would indicate the direction of the signal which it was receiving. I had two ADFs installed on the panel of my Mooney because I knew I wanted to do some long-distance flying and of course, I had installed a new engine after the eventful trip back from Caracas in 1971. As I said before, the plan was to fly from Canada in the general direction of England until about halfway across the Atlantic Ocean, where I should begin to pick up BBC (British Broadcasting Company). In the beginning, the direction-finding needle would swing from one side of the dial to the other, but as you got closer, the needle fluctuations would get smaller and eventually point toward the transmitter. George Reed told a story about a ferry pilot who planned to fly to England and landed in Spain. The most frequent problems of flying a single engine plane over the ocean at that time were not engine problems, but navigation problems.

In August 1975 I flew from Florida back to Johnstown, Pennsylvania, a trip of 1,000 miles. I had often made this trip and always made one refueling stop. This time I flew nonstop on the ferry tanks. I already profited from George Reed's good advice since he had told me to take a mason jar with me in case I should have to urinate.

Two days later I left Johnstown for Moncton, New Brunswick. There the inspector checked my airplane for life raft, life vest, emergency locator transmitter, and two functioning ADFs. He gave the short written test on emergency procedures and made me sign a waiver releasing Canada of any liability. I was then authorized to fly solo over the Atlantic Ocean.

Gander was an important fueling stop for aircraft leaving for Europe during the Second World War. Now, with the advent of long-range jets, the long runways don't get much use. The controllers and meteorologist were accustomed to briefing pilots of small planes prior to crossing the ocean. The weather forecasts over the Atlantic Ocean are more accurate than the forecasts over land because the surface of the ocean is consistent, whereas the mountains and other terrain features cause greater variation in the weather patterns. This was before weather satellites were used as extensively as they are now. Instead, the wind and weather information came from airliners who reported the actual conditions during every crossing.

Preflight preparations for an ocean crossing in a small plane can take some time. First, the pilot fills all of the tanks with gas and oil. After running the engine for all of the preparatory checks, the tanks will be again filled to the absolute top prior to takeoff.

Next he swings the compass. You taxi out to the compass rose and align the nose of the aircraft to true north. You then record what the magnetic compass reads. The difference between true north and what the magnetic compass reads is called the magnetic deviation. Electrical equipment creates magnetic fields which can affect the compass. For this reason, three measurements of the deviation are recorded, the first with all of the equipment on which you will have on during daytime on the flight, the second adding the navigation lights simulating nighttime, and the third with the master switch off simulating electrical failure. Unlike an automobile, the engine of an airplane will continue to run because the spark is generated by a magneto. Each of these three readings is recorded at 45-degree intervals around a circle of 360 degrees. At 48 degrees north latitude, where Gander is located, the magnetic variation is large. It becomes less important near the equator.

A transoceanic flight plan must be filed. All oceanic flying above 5,000 feet is by instrument flight rules (IFR), so it goes without saying the pilot must be instrument rated and the aircraft IFR equipped and certified. When filing a transoceanic flight plan, you must give estimates for what time and at what latitude you will cross 45 degrees west, 30 degrees west, and 15 degrees west. It is unlikely that you will be exactly at these points at the estimated time, but you must write them down anyway. The winds are very important. They will vary in intensity and direction as you proceed.

The magnetic deviation will also change as you progress over the Atlantic. Your airspeed will increase as you burn off fuel unless you reduce power. All of these things must be incorporated into the calculations of your flight plan. In addition, you must clear customs and pay airport fees.

When I went to the metrological office the briefer said, "Oh, you can't go there now; there is a strong low in mid-Atlantic with storms and major headwinds. They usually move northward by the next day. Then you will have tailwinds the entire way." George said, "Don't worry. Just stick with us. When we leave, you leave." The next morning we checked into the weather bureau. The low had not moved. The meteorologist said that it was unusual, but it should move northward soon, and then we could have a quick trip over the Atlantic. During the day, I was continually beguiled by stories and advice from the ferry pilots. The next day it was the same. The low had not moved. George began to talk with the meteorologist about pressure flying. This is where you follow the best winds, then change direction as the winds change.

The briefer advised, "You will never make it." On the morning of the fourth day, the briefer said he had never seen a low remain in the same position this long without moving. The theoretical reason for my trip was to attend a medical meeting in England so that I could deduct a portion of the trip from income taxes as a business expense. I had scheduled myself for a limited time out of my office, and I had to be back for surgery. If I didn't leave soon, I couldn't go. George explained to me, "You can fly southeastward toward the Azores. Since the winds circulate counterclockwise around a low, you will have tailwinds. We have to deliver these airplanes by the most economical route. We would use too much fuel to fly such a devious route." So I filed a new flight plan for the Azores, and, after an extensive preflight inspection, the new inexperienced pilot departed, leaving four or five highly experienced ferry pilots waiting for the weather to improve.

After a long takeoff run the heavy aircraft lifted off the end of the runway, which ended at the ocean's edge, and the trans-Atlantic flight was underway. I took my immediate heading from the outbound beam of the VOR at Gander. For about 100 miles, my direction would be accurate. I carefully monitored the heading on my magnetic compass until the VOR signal was lost. From here on

I was to continue in the same direction until I came close enough to pick up the ADF signal from the tiny Azores Island group. This would be easy if the winds did not change and the magnetic deviation did not change. I set my gyroscopic compass to read the same as the magnetic compass. The magnetic compass fluctuates wildly with the slightest movement of the plane, but the gyroscopic compass remains steady during turbulence. However, the gyroscopic compass suffers from a defect called precession, meaning that after a period of time it would no longer match the heading of the magnetic compass. For this reason I reset the gyro to match the magnetic compass every 20 minutes.

It is 1,736 statute miles (1,500 nautical miles) from Gander to the Azores. In calm air, I calculated it would take me 13 hours and 38 minutes, but I expected some help from the tailwinds on the bottom side of the low. I would fly about ten hours with no navigation other than my own calculations. The winds were forecast to change as I moved across the ocean, and the change in the magnetic deviation was known assuming that I was where I thought I was. I would fly about 1,300 miles, then I must hit a circle of about 100 miles radius around the islands in order to pick up their signal and home in on it. If the forecast winds were incorrect or I made a mathematical error, I could miss this circle of the radio range and miss the islands. It was not the same as flying eastward toward Europe. In this case, even if you missed your planned point of land crossing, you would eventually get to Europe somewhere.

It takes quite a while to prepare a plane and do all the paperwork before taking off. I began the process about 8 AM. My actual takeoff was about 2 PM. To get the longest range, the aircraft was throttled back to low power and I made a long slow climb, taking almost an hour to reach 14,000 feet, then pulled the power even further back. The air was smooth and I flew above a cloud layer and rarely saw the ocean. After passing five degrees of longitude from Gander, I was to call oceanic control and report my position and my estimated time for the next crossing. All of this was kind of a farce because I really didn't know if I was at the point that I was reporting or not; I was just estimating that I was there. I released the brake on the antenna reel and the coffee cup pulled out the wire. I turned on the power switch and dialed up the frequency assigned to me. After about ten seconds, some indicator lights began to glow on the big black box, which contained a high frequency radio powered by vacuum tubes and had been installed by Globe Air. I pressed the microphone button, took a deep slow breath, and began my broadcast, assuming the deep calm voice that I heard the airline captains using: "Gander oceanic, this is Mooney November 300 Mike Delta reporting 45 degrees west, 45 degrees north, this time, 14,000 feet." ......Nothing but static as a response into my earphones. I let out about five more feet of wire and called again..... The response—only static. I began to reel in the wire about five feet at a time and called each five feet. I found the coffee cup pulled rather hard on the wire, and I had to use some muscle to retract the wire.

By this time I had forgotten about the deep, calm airline captain's voice and the tone was about an octave higher. I was wearing a mask that fed me some oxygen from a tank, which was by my side because I was flying above 12,500 feet. If a pilot remained at this altitude for some time without supplementary oxygen, it is possible that mental powers would deteriorate. This is a fancy way of saying he would act as if he were drunk and could easily make a dumb mistake. As a new pilot on this trans-Atlantic route, I figured I might make a dumb mistake without the help of high altitude oxygen depletion, so I better use supplemental oxygen. With each of the radio call attempts, it was necessary that I remove the oxygen mask, speak into the microphone, then put the mask back on.

Oh well, George told me to call on 121.5 and an airliner would answer and relay my message.

I called on 121.5, "Anyone reading me, I would like you to

relay a message to Gander oceanic." I waited for the answer that George said always occurred. Nothing.... At least there was no static on the VHF frequencies. If you are flying from Gander direct across to England, there is heavy airliner traffic and you almost always get a response, but there was little traffic flying southeasterly where I was heading. I tried a few more times, then returned to the HF set.

Eventually as I'm winding the antenna in and out, I hear a faint voice within the static. "November 300 Mike Delta, do you hear me? This is Gander oceanic. You have given no position report."

I immediately called back without changing the antenna length. The voice crackled, "I will give you a count so you can adjust your antenna. One, two, three, four, five, six, seven, eight, nine, ten. How do you read?"

I had adjusted the antenna length as he spoke, and when it was at maximum volume and clarity, I put on the brake. The voice on the high frequency radio came in louder and clear enough to understand over the static: "This is Gander oceanic calling November 300 Mike Delta, when you failed to report in we were looking for you."

"This is November 300 Mike Delta. I attempted to contact but was unable. Mike Delta reporting 45 degrees west, 45 degrees north, twenty-one-30 Zulu, one-four thousand. Estimate 40-40 twenty-three-thirty."

I had just told Gander that I had crossed the point 45 degrees west longitude, 45 degrees north latitude at 21:30 Greenwich time and estimated that I would cross 40 degrees west, 40 degrees north at 23:30 Greenwich time. I had been flying three and a half hours.

The ferry pilots like to depart in the evening and cross at night so that their arrival is in the daylight. I had departed at 2 PM local time so I would be arriving in the Azores in the middle of the night. One advantage to night flying is that the high frequency radio with the trailing antennae works much better at night. I was motoring along above the overcast with very little turbulence. The plane was working well, but you can be sure that I checked the engine gauges frequently.

Slowly the night fell, and I was under a starry sky above the overcast. Now my calls to Gander oceanic were answered immediately and the voice was loud and clear. I could turn the volume down so the static was barely noticeable. I flew for nine hours with no navigational help. I had to hit the circle with a radius of 100 miles for the ADF to be effective and find the Azores. This allowed me a maximum error of four to five degrees on either side of my course. Eventually, my ADF needle began to quiver and fluctuate over the entire dial. As I flew on, the fluctuations became shorter, and when the needle settled down it was right on the nose of the heading I was holding. It would have required 13 hours for me to fly to Santa Maria without tailwinds, but I reached the Azores in 11 hours. I was still flying on my ferry tanks. I had not used any fuel from the aircraft's main tanks. I was tempted to continue to Lisbon, but I thought, "No, this is my first flight and I better land and refuel." In retrospect, I'm glad I did.

It was pitch black when I landed at Santa Maria. A few years later at this airport, two 747s would collide on the ground and nearly 1,000 people would be killed. This is the most lives lost in any airplane accident. The refueling truck came to the plane and I filled the tanks. I filed a flight plan, paid the fees, and took off for Lisbon—which everybody called Lisboa.

It was only 851 statute miles (735 nautical miles) to Lisbon, and I calculated 6 hours and 40 minutes. Even though the weather was good it seemed longer, probably because I was tired. When I approached the shore of Portugal, it was daylight and I was ready to land and head for a hotel for some well-deserved rest, but I was surprised that they vectored me a long distance from the airport. They required me to fly a wide circle to the other side of the airport, taking me 50 to 75 miles longer than it would have been to fly directly and adding 30 minutes to my flight time. Finally I was cleared to land and had successfully flown solo over the Atlantic.

I found a hotel and had a good meal, and the next day filed a flight plan for Marseille, France. I love the French Riviera and had spent time there when I was in medical school in Belgium. All went well until I was halfway over Spain. Suddenly the tachometer, which measures the revolutions of the engine, dropped to zero. The engine was running fine, so I recognized that the cable to the instrument had broken. It is difficult to properly control an airplane without a tachometer. It had been set at 2,300 RPM, so I didn't touch the propeller control until I landed. I asked for a change of destination to Barcelona, Spain. There I landed and, after clearing customs, taxied to a local FBO (fixed base operator). They said they did not have the part, but I might be able to use an automobile cable. It was Saturday morning and everything would close shortly and not open until Monday. They gave me the address of a speedometer shop and he called them. They were still there and would wait for me. The mechanic removed the broken cable and I took it in a taxi to the speedometer shop. They had one which would work, but it was longer than the one on my airplane. This was to my advantage, as the reason the cable had broken was it had too sharp a bend. I brought it back to the airport and the mechanic was kind enough to immediately install it. It worked perfectly. The FAA (Federal Aircraft Administration) would not approve of putting an automobile cable in an airplane, but the part was better than the original, and I never got around to telling them about it. The automobile cable stayed in my plane and functioned perfectly as long as I owned the plane. Everybody in Barcelona was wonderful and very helpful, and I lost only one day and could continue the next morning, which was Sunday.

Now I was getting short on time, and I elected to give up the Rivera on this trip and filed a flight plan for Stockholm. I had been to Sweden before but never to Stockholm, and I always wanted to visit it. The European control marveled that I flew the entire distance from Barcelona to Stockholm in such a small plane without refueling. They didn't know I had just flown much longer distances over the Atlantic.

Ah, Sweden—the people are so nice, the clubs are so much fun, and the girls are so pretty. It was everything that everybody said it was.

After two days I sadly departed for Bergen, Norway, to refuel to begin my return over the Atlantic. From Bergen to Reykjavik, Iceland, was about seven hours. This now seemed a short flight compared to my previous flights. I had been to Reykjavik many times before. When I was a medical student in Belgium, I often flew back and forth on Icelandic Airlines because they were cheaper than any other airline. They stopped in Iceland and then continued to Europe. I had never had the opportunity to see much of Iceland, so this time I stayed overnight and toured the region.

A day later I filed a flight plan for Narsarsuaq, Greenland, with the intention of continuing to Gander if fuel and weather allowed. About six hours later, I crossed the lower part of the Greenland icecap and realized I had plenty of fuel for Gander. Another six hours and I was over Gander once again with adequate fuel. I cancelled IFR and continued VFR (visual flight rules). I figured that now I was over land and had plenty of options to land before my fuel was depleted, so I continued to New York City. Landing at an international airport with customs was required; I decided to land at Kennedy. I had often landed at LaGuardia and Newark, and I wanted to land at Kennedy just once. At the present time none of these airports would welcome small planes, but they cannot legally prohibit us from landing. The airports are supported by tax funds from all citizens, and are not designed only for the airlines to make money. We do, however, greatly slow down the takeoffs and landings because we have a slower airspeed than the jets.

Well, it was the middle of the night and I landed at Kennedy. I kept up my airspeed until touchdown, but it still slowed traffic flow. I was cleared to taxi to one of the same gates the airliners use. The reason for this was I had to clear customs, and this was where customs was located. It took me about an hour to clear customs, and I had to pay 100 dollars for the privilege of using this commercial gate with a jet-way during the hour. I suppose that is how they dis-courage small planes from landing—charge one hundred dollars an hour for parking. This was a lot of money to me in 1975. I'm glad that I landed at Kennedy this one time, but I wouldn't do it again. I had flown 21 hours from Reykjavik to New York City.

Greenland

"If you haven't landed at Bluie West One, you have missed one of life's biggest thrills. BW-1 is 52 miles up a fjord with walls several thousand feet high, numerous dead-end offshoots, no room to turn around, and usually an overcast below the tops of the walls. You have to get it right the first time." So writes army pilot George James about his ferry flight.

One year after having survived my first round trip to Europe in a single-engine plane, I decided to do it again; this time I would take a passenger and visit Europe and Africa.

Pat, my girlfriend at that time, officially was not a passenger. Since we had permission to take off ten percent over gross, passengers were prohibited. A copilot, however, was allowed. This copilot could possess only a student's license. That made it simple. A class-three aviation medical examination issued by an Aviation Medical Examiner is also a student pilot's license. And I was a medical examiner.

When the mechanic at Globe Aero who removed the rear seat in the Mooney and installed a 55-gallon drum as a ferry tank heard that I was taking a girl to Europe, he said, "That's like taking a ham sandwich to a banquet." The avionics department put in a

H.F. (high frequency) transmitter and receiver with a 100-foot wire antennae on a reel between my feet. We pulled the wire through the hole in the floor and attached the Styrofoam coffee cup.

This time we would follow the route across the Atlantic, which was built to supply the troops during the Second World War. After I repeated my written test in Moncton and the aircraft was inspected, we headed for the first station of this route, Goose Bay. This airport, as well as Gander, was built to refuel aircraft starting their journey across the ocean to join the battle going on in Europe. Goose Bay, Labrador, is one hundred miles from the open ocean up a body of water called Hamilton Inlet. Gander is to the south on Newfoundland Island and is on the ocean. Both airports have long runways to accommodate overloaded bombers leaving for Europe. The military route is Goose Bay; 777 statute miles to Bluie West one in Greenland; 770 statute miles to Reykjavik in Iceland; and 844 statute miles to Prestwick, Scotland. Thousands of planes, including those that bombed Germany, traveled this route during the early 1940s. With the development of jets that have the range of crossing with no refueling, both Gander and Goose Bay have lost their traffic and value.

We topped the tanks, spun the compass, and did the paperwork in Goose Bay. The weather was satisfactory. The navigation to Greenland was much simpler—follow the VOR outbound for about 100 miles, and by that time you can pick up the ADF beacon in Greenland and follow it in. The fun begins when you get to the coast. We were flying at 12,000 feet above a light mist, spotting an occasional iceberg below. You can see the mountains of Greenland through the mist more than one hundred miles away. They are very high. As we approached the largest island in the world, the icebergs became more numerous. This is the time you must pray for good weather because the weather can change in an instant. Bluie West One is sixty miles up a winding fjord. Ernest Gann writes in his bestselling book *Fate is the Hunter*, "There are three fjords. You will notice that they all look exactly alike. But only one is the right fjord which leads to the field. The others are dead ends and you are advised to stay out of them unless you have learned how to back up an airplane."

Navigation became slightly better when on July 6, 1942 the supply ship s/s Montrose hit the wall and sunk in the fjord. "It is about thirty miles up the correct fjord on the north side," Gann continued. "If you do not see that freighter you are in the wrong fjord... You will not actually see the field until you have made the last turn around that cliff; then it will appear all of a sudden so you'd better have your wheels down early. It's a single runway with quite an incline.... You have to land whether you like it or not."

This is the terrain into which we were heading. The ADF brought us to the coast, but it would be no help in choosing the inlet. The advisors had said there would be three fjords. Take the middle one. But I saw more than three. I saw four—or is that another one? Could there be five? There were three that looked wider and looked like they went further back than the others. I guess they don't call those others fjords, just deep crevices in the mountain. Well, here we go. They say there is no room to turn if you later determine that you are in the wrong one. That's what they call "being up the wrong fjord." The predicted overcast covered the tops of the cliffs on each side. We were flying in a tunnel. Four eyes close to the windshield stared ahead, watching for turns in the stony tunnel and looking for a sunken ship. It would be fifteen minutes before we would know if I had chosen the correct tunnel. When that rusty hull, stern sticking upward, came into view I had never seen a prettier sight. From here on all we had to worry about was, don't hit the walls. We then came on a wider area and turned right and there she lay; right in front of us was the runway threshold. The rollout was short on the steep uphill grade. No brakes were required. We used moderate power to taxi uphill to the gas pumps.

We crawled out, stretched, and headed for the restrooms. We had flown six hours and twenty minutes. Fuel in Greenland is not cheap. Neither was the food, which was served cafeteria style in the army barracks, which had been converted to a hotel. However, the food was filling and tasty. The Eskimo name for Bluie West One is Narsarsuaq. There are several spellings. You might wonder where the name Bluie West One came from. Before the Second World War, the U.S. Navy gave code names to areas all over the world. Iceland was named Bluie. In anticipation of the war, and planning for a transatlantic aerial supply line, the navy surveyed the coasts of Iceland for possible locations for airstrips. They found eight on the west coast and named them Bluie West one through eight. Narsarsuaq was the first one as you headed northward.

We filed a flight plan to Reykjavik, the capital of Iceland. Two hours on the ground and we were ready to go. The landing at Narsarsuaq is always uphill, and the takeoff is downhill. You accelerate fast and take off early. We could see light above, so we circled and climbed through the overcast over the lagoon. Soon we broke out in the sunlight. We squinted our eyes in the brightness. We were 61 degrees latitude, only five degrees below the Arctic Circle. At this time of the year, above the Arctic Circle there could be 24 hours of daylight. We would have only a brief period of darkness. We climbed above the coastal mountains and headed eastward over the Greenland Ice Cap.

Over 80% of Greenland is covered by an ice sheet, commonly called the ice cap. It is almost 1,500 miles long in the north-south direction and 684 miles wide at its widest point. It averages about two miles thick and is three miles thick at its deepest point. We would cross it in the south where it was narrower. In the right light, the ice blends into the sky and there is no horizon. It is nearly flat with a mean height of 7,000 feet. But it is domed and rises to 9,800 feet at its highest. There are mountain ranges on the east and west coast. In effect, this acts like the sides of a giant cup. The weight of the ice has caused the ground under it to sink below sea level. There are many stories of aviators being marooned on this icy wasteland. One light plane was flying above the cap when the pilot realized that the plane was not moving. The surface had gradually risen to meet his altitude, and he had "landed" with his wheels up in the soft snow. He claimed that he was not aware that he was no longer flying for a period of time. According to legend, this has happened more than once.

The story of the "lost squadron" is absolutely true. On July 15, 1942, six fighter planes and two B-17 bombers set out for England but never completed the journey. Due to bad weather and low fuel, they crash landed on the ice cap. All 25 crew members were rescued, but the eight planes were left behind and were gradually entombed in ice. One of the planes, a twin engine P-38, built at Torrance airport within walking distance from my present medical office, was recovered from its burial site about 250 feet below the surface. It is now flying again. The project required seven expeditions over 11 years and several different aviation explorers to pull the plane, piece by piece, out of the glacier. Years ago, when the project was just beginning, our Flying Physicians Association had held a meeting in Atlanta, where the organizer of the undertaking lectured to us about his dream. At that time they had already reached the plane using ice melting heated drills. It appeared to be intact.

As predicted, it was very difficult to discern a horizon. The sun was behind us, which is the worst angle for vision. I climbed to 11,000 feet and flew on instruments. At that time, nobody knew accurately how high the ice was. Now satellites can measure it to within ten centimeters, and it is constantly changing.

The ice pack gradually became lower, and, as we came to the west coastal mountain range, we left this weird landscape and were once again over water salted with icebergs. Another six hours and we were in Reykjavik, Iceland. The night in the Icelandic Hotel at the airport was actually a day because it was always light. After our rest and food, we flew southbound seven hours to the warmer climate of Prestwick, Scotland.

Casablanca – 1976

Suddenly a convoy of police cars, red lights blinking and sirens screaming, accompanied by military vehicles, raced to our holding point and surrounded the aircraft.

A few hours before, we had begun preparations to depart the Casablanca International Airport. The afternoon before, Pat and I had flown there from Spain in my single-engine Mooney airplane. The inside of a Mooney is about the size of the inside of a Volkswagen beetle; the engine is a four-cylinder, 200-horsepower Lycoming. I had removed the rear seat and replaced it with a 55-gallon drum. This provided us with enough fuel to fly from Canada to Greenland, then Iceland and Europe. Now we were going to fly to Marseille, France.

The departure formalities are always complicated and time consuming for international flights at all airports, but here they appeared much worse than usual. File the flight plan, check the weather, fuel the plane, pay the landing fees, pay the parking fees, pay the departure fees, report to the airport administration, get their stamp on your flight plan, report to the police, get their stamp, report to customs, get their stamp, report to passport and immigration, get their stamps. Everybody appeared gruff and suspicious. We had our luggage thoroughly inspected several times. Sometimes we were sent back to previous offices for further paperwork. After about three hours of this, we were eventually given permission to leave. We climbed into the plane, started the engine, and got taxi clearance. I taxied out to the runway, did the engine run up, and reported ready for takeoff.

From a distance I heard the sirens. The police and the soldiers poured out of the cars and trucks with their weapons out. The soldiers surrounded the plane with automatic rifles, and the police had their pistols out of their holsters. A loudspeaker blared, "STOP THE ENGINE AND GET OUT." Of course we did as instructed. Two policemen in plain clothes instructed us to stand at a point about fifty feet away from the airplane. He left three soldiers with machine guns to guard us. They stood around us with their guns pointed approximately at our shoes and their fingers on the triggers. After standing still for a long time, I made one small step toward the plane to shift the weight on my feet. All three of the soldiers raised their machine guns to their shoulders and pointed them directly at us. I didn't take a second step.

They proceeded to essentially take the airplane apart. They removed our bags and took everything out. Every piece of clothing was taken out, felt completely with their hands, and shaken. Every item was given the same inspection. When I protested that we had already been inspected several times, I was told to keep quiet and the guns were raised. They opened all of the inspection plates on the airplane with screwdrivers and inspected inside the wings and inside the fuselage. They opened the battery. They crushed every one of Pat's Tampax into powder. They asked us no questions. When I asked what they were looking for, I was told to keep quiet.

For at least forty-five minutes this continued. They just didn't want to give up. They were determined to find something. Whenever any of the search crew would pause in the search, the chief would shout further instructions for a deeper and deeper search. About an hour after they had begun, even the supervisors began to real-ize that they were not going to find any contraband. They couldn't believe that we were clean. The chiefs held a conference and the entire troop, police and soldiers, departed. There was no apology, no explanation. One of the lesser officers handed me a part of the airplane that he had dismantled before he got in the car with the others and left; I was able to put the plane back together and reload it in about an hour. We departed as soon as the plane was ready to go without rechecking the weather, although officially the forecast which we had was no longer valid. They couldn't believe that we had flown to Africa, and stayed less than 24 hours, just to say we had landed in Africa.

Round the World in a Mooney

After crossing the Atlantic Ocean four times in the airplane which I had bought for $12,700, I wanted to do the ultimate—that is, fly the Pacific. Besides my good friend, Henning Huffer, who had done it several times, had enthralled me with tales of cruising the balmy South Sea Islands in a light plane and about the enticing females who inhabited the region. With good tailwinds, I could hop over the Atlantic in 16 hours and arrive in time for a late evening dinner, but the Pacific—well, I'll have to play hopscotch on the islands.

I flew out to Flo Air in Wichita and discussed the problem. The owner and manager grabbed a flexible ruler and took me down to the guy who made the tanks. He began to measure the interior of the Mooney, which is about the size of an old Volkswagen beetle. After a few minutes he put his head outside the door and spoke to the head honcho. "How much fuel does he want to put in it?"

"As much as you can."

"OK, but he'll have a hell of a time getting in the door."

"That's OK, he's kind'a skinny."

So they built tanks that went from floor to ceiling everywhere but the little left seat where I was supposed to sit. They had to build them in sections just to get them through the only door, which was on the right side of the airplane. Of course, the back seat was taken out and replaced with tanks that went from floor to ceiling. The right seat was also removed and a tank went from the floor to within ten to eleven inches of the ceiling. For me to get into the pilot's seat, I had to shimmy through a slot, ten to eleven inches wide, feet first. I learned to take off my belt just to narrow my body the width of the belt buckle, and also to exhale, and I took off my shoes, pushed them in ahead of me, and put them on after I had squeezed through my slot. This ten-inch opening was also to be my escape hatch if I should ever want to get out of the plane in an emergency, including exiting in the water onto my life raft. My life raft and emergency equipment including flares, portable emergency locator transmitter, and life vest, I would position on the wing while I crawled in. I put a short rope on each piece of emergency equipment and laid the ends of the rope on the tanks in the slot before I entered. Once inside, I would use the ropes to pull the equipment close enough that I could reach through the slot, grasp the equipment, and pull it into the slot above the tanks. It was necessary to close and latch the door from the inside. I could swing the door almost shut with the tips of my fingers, but latching it was more difficult. I had to reach over the front tank and blindly find the door handle and latch it. Once again, by exhaling and reaching as far as possible, I was able to close and lock the only door. Then I stuffed the space where I entered with my life-saving equipment.

The front tank occupied the entire space where a copilot would sit and also covered the right side of the instrument panel. Many important flight instruments are on the right side of the panel, including the tachometer. To solve this dilemma, I held a mechanics mirror between the tank and the instruments when I wanted information from them. A mechanics mirror is similar to a dentist's mirror except that it has a hinge on the mirror and a small lever on the handle to change the angle of the mirror when it is in place. The instruments, of course, read backwards when viewed through a mirror, but I adjusted to that after a short time. Crowded also into this space was the oil addition pump, which allowed me to replace engine oil in flight. Completely filled with fuel, the plane would be 25% over legal gross weight with a center of gravity just at rearward edge of the envelope. To move the center of gravity forward, to put it within the limits, a 15 lb. sack of buckshot was wired in the forward engine compartment. Permission to take off at 25% over gross was obtained from the engineering department of the Federal Aviation Agency in Oklahoma City. I had gotten permission to take off at 10% over gross on my previous trips over the Atlantic. This can be issued from the local GADO (General Aviation District Office).

We installed a HF (high frequency) set with a reel for the antennae between my feet. The antennae, which would trail 100 feet behind the plane, had a Styrofoam coffee cup on the trailing end just as we had for the other trips; but for this trip I rented a primitive portable loran-A, which in theory should help me find the islands. At least it would keep me amused watching all the sine waves dancing around on the cathode ray tube, and it might even help me to navigate.

With all this equipment, it looked like I was ready to fly around the world. Packing was no trouble, as I had almost no place to take personal items. A change of clothes and a toothbrush pretty well filled up the space allotted to my stuff.

In the morning of August 19, 1977, I took off from Johnstown for Bangor, Maine, to clear U. S. Customs. Next stop was Moncton, Canada. After clearing customs, I reported to the Canadian Aviation Office to take the same written test which I had done two times previously when I flew the Atlantic. The pleasant official also inspected my plane for adequate safety gear and communication and navigation equipment. He said I passed and issued me a permanent clearance. I would no longer have to stop at Moncton and take the test. After three trips, pilots are issued permanent clearances. He said my clearance was very rare because it was issued to me as an individual. Most ferry pilots worked for ferry companies, and their clearances were only valid as long as they continued to work for the same company. Mine had no such restriction. I took advantage of this about nine months later when I flew to Europe again. I didn't have to stop at Moncton and be tested and inspected. After Moncton, it was Gander again. I left from Goose Bay whenever I was flying the northern route to Greenland and Iceland, which I did when I had a passenger on board. But I left from Gander if I was going nonstop across by myself. This time I didn't fill my ferry tanks when I left Gander, and I flew nonstop over Ireland, over England, over France, landing at Karlsruhe, Germany. This was because Henning Huffer lived there. Henning is by vocation a lawyer and by avocation a pilot and adventurer. I first met Henning at Kerrville, Texas, at a Mooney Convention. He was flying around the world at that time in a Mooney, and I had just completed my first trip to Europe and back. Henning had flown from Germany to the Fiji Islands eastbound via Asia. He had spent about a year and a half there wandering around between the islands until he ran out of money. Now he was on his way home. He had stopped at the Mooney convention to see if he could raise some money—possibly from the Mooney Company—to continue his trip. We immediately became friends because of our common interests, flying over oceans in Mooneys, adventures, and girls. Henning had left his aircraft at Houston, Texas, some distance east of Kerrville, and on my way back to Pennsylvania I dropped him off.

Kerrville 1975. My first meeting with Henning; The motorcycle has the seat removed to put in the plane. It is a 180 cc Suzuki and is freeway legal.

The motorcycle is now in the Mooney and Henning and I will fly to Houston, Texas.

There are many tales about Henning, some true and some maybe stretched a bit. On one of his trips, he flew to the Fijis from Germany via Asia. This Henning could do with the plane's wing tanks or a small ferry tank. After a stay in the islands, he wanted to continue back to Germany by crossing the Pacific. He needed larger ferry tanks. He found a round 55-gallon oil drum but it wouldn't fit through the door of the Mooney, so he took it somewhere where they had a hydraulic press and partially smashed the oil drum, then passed it through the doorway and used it as his ferry fuel.

Another story is that he flew from Pago Pago to Honolulu and was directed to a parking place at night. The next day when he returned to the plane, he had a note from the FAA (Federal Aviation Agency) to report to their office. When he parked at night, he was right under the window of the FAA office. His airplane had United States registration. The officials couldn't believe what they were seeing. He had used a number of square plastic containers like you might buy from the hardware store, grocery store, or auto supply store to carry fuel. He would put a plastic hose into one container and run on it until it was dry, then take out the hose and put it into the next jug, and so on. The FAA said you can't fly like that. Henning protested that he had just flown ¾ of the way around the world like that and had only one long flight ahead, to San Francisco, to complete the journey. The FAA officials were astounded but decided to look the other way, and Henning completed the trip using his homemade fuel system.

Henning and I have remained friends. He has visited me when I lived in Pennsylvania and after I moved to California. I have visited him several times in Karlsruhe, Germany. Henning later became a very successful lawyer, and he married a Fiji girl, Sulu. They have four children. In spite of this, Henning never lost his lust for flying adventure. He made far more transatlantic flights in light planes than I did; I crossed seven times and Henning crossed many more in various aircraft. He started ferrying aircraft for fees over the ocean. He flew around the world at least three times and probably more. He began his first round-the-world flight in a Mitsubishi shortly after he got his private pilot license. He still occasionally flies to Fiji and usually completes this trip by circling the globe. He stayed with me while he got his airline pilot rating in America because the training is cheaper there. He flew airliners for Lufthansa for a while and practiced law at the same time.

I always liked to have a surplus of fuel. Henning is an expert in making long distances on small amounts of fuel. He flies all day at 1,900 rpm, with the mixture lean of peak. To me, this feels like idling the engine. But he has often flown a Mooney and other light planes across the Atlantic and back with no ferry tanks. He stops in the Faros and two times in Greenland, once on the east coast and again at Narsarsuaq, on the west coast, and sometimes goes the extreme northern route stopping at the airbase, Sondestrom. These are all short legs, which can be flown on the plane's wing tanks if you ration your fuel as stingily as Henning does.

Henning says no more winter ocean crossings via this route. On one eventful trip, he was flying a new airplane in midwinter from North America to Europe via the northern route. He stopped in Goose Bay and received a good weather forecast, so he set out for Narsarsuaq on lower western Greenland. Here you fly for about 100 miles up a fiord to an airfield with an uphill runway and no go-around possibility. He was flying after dark between the stone walls of the fiord when without warning, it began to snow. Within a few seconds he could see nothing. He was in solid instrument conditions below the walls of a winding stone canyon. He said to himself now I am going to die. Then he caught a glimpse of a light below. It was Eskimos fishing on the ice. He cut the power and landed wheels up on the ice. The airplane was a total loss, but Henning only had a few bleeding scratches on his forehead. He was only a quarter mile from the threshold of the runway, but there was no way that he could have landed. The next day he retrieved some of the plane's radios.

Upon landing in Karlsruhe, Germany, a small airfield, the people there knew Henning. They telephoned him and he drove to the airport to pick me up in a short time. I had to clear customs. There was a customs office at the Karlsruhe airport, but they had never serviced a plane which had arrived from America. I then took Henning to the Mooney, asked him to open the wing tanks, and took a picture of him looking in amazement. The wing tanks were full! I had taken off with my ferry tanks not completely filled; I had flown 2,898 statute miles in 19.5 hours and had never switched to the plane's regular fuel tanks.

We partied for two days, and by the third day I was having so much fun that I knew I had to leave or I might not get the whole way around the world in two months. At the airport, we met a gang of girls and boys crowded in an old German vehicle, which I think was a surplus military vehicle. It had no top and was a dull khaki color. It looked something like our army jeeps but it was bigger. I think they called them troop carriers. This mixed crew of people was drinking beer, singing, and yelling at people on the streets and in other cars. They were following our car and yelling at us. Henning yelled back. Soon we were partying together. When they found out I had just come from America, they invited us in. Their vehicle was overcrowded, so a few got in our car, and later I went back and rode and drank beer with them in their contraption. Eventually, some of us ended up at Henning's place. People were coming and going all the time. I had had no sleep for well over 24 hours and was glad when eventually everyone wound down and went to sleep. When I woke up, there were people sleeping everywhere. The beds were crowded as well as the couches and the floor.

Karlsruhe, Germany 1977. I have just landed from flying non-stop from Gander, Canada, 2898 statue miles in 19.5 hours. The wing tanks are full because I only used the ferry tanks. The ferry tank can be seen and my slit entry is on the plane's right side. The other fellow is a new acquaintance we met and the airport.

I got in the "troop carrier" and we followed Henning's car to celebrate.

The next evening, Henning said his friend wanted to take us for a ride on the Rhine in his yacht. That sounded like a pleasant diversion from the night before. Henning said he had this large yacht and we would sail down the river, stop and have our evening meal, and return. We would have a great time. About six o'clock in the evening, we went to the harbor to sail away. The yacht was a retired tugboat that had pushed and pulled barges on the Rhine until it was too old to work. True, some tables and chairs had been placed on the aft deck, and maybe some curtains on the windows, but the boat was designed for work and there was very little room for people. In spite of this, it was quite pleasant. There were two German men, slightly older than Henning and me. One was the boat owner and the other was his friend. We had all brought food and, of course, beer and wine. A trip down the Rhine is a pleasant, colorful experience. I had cruised on the Rhine before when I'd spent two years in Frankfurt am Main, but one never tires of it. We sat in the back and the old men smoked their pipes, and we drank from the wine and the beer. About ten miles downstream, the captain announced that we would stop and have our evening meal. The last light of day was just dying when we dropped anchor and the meal preparation began.

Our hosts prepared bratwurst, bockwurst, sauerkraut, kartafelen, and salat, a delicious meal which we washed down with more beer and wine. Then we sat and told stories. Each of us had true adventures to relate, which the others had difficulty believing. I particularly enjoyed the evening because we all spoke German all night. And I got a chance to utilize the language, which I might forget if I didn't exercise it. Henning speaks English just like an American, and we usually converse in English.

About midnight, the captain said it was time to pull up the anchor and head back. Before "up anchor," he would start the diesel engine which powered this huge ship. When he pushed the starter button, only a weak noise emanated from the engine room. The battery did not have enough power to turn the engine. German curse words are very colorful. They set out to find the reason. In a short time, it was determined that I had gone to the head about an hour and a half ago and left the light on. The light bulb in the head is about 25 watts, and burning for an hour and a half should not, in my opinion, be enough to drain the battery on a ship this large. This is what I thought, but I didn't say it, as clearly it was to be blamed on me. What can we do? The captain said an automobile battery would not do. This was a big diesel and would require a more powerful source. Henning came up with an idea. We had just passed a Mercedes factory before anchoring. There were a large number of new trucks waiting to be shipped. We would go over there and ask the watchman to borrow a battery.

Excellent idea—there was nothing else.

Henning and I crawled into the dingy, which we had been towing behind since we left Karlsruhe. We had the oars and wrenches to remove the battery. In the distance we could see the faint neon sign of the Mercedes factory. Henning rowed, and when he tired I rowed. We wanted to move fast because the others wanted to get back to get to work the next day. At the Mercedes factory, I felt like I was in a James Bond movie where the heroes land quietly on the shore at night and sneak to attack. The shore and the boat were in pitch blackness, and only a neon sign which spelled out Mercedes cast a pale blue glow on the storage area, where the new trucks awaited shipment. We called for a guard. We shouted at the top of our lungs, but nobody responded. After some time Henning said there was only one thing that we could do—climb the eight-foot fence, borrow a battery from one of the trucks, start our engine, and return the battery. So with considerable difficulty, and with each of us helping the other, we scaled the fence carrying the wrench. We opened the hood of a massive truck and there it was—our prize—a big battery. With our wrench, we removed the battery and disconnected the cables. Then we closed the hood.

This battery was no small prize. One person could carry it a short distance, but it was easier with two. Now we had to climb the fence with the battery and lower it down the other side. Henning climbed to the top. With all my strength I hoisted the battery above my head, and Henning took it and balanced it on top of the fence. I climbed the fence—this climb we had to do with no assistance from the other person—and let myself down the other side. I then reached up and Henning eased the load into my upraised hands. We now had the battery over the fence. It was nothing to move it into the dingy and row back to the boat. We were gone one hour.

The whole Rhine and the boat were in black darkness, but we could locate it from the lights on shore since we knew which lights we had sat by during dinner. When we rowed up, the two men didn't hear us until we were in contact with the boat. They shouted, "Did you get it?"

Henning decided to make a joke: "We came back to get a different size of wrench." The men moaned. But when we showed them the battery, they were ecstatic.

Eight arms lifted the battery, and the men soon connected it to the electrical system and the diesel started immediately. Now Henning and I had to return the borrowed battery. We loaded it into the rowboat and rowed back. We were getting good at this; we now had some experience. We landed the dingy, carried the battery to the fence, and Henning climbed to the top. I hoisted the battery, climbed the fence and down the other side, and Henning again passed the battery into my upraised hands. We opened the hood, lifted the battery into the truck, and were tightening the retaining lugs. THAT'S WHEN THE POLICE ARRIVED!

That is also when I realized that Henning was going to have a highly successful career as an attorney. Henning Huffer talked the notoriously strict Deutsche Politzi into believing that we were not taking out a battery to steal it, rather that we were putting it back in. So instead of handcuffing us and taking us off to jail, they let us go back to our rowboat and return to the ship.

We got back to port at about 4 AM, and that's when I decided to leave the next day.

Karlsruhe to Ankara, or rather to Athens ━━━━━━━

I slept a while but got up early enough to file a flight plan for Ankara, Turkey, about a ten-hour flight, which I should be able to do all in daylight. The weather was good, and surprisingly I felt rested because I had slept most of the trip back to Karlsruhe in the boat. Everything went fine; I was carrying less weight than when I left with on my last leg. On such a nice day, nothing could go wrong—that is, until I followed my flight plan, which crossed over communist Yugoslavia and Bulgaria. VFR (visual flight rules) flying in Europe is more like IFR (instrument flight rules) in America. The controllers order you around, tell you to turn here, climb now, or descend. They also ask you often for your estimated time of arrival at your next point and perhaps the point after that. You better have all that calculated when they ask, as they want it immediately. When I got to the point where my last controller wanted to hand me off to the Yugoslavian controller, the Yugoslavian controller would not accept me. I protested that I had paid for an over-crossing permit, but he was not to be budged. The permit gave an exact time to the minute to enter their airspace and to leave it, and I was off by several days. What to do now? I got out the maps and decided to continue down the Adriatic Sea and go around Yugoslavia and Bulgaria. Athens was down there and I had never been to Greece, so I decided to land at Athens. Now I'm glad that they didn't honor my over-crossing permit. I've been to Athens several times since that, but the first time is the most impressive.

It is best not to fly directly across Greece to Athens because you have to keep your altitude up to cross the mountains, and the airport lies near the base of the mountains just after crossing them. Best is to approach Athens low over the Mediterranean Sea from the south.

The next day, after a brief tour of the city including the Parthenon, I prepared for a flight to Ankara, where I'd thought I was going when I left Germany.

I made an early morning takeoff from Athens for the 520 sm. flight to Ankara, Turkey. The weather was perfect and visibility was unrestricted. Beneath me, the blue Mediterranean Sea was dotted with Greek Islands. Ships cruised on the surface, leaving white trails on the dark water. Smaller boats did not move and had nets spread in circles near them to entrap the fish. When I crossed the western shore of Turkey, the Mooney was flying for the first time over Asia.

Four hours later I landed at Ankara International Airport, parked, and cleared customs. The taxi driver that took me to an economical hotel suggested that he wait and offered me a very reasonable price for a tour in his cab of the city. I accepted his offer.

Ankara is the capital of Turkey and probably the most European city in Turkey. It is also well known for the University located there. On this sunny afternoon, clusters of students streamed the streets and clogged the bars. The cabby gave an interesting running commentary and eventually dropped me off at a pleasant outdoor restaurant for my evening meal.

The next morning I repeated my itinerary, arising early for a prompt start. By eight AM I was flying eastward toward Tehran, in Iran, a distance of 1,092 sm., which would take about eight hours. The majority of the flight was over mountainous region. I flew at 14,000 feet, breathing from my oxygen tank but conserving the gas because I would rarely have an opportunity to refill the tank.

(Italics written in flight) *About one and a half hours ago, heard a Scandinavian airliner calling Tehran of 119.3, and he didn't get an answer either. He is much higher than me and should have a better chance of getting through. Hope the anoxia is not getting to me. Have my oxygen turned low at flight level 14.0 (14,000 feet). Try to do everything legal—have checked by adding my distances in my head, then checking with the calculator. I appear to have a clear head but one can't tell. Anoxia can creep up unexpect-*

edly. That is, it's tricky; you can't really tell. I recall listening to the tape-recorded voice of Elgin Long, the first person to fly around the world via the North and South Poles. He installed an inertial navigation system in a Navaho and flew solo. He then had a constant digital readout of his position on earth at all times. He passed over the North Pole and over Greenwich, England. He took photos of the digital readout at zero north and zero east and over the South Pole as well. He also took a photo crossing the equator at 180 degrees. Passing over Antarctica, he too was on oxygen, but being very conservative. His voice tape recording at that time showed definite anoxia in his slow drawled speech and his inability to make up his mind. This anoxia can kill you.

Why did airline Captain Elgin Long fly around the world? He was an airline pilot with a comfortable position and a good income, yet he took leave of his position and spent $50,000, admittedly wrecking the family's finances to carry out this seemingly worthless feat. His answer was this: "Aviation had given a lot to me, and I felt that in my lifetime I must give something back to aviation."

Max Conrad had tried this pole-to-pole, around-the-world flight. Max, who had set scores of long-distance flight records, the "flying grandfather" with the largest number of hours of any human being, 55,000 logged hours in 1974. He probably knew more about light plane long-distance flying than any other person on earth. Yet this soft-spoken grandfather lost his chance at the first pole-to-pole, round-the-world flight by one day. He arrived at the U.S. station at the South Pole. He was ready to depart, completely refueled on a beautiful sunshiny day, but the South Pole crew insisted that he remain for a celebration to take place the next day. Against his best judgment he stayed, and the next day had complete "white-out." He caught a wing on takeoff in zero-visibility conditions. His plane was severely damaged and remains at the South Pole, but Max was not injured. This just about ruined Max's spirit.

Just have been able to relay a position report to Tehran by an airliner. Nothing but sand below me now—drifting sand. The mountains appear gone, but the visibility is poor due to haze— apparently white sand. Sandstorms can ruin an engine.

Something below I never heard of—"sand glaciers."

Trying to determine if I'm becoming anoxic. Handwriting very bad but [it is] also very turbulent. I'll never forget the impression which the altitude chamber made on me. Take off your mask at 23,000 feet and try to do calculations. What a disaster.

Being in good condition helps minimize anoxia. I try to run five miles a day, often ten. I've run 20 miles several times but have never been able to make the twenty-six miles which constitute a marathon. Several times I've tried to bring myself into "marathon condition," but I've never been quite able. After twenty miles, something happens; my legs get too weak and I get sick in the stomach. My willpower appears absolutely gone. Each time the marathon comes up I'm conveniently out of town, thus been unable to run. But the truth is that I was never in good enough condition to complete the race. Rather than disgrace myself, I'm conveniently away. In spite of this I maintain myself in relatively good condition. The trend now in the nation is to be physically fit. It is no longer popular to be out of condition. I look forward to the time when the desire for fitness will reach that of the Scandinavians, where it is rare to see an obese person, young or old.

The high altitude and clear air allowed me to see a lake far in the distance to the north, which I think was Lake Sevan in the center of Armenia. Two years prior in 1975, I had flown commercial into Yerevan, the capital of Armenia, and had taken a bus about 50 miles to Lake Sevan, a beautiful mountain body of blue water. That evening we dined at a shoreline restaurant on fresh trout caught in the lake. The last quarter of the trip paralleled the south shore of the Caspian Sea, separated only from my flight path by a few high mountains and some low hills. Between the hills at my altitude, I could see the Caspian Sea. In 1975 as part of a medical tour of the Soviet Union, I also visited Baku, the capital of Azerbaijan. Baku lies about 200 miles to the north of my route, and I had gone out on the piers to the oil derricks. The Soviets wanted to show off their petroleum production. The oil from the Caspian Sea was clear and light yellow colored. According to our guides, this oil could safely be taken directly from the ground and directly put in the crankcase of an automobile engine without further refining. I peered into the distance and attempted to spot one of the oil derricks, but I never identified one. On the 1975 trip we also visited Tbilisi, the capital of Georgia, and Kiev, the capital of Ukraine.

I landed at the major international airport at Tehran. The Shah was still in power in 1977, and there were no international problems. The city was congested with automobile traffic, and heavy smog filled the air. I crossed the downtown streets very cautiously as the vehicles sped past from all directions and paid little attention to a pedestrian who might want to get to the other side. The city appeared to me to be a busy metropolis with no adversity toward Americans.

In the morning there was no trouble getting 100-octane gasoline, but when I asked for a liter of oil for my engine, it created quite a problem. Nobody seemed to have a can of oil. Various personnel at the airport discussed it in Farsi. This country is one of the major oil producers in the world, but it appeared to be a major problem for me to get a liter of oil. Eventually they went to another office and brought papers for me to fill out. The form asked extensive information, including my name, address, pilot's license number, flight plan including where I came from and where I was going, and my signature. After the paper was signed, I was brought a can of oil, which I put in the engine.

I took off for Karachi, Pakistan, flying southeast at 15,000 feet and rationing my breathing oxygen by keeping my breathing rate lower than normal. I would take a breath of the oxygen, then hold my breath for as long as I could, then take another breath. This is the same method that I use when I scuba dive and which has allowed me to get much longer dives from one tank than most divers. Even the professional divers who guided our underwater tour would empty their tanks before me. In the plane, I did not have a demand system like a scuba regulator, but I could turn the flow down and slowly fill the balloon, then take a breath and hold it until the balloon filled again.

(Written in flight)*Just entered into Pakistan. Passing near the Himalayas now. No contact with Karachi radio. Tried VHF 127.3, also HF 6624 and HF 13336; 6624 is so full of chatter, talking to Bombay, other stations can't get in. Everybody's talking at the same time. 13336 is dead, no response. Guess I'll wait till I'm closer. Getting dark—fun flying near Himalayas in the dark. Mountains certainly much higher than my flight level. Now is the time to hold the course well. Suspect, but am not sure, that the mountains are to my left and lower terrain to my right. Safest thing is to hold a good steady course. But what happens when the VHF station fades away and the other has not yet come on? Best hold the course that I have when Zahedan fades and hope the winds don't change until I begin to pick up Parjgur.*

Flying at flight level 15.0[15,000 feet] now. I think I can spare a little more oxygen. Oil and cylinder temperature just barely in the green. Don't really like this. Think I'll change back to W 100 [oil density] as soon as I get the chance.

VHF from Zahedan getting weak now. Needle flickering. Apparently must dead reckon for a while. But the ADF needle at Parjgur seems to be showing a little life. I shouldn't be too long in the mountains without navigational signal. Moon is out. That's nice. Moon has been out every night in a clear sky since Athens. No lights at all below. Apparently this area is completely unpopulated, or if anybody is within my range of vision they have no lights.

VHF starting to flicker now. Making 140 knots. Have been lucky, almost all tailwinds.

One of the toughest things about being a pilot is sitting so long at one time. I just have not been able to get used to it like a cowboy does. After a while, he doesn't get saddle sore. But I never get used to it. After the Atlantic, there was a vertical abrasion over my sacrum when I looked in the mirror. I thought I must have scratched it and, believe me, it hurt. It was from the pressure of the seam in my blue jeans. From all my years of sitting in a school room, I never knew of the middle seam of one's trousers to cause an abrasion. This merely indicates how long one sits in one place. I put a Band-Aid on the strategic spot right between the buttocks, and there it has remained through soaking in numerous bathtubs in the Middle East capitals. But this was not the worst. The greater trochanters, or the bones which stick out the furthest in one's butt, are acutely tender. Indeed, sitting on my butt is one of the most difficult problems of the entire trip, as my butt is acutely tender. I am determined to buy a soft pillow. In Tehran the streets were nearly deserted at 11:00 PM, and after going to a restaurant and trying to walk home, I suddenly found myself face to face with a drugstore which I later discovered is well-known. There are picture postcards of this Tehran drugstore for sale at card shops and on the street. But the drugstore had no pillow.

During the first part of the flight in Iran, the land below me was unusual; a very high rolling desert plain. The surface was between 7,000 and 10,000 feet above sea level. I had never seen relatively flat land this high. Only the snowcap covering Greenland had similar terrain. There were large areas of dry salt beds with little or no vegetation. The trip began with scattered clouds, but the cloud layer gradually increased to 85% coverage. Tehran to Karachi is 1165 sm. I would make it in about eight hours with a light tailwind. Near the end of my flight, I began flying over the Arabian Sea, following the shoreline of southern Pakistan to Karachi.

Karachi is a seaport and is one of the largest cities in the world, with a population of about nine million and a traffic problem. It is the economic hub of Pakistan and was the capital until the mid-sixties when it was moved to Islamabad, which is located nearer to the center of the country. Once again, the persistent taxi drivers approached me as soon as I exited the airport, touting their services of a tour of the city which was to be included with a ride to a hotel. I accepted one man's offer and we were off. The best known landmark of Karachi is the Tomb of the Founder, Mohammad Ali Jinnah. He posed me in front of the monument and took my photo. I carry a small camera on my trips, but I take few photos. In my early travels, I carried no camera. I preferred to blend as much as possible into the native inhabitants. I felt that I could learn more about the people if they did not, at first glance, identify me as a tourist. I had traveled a good bit of the world, and I liked to feel that the memories in my mind were my photographs. I enjoyed studying the other cultures, but I didn't want the natives to realize that I was closely observing them. In retrospect, I realize that I live and enjoy the present moment more than the past or the future. But I made an exception and did allow the taxi driver to take my picture standing in front of the Tomb of the Founder like a common tourist.

The next morning I crossed India. I had gotten landing permission for Bombay (now Mumbai), which is on the west coast, as well as Calcutta, which is on the east coast. However, because I was behind my loosely planned agenda, I decided not to stop at Bombay and to continue to Calcutta.

(written in flight, August 29, 1977) *Flying across India. Moon now peaking through the clouds. No turbulence at this time, and I'm out of the instrument conditions at this time. Listening to Indian music on the ADF. It is just getting dark and I can steer directly to the moon to hold my course. I check for my flashlight, which should always be available in case of power failure at night, and realize that both of them are in the baggage compartment. I don't like that. You can't get into the baggage compartment in flight. You must plan for everything possible and put it up front in the cabin prior to takeoff. I decide that in case of power failure, I can get* enough of a horizon from the moon, and I will follow in the direction of the moon.

The moon peaks out from the clouds—it is full!

THE ENGINE JUST QUIT. [This simply means that I must switch tanks, but it always gives me a thrill.]

It is the monsoon season in India, and I get my first taste of flying in it. This is a big low in the center of India. I asked the meteorologist in Pakistan which way it is moving. He answered, it doesn't move; it just stays there. It is "the season."

One of my main worries was the monsoon weather. I had questioned most everybody I knew who was an authority. Phil Waldman said it doesn't stop flying—just makes it more difficult. The pilots at Flo Air said it was merely heavy rain—turbulence was not that bad. They said there could be some cumulonimbus but usually not thunderstorms. I asked the Air Pakistan pilots and they said it was just heavy rain.

The lower part of the Indian subcontinent is flat; it was summer and monsoon season. The trip from Karachi to Calcutta via Mumbai is 1,553 sm. and required 11 hours, most of it in IFR conditions. The majority of it was in solid monsoon rains. I had little or no winds or turbulence, but the rain was continuous and heavy. The rain poured in such volume that it was easy to imagine that all this water would drown out the engine. But the Lycoming ran steady through it all. The heavy rain fell from the sky vertically. There was no wind to make gusts. Of course, I flew through it and the water struck the aircraft at 140 mph. I usually flew slow even over land for most of this trip, not because I had to extend my range, but because the price of fuel was so high. I flew less than my usual cruising speed to conserve fuel. I rarely saw land this leg, and I rarely saw sky. In general, I just cruised along with always the same weather conditions.

Flying by instruments is a skill to be learned which gives the pilot a very satisfying experience when all goes well. I can remember taking off from Johnstown in the Mooney, climbing into the clouds cruising in a consistent cloud layer with no turbulence, no sight of land or view of the sky, and descending into Indianapolis, breaking out at 400 feet with the runway directly ahead of me. This gives a feeling of accomplishment. Your own skill and intelligence brought you across three states with no visual clues.

But sometimes things don't go as well. I remember one time returning home between layers on a dark night with no stars or moon and, of course, no lights to see on the ground. I sensed something was wrong but I didn't know what. I felt G forces on my body, but I was hand flying the plane and had the attitude indicator perfectly centered. I looked at the turn and bank indicator and saw that the plane was in a 45 degree bank. A glance at the vacuum gauge told me that the vacuum pump had failed. I moved the controls to stop the turn and pulled back on the yoke to arrest the descent. The plane had been in a steep descending spiral, just short of a spin, but I had been following the artificial horizon as a pilot usually does on instruments. I centered and stabilized the altitude. Everything outside was black. My body was shaking, but I had the aircraft under control. Now just fly it without losing it. I knew that there was plenty of room below the clouds and I was over flat land, so I asked the controller for a non-gyro descent through the overcast. I didn't care what direction I went as long as I got under where I could see lights on the ground. I had to cover the attitude indicator with one hand. I found it impossible to fly using the compass and turn and bank indicator with the artificial horizon at a 45-degree angle. All of simulation for partial panel instrument flight is done by blocking off the faulty instrument. With my left hand covering this gauge, after a while I held a steady heading during descent. When I saw lights below and excellent visibility, I cancelled instrument flight plan and continued home visually.

It was after dark when I landed at Calcutta International. After parking my plane, an attendant put a chain and a padlock on the door handle so that nobody could open it, including me. I had gotten my overnight case out, but I wasn't sure that I had everything that I wanted. This didn't matter to him. When I said that I might want to get something out of the airplane, he said that was not possible.

I found my way to a hotel, and this time I didn't take a tour of the city. Calcutta is an extremely poor city noted for its poverty. Mother Teresa worked with its poor citizens and there is the infamous Black Hole of Calcutta, a prison where in 1756 a large number of prisoners died from being confined in a small space with little or no air. It was dark when I left the airport, so I stayed nearby and left early the next day.

I had obtained permission to land in Myanmar (previously Burma), but once again I decided to over-fly it. The government was not very pro-American, and the place was notorious for the price of fuel. It would have been interesting to me, but not enough to invest the time and money. So I filed my flight plan for Bangkok, 1035 sm., about a seven-hour flight.

Thailand is known as the land of smiles, and with good reason. During my stay, I cannot recall a single person who was impolite or appeared to be in a bad mood. I landed at Don Muang International Airport and found an inexpensive hotel. The prices in Thailand at that time were very reasonable. Don Muang is now replaced by the new Suvarnbhumi (pronounced su-wan-na-poom) Airport. I had visited Bangkok before and had seen many Buddhist temples and had taken an elephant ride and a tour up the river. This time I settled into a slow pace after the hectic days of daily flying. I spent a good bit of time by the river shore, where hundreds of wooden skiffs lined the banks, many of them selling vegetables, fruit, and other foodstuffs. Other boats sold most anything imaginable, including clothes. This was known as the floating market. The shore was lined with open air restaurants and bars. I could sit at an open air restaurant for hours, nursing a beer, observing the throng of mankind.

One day I met a young girl named Lila in one of the restaurants, and I asked her out for the evening. She accepted, and we had a long pleasant dinner while she told me tales of Thai culture and stories about Bangkok. She said she was going to go home on Sunday, the next day, to celebrate the birthday of her uncle, who was a retired navy admiral and somewhat of a celebrity, and asked if I wanted to accompany her. I took her up on her offer, and the next day we caught a train northward. After about 20 miles, we exited and walked about a mile and a half to her home. It was on stilts to keep it dry during the rainy season and had a thatched roof.

About 20 people had gathered to celebrate the birthday and, like me, most had brought a present. The group sat cross-legged in a circle on the floor. The admiral sat at the head of the circle. He wore the coat of his naval uniform and a sarong. The food was served from a large pot in the center. The family suggested that I sit on the couch because they felt that I would have trouble sitting cross-legged. They were right. I felt quite comfortable with the jovial crowd, and we laughed at many things even though we understood only a small amount of what we said to each other. As evening approached, Lila and I caught the train back to Bangkok. After three relaxing days, I reluctantly prepared to leave.

Singapore was my next stop—906 sm. almost due south and on the equator. The view from my cockpit was marvelous. I followed the east shore of the Thai Peninsula. White beaches edged with palm trees alternated with rocky shores, and lush green jungle grew almost to the water's edge. Seabirds soared below me. Six hours of impeccable flight landed me in Singapore.

Singapore is one of only four city-states remaining in the world. It is a progressive modern country of only 267 sq. mi. on an island at the end of the Malaysian Peninsula. There are two modern airports in Singapore, a large international airport, and a smaller airport for private aviation named Seletur. My advisors at Flo Air had recommended that I stop at the Piper dealer and have a checkup before starting over the Pacific Ocean. The service there was excellent. I was not yet due for a hundred-hour inspection, so I asked them only to give my plane a thorough examination. They changed the oil and checked the plane, finding nothing that I should be concerned about. I felt very comfortable with their service. I was even able to refill my oxygen tank.

While I was in Singapore, I called home and was distressed to learn that my mother, who was 85 years old, had fallen and broken her hip. This is a tragic thing for old people because they must be bedridden, and it is important that the elderly keep moving or they deteriorate rapidly. She had always been active and never been ill. She had lived by herself, taking care of her own house and preparing her own meals. I made the decision to speed my progress around the globe to return to care for her.

From Singapore, I flew southeastward following the Indonesian Islands of Sumatra and Java. I had obtained permission to land at Jakarta, the capital of Indonesia, but I decided to eliminate this stop to arrive home sooner. Instead, I made another long flight of 2.200 sm. in 15 hours and 40 minutes from Singapore to Darwin, Australia. Darwin is on the north coast of Australia.

After a night's rest, I flew to Mount Isa in central Australia a distance of 776 sm. in a little less than six hours. I refueled and bought a few opals to take home as gifts. The region is noted for excellent opals, and there is a shop in the small terminal which sold un-mounted stones. I could not take anything in the plane which had any significant weight, and this appeared to be a good solution to how I could bring gifts home with essentially no weight. From there I headed northeast to Cairns on the Great Barrier Reef, a distance of 427 sm., which I completed in three hours. Both of these legs totaled nine hours of flying. This seemed like an easy day compared to the Singapore-Darwin marathon. I completed both legs in daylight in spite of the fact that I was now in the southern hemisphere in mid-winter and the days were shorter than the nights. I flew slightly out of my way to go to Cairns because one of the things that I really wanted to do on this trip was dive on the Great Barrier Reef. The following morning, I took a boat out to Green Island and rented mask, fins, and snorkel. I got to snorkel all day and took the boat back in the evening. The reef was everything that I had dreamed. This day gave me a memory that will remain with me the rest of my life.

Now it was time to get home. Brisbane was to be my jumping off point for crossing the Pacific. Cairns to Brisbane is 910 sm. following the coast of Australia southwesterly. It took me six hours.

The Blue Giant

Now the fun would begin. When I left the shoreline behind at Brisbane, I had 5,692 sm. equivalent to 82 degrees of longitude or almost 23 percent of the diameter of the earth at the equator, until I reached any solid ground other than small islands in the Pacific.

I must confess my heart was beating faster as I left land behind and steered northeastward. I had 1,294 sm. to go before landing at

Suva in the Fiji islands. I flight planned for 9 hours and 15 minutes. Halfway there, I spotted New Caledonia and the Loyalty Islands off my port wing.

The typical flying weather in the South Pacific is different from the North Atlantic. Unless there is a tropical storm, when I have no business flying, the weather is generally balmy with scattered fluffy clouds. There is always a cloud over an island because the land warms faster than the water in the sunshine, causing the air above to heat and rise. The winds are usually light and the ocean below is clearly visible and calm. The word *Pacific* means calm, and that is what the water and the weather is like unless it gets angry in a storm, in which case it gets extremely angry.

Flying direct across the North Atlantic to Europe is different. On the typical crossing of the Atlantic, a low marine cloud layer blocks any view of the water and you fly above it. The winds can be stronger and affect your speed and direction. The winds are usually steady, thus turbulence is rare. Taking the northern route from Goose Bay to Greenland and Iceland is different. Apparently, the cooler temperatures inhibit the marine layer, and the ocean with its icebergs can usually be seen from the plane. I am glad for this because you must find the fiord at Narsarsuaq, Greenland.

Everything went well on this leg, and I landed at Suva airport before dark. Henning had asked me to do him a favor when I got to Fiji, which I did. He asked me to look up one of his past girlfriends and give her a message from him. I had considerable difficulty locating her because everywhere I went, the neighbors said she had moved to another location. Eventually I was successful in tracking her down and passed Henning's message.

As for myself, I stayed at the Holiday Inn near the airport. This was a small motel-like accommodation, not the large Holiday Inn resort which has been built since 1977. The girl that worked in the gift shop was pretty. I invited her to dinner that evening. It turned out that she was Miss Fiji in the Miss Universe pageant. Between hunting down Henning's ex-girlfriend and Miss Fiji, I stayed two days in Suva, then left for Pago Pago, a distance of 595 sm. which I planned to cover in 4 hours, 25 minutes. Shortly before landing in Pago Pago, I would gain a day because I would cross the International Date Line.

Pago Pago (pronounced pang-go pang-go) is in West Samoa. I landed and took a room at a small hotel near the airport and got some rest because the next leg from Pago Pago to Honolulu was the longest flight completely over water. It was 2,500 sm. (about 18 hours). I had made nonstop flights greater than that, but not all over water. For the first time ever, all of the tanks were filled to the brim. The aircraft had never been tested nor flown at this weight, or with the center of gravity this far aft. The temperature was 100 degrees. I waited until evening when the temperature was lower, and then I backed my plane into the grass before the approach area of the runway, ran up the engine, and released the brakes.

(My original intention was to slow the pace of my travel and spend some time in the South Sea Islands sitting on the beach and writing the story of my trip. When I found out that my mother was in the hospital, I made the decision to proceed home with no undue delay. I did, however, do some writing both on the ground and while flying. I have put in *italics* the portion of this story which was written at the time that it occurred.)

(This description was written in 1977 while flying.) *I had gotten up early enough and taken a taxi from the hotel to the airport, but like many of my takeoffs, the preparation took the largest part of the day. First the refueling was typically slow; an hour's wait for the gas truck followed by the slow refueling of the three cabin tanks a liter at a time. The big nozzles which pumped so rapidly into the wings of the airliners wouldn't even fit into my cabin door. Also, the size of the tanks left only a tiny space between the cabin roof and the top of the tanks. So we fitted a plastic tube into the filler spout and dripped the gas from the huge nozzle into the plastic tube. The largest cabin tank held 55 gallons and sat where the copilot usually sat. The control yoke and* pedals had been removed to facilitate this. The fit was so critical that only an inch remained between the instrument panel and the tank. Thus, to read my engine instruments and set the highly critical manifold pressure and engine R.P.M., I used a long-handled mechanics mirror, a rather ingenious device in which one end was constructed like a hypodermic syringe with a loop for the thumb and a loop each for the middle finger and the index finger. By pushing with the thumb, the angle of the mirror on the other end varied. With a bit of practice I could read these instruments accurately, even though the numbers in the mirror were backwards.

With a sweaty hand, the throttle was eased forward and the fuel-injected Lycoming sprung to life. In spite of the fact that she developed all of her rated 200 H.P. eight feet above sea level, the Mooney began to move forward only very slowly. Every tuft of clumped grass under the half inflated tires was felt in the cabin, and all too often the shock absorbers on the landing gear hit bottom on a tuft of grass. The 1965 Mooney was 25% over gross and loaded at the most aft portion of its center of gravity envelope. The tail nearly touched the ground when sitting on the apron.

Every ounce of unnecessary weight had been trimmed. Every chart which was not necessary for the homeward flight had been discarded. My personal belongings had been reduced to a toothbrush and the smallest tube of toothpaste. The few clothes that I carried were loose(no suitcase for me) and stuffed as far forward in the cabin as possible in a desperate attempt to add forward weight and keep the center of gravity within the critical envelope. Now I added the weight of my torso; I leaned forward as far as possible.

The small area under the panel which normally held the co-pilot's foot pedals and feet now contains the oil addition system. Unfortunately, I have access to this only with the tips of my fingers when I strain to the utmost. Once again, with practice, I have become quite adept at adding oil. With the very tip of a finger, I can ease a can of oil from the storage area beside the oil addition apparatus. It was kept there for a dual purpose, first to keep all possible weight forward, and second because there simply was no other storage area. On my other transatlantic flights, I had access to the rear baggage compartment by crawling over a 55-gallon drum in the back seat area. On this flight, however, this was impossible as the cabin tanks extended all around me to within a few inches of the ceiling.

After obtaining the can of oil from its storage area with the tips of my fingers, it was dropped into the apparatus with the tips of my fingers. Then I took the hatchet, which was also in this area, and gave a few sharp raps on the oil can. The apparatus is so designed that the points on the bottom of it made two holes in the can and poured oil into a hopper. I then pumped it into the engine using a mechanical pump. The oil would enter the engine where the dipstick usually was, but now had been removed. The hydraulic pump, which took 20 to 30 strokes, was (you guessed it) operated with the very end of my fingertips in the narrow space. All of this gives me a 15 to 20 minute diversion and physical exercise every several hours from an otherwise tiring flight.

This brings back memories of another flight when returning from Caracas, Venezuela, after flying into the jungle for the first ascent of the face of Angels Falls. I flew across the Caribbean at night in torrents of rain with lightning all around. So much rain hit the windscreen and motor, I had to wonder how a healthy engine could keep running. But this was not a healthy engine. Its oil consumption was so high that no oil could be found on the dipstick after an hour and a half test flight. I had made three separate trips by Pan American from New York to Caracas in an effort to ferry this aircraft home. On Saturday or Sunday I would test fly the plane, and its oil consumption was just as bad as it ever was. At each stop—Grenada, Puerto Rico International, South Caicos, and Nassau—I bought a case of oil. From Fort Lauderdale northward, things got worse. I eventually had no working radios, either navigational or communication, was in the middle of a rainstorm solid

IFR. This was in the days before transponders or radar in-route guidance. I just continued my flight for several hours northward. Eventually I caught sight of a few lights on the ground and shortly thereafter, the engine quit. I spotted a light, which I recognized as an airport beacon a few miles ahead. It was a marginal glide to say the least. The propeller was still windmilling and I switched the tanks and leaned the mixture. Shortly thereafter, the engine kicked on again and flew with somewhat reduced power. I was able to make a normal approach and landing. The airport was dark and deserted, and I didn't even know what state I was in. Running the engine on the ground with the mixture leaned produced full power, and I was able to take off and land at Linden, N.J, at about 6 AM where I hangared the plane, just time to make it to my scheduled start of my hospital training schedule. When I was asked at the hospital what I'd done on my weekend off, I replied, "Nothing special." The cause of the engine problem was the infamous slipped main bearing in the Lycoming IO-360.

Leaning forward, forehead almost touching the windscreen, may have added little to keeping the center of gravity within the envelope, but at least if the airplane rose into the air only to fall back on its tail as a rearward-loaded airplane is prone to do, I had done everything possible to prevent it.

This was the first time all five fuel tanks were totally filled. The flight from Pago Pago in Western Samoa, 2,500 statute miles, crossing 36 degrees of the earth's surface, one tenth of the circumference. It is the longest over the water leg of my trip around the world, 100 miles further than Honolulu to San Francisco. The flight is more south to north than west to east. When I cross the equator, perhaps 8 hours out, I will be less than halfway to Honolulu.

The plane lumbered forward, climbed onto the hard 8,000 ft. runway, and accelerated. I was concerned to see if it would fly, but it lifted off at the first quarter of the 8,000 ft. runway. I flew very carefully. I talked to myself: "very gradual turns, keep the airspeed up, climb slowly." She flew well, but I didn't want to challenge it. Very slowly, I turned around the mountain and headed nearly north for Honolulu 18 hours away. I left in the evening and flew through the night to have a daylight arrival. I took the first heading from the outbound VOR radial. About 100 miles out, the VOR could no longer be received. Now it was my job to hold this heading.

There is an emergency airport about halfway, but several hundred miles to the east of my course, on an atoll called Christmas Island. There are two Christmas Islands—one in the Indian Ocean and under control of Australia, and this one in the Pacific. George Reed, one of the ferry pilots whom I became friends with, told the following story: The ferry pilots like to keep a map into which they stick pins to show where they have been. George had flown delivery flights that went from Honolulu to Pago Pago several times. This time he decided to stop at Christmas Island just to be able to put another pin into his map. He filled a flight plan for there. He was following the ADF signal when it suddenly went off the air. The electricity on Christmas Island comes from a gasoline generator, and they turn it off to save fuel when they don't have a plane scheduled to land. He turned toward Pago Pago and flew for a while, then the ADF from Christmas Island came back on the air. He turned back toward the signal, then it went off the air again. He turned again toward Pago Pago, but now it was a question if he would have enough fuel to make it. He made it, but with little fuel to spare. I made no plans to land on this atoll.

(Written on the trip) *In case of a water ditching, a hatchet was carried. The normal entrance into the plane was made by taking off my shoes and passing them through the slit between the 55-gallon tank and the cabin ceiling. Following this, I put my hands on the wings and my feet through the slit. Then I inched my body through the slit; my belt buckle scraped the ceiling and, much like a limbo dancer, it was necessary to turn my head sideways to pass through the opening. This type of entrance and exit was not* designed to encourage much weight gain in these exotic parts, or to give confidence that one could escape rapidly in case of ditching. The original plan behind the hatchet was to hack my way out of the left side window and the side of the plane in case of an unscheduled landing in mid-ocean. Whether I could pull my body through this opening and pull my lifeboat and emergency equipment behind me had not yet been tested.

Nevertheless, I was glad I had not yielded to the tank designer's suggestion that they remove the inside door handle to allow an inch more for the tank. This would have necessitated someone from outside to open and close the single right-sided door each time. After landing in some exotic port in the middle of night, I might have to sit for hours for an oriental line boy to show up at daylight, then teach him in a strange tongue to open the door because I was a prisoner in my own airplane.

You might wonder what I thought about the risk of flying 18 hours over the ocean without any sight of land in a single-engine airplane with four cylinders. The most severe emergency, of course, is engine failure. The odds of spontaneous sudden engine failure in a properly maintained piston-driven aircraft engine are infinitesimally small. Most engine failures are pilot errors; for example, in switching fuel tanks, fuel contamination problems, or poor preflight inspection, something that the pilot or proper maintenance could have prevented. N-300 MD had won first place as the best single-engine aircraft at the Reading Air show. This, at that time, was called the National Air show. She won against large numbers of newer and more expensive airplanes. In theory, this represented the best single-engine aircraft in the United States. Part of the judging was a detailed examination of the maintenance records which were good enough to win first place. I considered myself to be flying the best maintained single-engine plane in America. I felt that the chance of this engine failing in the next 18 hours was so extremely tiny that I was willing to take this risk for the thrill of making this journey. Navigation problems were more likely.

Navigation over 2,500 miles of trackless Pacific to find an island is a serious matter. There was no GPS on which to rely, but I did have an early Loran. When I considered this trip, I regarded the Loran as superfluous. The word *Loran* is an acronym for long range navigation. Up until now, I had always been able to head in the general direction of my destination and pick up the ADF as I approached it and home in on it. The last 100 or so miles would be directed by the VOR. In general, the ADF was easier to pick up at night, as was the HF communication frequencies.

I flew northward, and in a few hours darkness fell. When you are at the equator, darkness really falls with a boom. It changes from light to dark within a few minutes. In contrast, when you are at high latitudes the evenings are long, with daylight gradually fading into night. Above the Arctic Circle and below the Antarctic Circle, the sun can never set at certain times of the year and never rise for other times of the year. At the equator when the sun drops below the horizon, the period of dusk which follows is very short.

In the middle of the Pacific, miles from land, there is no smog problem, and no lights on land to compete with the light of the stars. Thousands of stars (could it be billions?) lit up the sky. I spotted the Southern Cross, which can't be seen in the northern hemisphere. It wasn't hard to recognize. There was no question what it was.

An airplane seems to run smoother at night. Turbulence is less because the earth doesn't warm the air and cause it to rise. But in spite of all my previous experience with night flying and trans-oceanic flying, I maintain a state of hyper-alertness. For example, I was always aware of how much time I had flown on each tank, and when to expect the tank to go empty. I would be expecting it. In long-distance flying, one allows the tank to run dry before switching. When the tank goes empty the engine quits, and I immediately switch to another tank, at which time the engine starts running again (I hope). Even though I would be expecting this to happen for 15 to 20 minutes, when the engine stops my heart jumps into my throat, and when I switch to a full tank and the engine restarts, I start breathing again.

I was disappointed because I was picking up little or nothing on my ADF at night when the reception should be the best. I would have to rely on the Loran. This was not the modern Loran, which you turn on and you read your location in a similar manner that you might read a GPS. This required 13 steps to acquire and confirm a signal. After this, you took the number that appeared on the digital readout and compared it to numbers corresponding to curved lines on a Loran chart. Then you repeated these 13 steps for a second station, preferably at right angles to the first line, and you would be at the intersection of these lines on the map. After playing with it for about half an hour, I had locked onto the Loran transmitter in Hawaii. Locking on to a second station at right angles to my flight path was not as easy. This did not matter to me because I only wanted to know was whether I was on the right track to Hawaii. The cross station would tell me how far I had progressed on this track, but I had a good enough estimate of that by knowing my time en route. All I had to do was keep the number in the window on the Loran stable and I would get to Hawaii.

Night changed into a beautiful daybreak, and I was still motoring on. The tropical weather god was being good to me. I was beginning to pick up Honolulu VOR. Another 10 minutes and the DME (distance measuring equipment) began to flicker. Within 10 seconds, it was stable reading 120 nautical miles to the airport. A normal approach and landing followed at busy Honolulu International, completing the longest unbroken over-water leg.; 2,500 sm. without sighting land. If I had not had the Loran on board, I would not have found Hawaii. I never picked up an ADF signal.

The Longest Hop

I found a room at the airport and called home. My sister, Eleanor, answered; she was distraught. She said, "You better hurry home. Mother is not good. She might not make it. You better get the next airliner back or you might be too late."

Of course I was troubled. I called the airlines asking the schedule of Honolulu to Johnstown, Pennsylvania. All of the connections were terrible. The first plane out of Honolulu would not leave for some time. Then I could go to San Francisco or Los Angeles, then long waits between planes, then stops and plane changes on the way to Pittsburgh, then a long wait for a commuter to Johnstown. I decided to fly the Mooney.

I slept six to eight hours, then began to fuel the plane. There were no customs to clear out of Hawaii to the mainland. This saved some time. Once again I began my flight from Honolulu to San Francisco in the evening. The temperature is lower and the night air is calmer. I would arrive in the United States and make my landing in the daylight. The distance is 2,400 sm. This is 100 miles shorter than my last leg.

On the last leg, I had not used any fuel out of the aircraft's main tanks. This time I wanted to see how far I could fly with the 199 gallons of fuel I had on board. The total weight of the fuel was 1,194 lbs, and the airplane would fly differently when it was 25% over legal gross weight than when the fuel tanks were empty. I could easily fly to San Francisco, then continue over land and, when I was able to calculate my maximum range, choose an airport just short of running out of fuel.

Shortly after takeoff in the early evening, it turned dark. This flight seemed easier because navigation would be simple. If I headed eastward, eventually I would arrive at the west coast of California. I certainly didn't expect to fly with no navigational information, but if I had to, I could arrive there without it.

I remember one time flying in the Mooney from Denver to my home base in Torrance, California. I was in clear VFR conditions when I lost all electric power. The engine in a piston-powered plane continues to run because the spark is generated by magnetos. I simply continued my journey over Utah, Nevada, and California until I came to the coast. I then followed it southward to Los Angeles. I crossed above the class B, controlled airspace which went up to 12,000 ft., went out over the ocean, descended, and returned under the class B airspace to the Torrance airport. I made a low pass over the tower, rocked my wings, and returned for a landing. The tower gave me a green light to approve my landing.

When I left Honolulu I had headwinds for the first 100 miles; then they turned into tailwinds. I flew through the night and into the daylight. When I was halfway between Hawaii and California, I was 1,000 miles from the nearest land in any direction. This is the only point on earth where this is true. You might wonder what it is like to be 1,000 miles from land in a single-engine airplane with four cylinders. Did I sleep? No. The adrenaline in my bloodstream would prevent that. I had an autopilot, but the altitude hold didn't work. Thus, most of the time I would allow the autopilot to control the heading, but I had to manually monitor the altitude. With the airplane trimmed the altitude stayed fairly steady, but not enough for me to trust it to go to sleep. I tried closing my eyes for a short time, but I couldn't keep them closed. After about 30 seconds, I would open one eye and look at the altimeter. Approximately 17 hours after takeoff, I crossed over San Francisco. At that point I cancelled IFR and continued VFR.

All the airspace above 5,000 ft. over oceans is controlled airspace. Flying in controlled airspace must be done by Instrument Flight Rules (IFR). IFR means theoretically that the controller on the ground commands the pilot in the air what to do. Over land, this is what actually happens, and the pilot is assigned an altitude and a flight path. The pilot has to ask the controller's permission to change altitude or heading. This is to avoid collisions between airplanes. You may legally fly over the ocean below 5,000 ft. without contacting the controller on the ground, but this is not practical for long distances. In reality, there are almost no other airplanes in the middle of the ocean at the altitudes that I fly.

I continued to fly eastward under visual flight rules with tailwinds at 13,500 ft. and was over Salt Lake City when my last ferry tank went dry. Now I was on the airplane's wing tanks. I had progressively pulled back the throttle and used less fuel per hour as the plane became lighter.

You might wonder how I took care of bathroom necessities. I carried a plastic jar to urinate into, and this was relatively easy. But what if I had to move my bowels? This trip around the world represented the fifth time that I had crossed the Atlantic Ocean, and I had made many other flights of over 12 hours and as of then, I had never had to move my bowels during a flight—but this time I did. However, I had always been prepared. I had stashed a plastic garbage bag and a small roll of toilet paper just for such an emergency. It is used like this.

(1) Roll the edges of the garbage bag down until there is only a circular roll around the flat bottom.
(2) Raise your bottom off your seat.
(3) Take down your pants to around the ankles.
(4) Put the garbage bag on the seat.
(5) Do your business and wipe yourself.
(6) Unroll the garbage bag and tie the top.
(7) Now you have your choice: you can stow it in the cabin. ......(or you might open the side window and throw it out.)

I had good tailwinds, and by this time I was flying the plane on long range cruise burning very little fuel. I calculated that I could comfortably make it to the Chicago region and decided to set my destination as Joliet, Illinois. The weather was good but I was flying above the clouds. When I checked the weather at Joliet, I found that the airport was below instrument conditions because of ground fog.

My mind flashed a few years back to when I was returning to Johnstown from a Flying Physicians Association meeting in instrument conditions. For two hours I had flown in thick clouds, and for two hours I had seen neither ground nor sky. I also had no turbulence. Johnstown at that time had only a VOR approach. The tower operator reported heavy cloud cover, at some places extending to the ground. He did say that a half hour earlier, Norman Mendenhal had made it in. Norman was at the same meeting that I had attended. I decided to shoot the approach to minimums and, if I couldn't see the runway, make a missed approach. Arriving over Johnstown, the VOR needle reversed direction, indicating station passage, and I turned outbound at the proper altitude. After five minutes on the outbound leg, I began a procedure turn which reversed my direction and theoretically placed me on a direct course inbound for landing on runway 15. I descended stepwise to the minimum altitude. During all of these maneuvers, I saw nothing of the ground. The luminous grey haze which surrounded our plane had maintained the same consistency for two hours, as though I had stayed in the same place. Only my instruments and the drone of the engine gave any sensation of motion. I continued inbound at minimum altitude, and just as I reached the missed approach point, I saw a bit of ground nearly directly below me. It was a hazy number 15, the runway identifier; painted on the end of the runway a scant 400 feet below, the first evidence that I had seen of the ground for two hours. My hand was on the throttle to apply full power and start the climb for the missed approach; instead, I chopped the throttle and descended rapidly to just above the runway. This gave me a good bit of speed, but I bled it off by holding the plane about three feet from the runway until it gradually settled down. Fortunately, the runway is 6,000 feet long and I touched down at about the middle. My friend operates a FBO (Fixed base operation) halfway down runway 15. He said he was listening to the tower and my transmissions because he didn't think I could make it in. He said visibility prevented him from seeing the runway 400 feet away, and all he heard was tweet, tweet as both of my main wheels gently kissed the concrete.

I felt competent to shoot an approach to minimums under normal conditions, but I didn't want to do it after six hours of pre-flight preparations followed by twenty-seven hours of flying. The controller said it would probably lift by the time I got there but I didn't feel comfortable with the term "probably," so I changed my destination to Des Moines, Iowa, and landed. I had flown 4,000 sm. in 27 hours and 20 minutes. I still had two hours of fuel. This is probably a distance record for a Mooney.

It was after dark when I landed. I told the tower operator when I was on final that I had just flown nonstop from Honolulu. He didn't seem to care the least bit. I had left at dusk and had flown in the opposite direction that the earth rotated—thus my days were shorter and I had to turn my wristwatch six hours ahead. I lay flat on a wooden bench in the terminal and fell asleep for four or five hours. Then I got up, refueled the plane, and continued on to Johnstown where I had started. When I landed, I had 183 hours of flying time in 29 days and had flown 25,280 sm. (21,983 nm.). I arrived home at approximately the same time as I would have if I had flown commercial from Honolulu.

After landing in Johnstown, I put my plane in my hangar, got in my car, and drove the 30 miles to Somerset Hospital where my mother was. She was OK but she couldn't walk. I spent most of the next few days with her, then moved her to a nursing home in Johnstown.

Above: September 1966, William Piper, founder of Piper Aircraft, between Paul and Marjorie. He was 54 years old before he ever flew in an airplane and is 87 in this picture.

Right: Scott Crossfield, famous X-15 test pilot, first man to fly two times the speed of sound, and the Mooney.

Paul and Buzz Aldrin

One Last Hop over the Pond

Toni, my new girlfriend, later my wife and the mother of my three children, had uncomplainingly tended to the home duties while I merrily circled the globe. For this munificent deed, it was my opinion that she should be given the opportunity to join that tiny set of adventurous individuals who were bold enough to cross the Atlantic Ocean with only one engine in their airplane. Toni, whose real name is Antoinette, a name of which I am quite fond, enthusiastically agreed with my proposition. This is a clear demonstration of her carefree love of life and adventure. We had previously spent many hours in the Mooney with nothing but blue water below the wings when we made multiple trips to the Bahamas and the Caribbean with destinations such as Saint Martin, Guadeloupe, Martinique, and Jamaica. It is a fascinating observation of femininity that Toni, who immensely enjoyed all of these over-the-water flights and two Atlantic crossings in a single-engine airplane, changed dramatically after bearing children, as illustrated years later by expressing a fear of flying the twenty-two miles to Catalina Island in my twin-engine Aerostar.

Nine months after returning from the round-the-world trip, we were off again to Europe via the northern route, refueling in

Greenland and Iceland. Once again, Globe Aero had installed the 55-gallon tank in the place normally occupied by our rear seat. The required HF set with the antennae reel between my feet was again in place. I took particular pride in overflying Moncton. This was the fourth time that I would use Canada as a springboard to begin a trans-Atlantic crossing. Three times before I had landed in Moncton, taken the short written test, and had my plane and emergency gear inspected. Now my chest swelled with pride when I stepped up to the briefing counter at Goose Bay and showed my permanent crossing permission license. This was, at least to me, more significant because it was issued to me as an individual rather than a ferry pilot, which was valid only as long as he remained an employee of his company.

The weather was good, including a light tailwind and a rare forecast of high clouds over Narsarsuaq. We expected to be able to see all three entrances to the three fjords at one glance, making it much easier to choose the correct one. True to the forecast, the entrances to the fjords were clear and the approach and landing at Bluie West One was as uneventful as possible. But BW-1 remains a tricky landing even under optimal conditions. We made the government of Greenland somewhat richer when we paid the high fuel prices and fees. And we splurged on the airport's expensive but delicious food.

Then we were off again, circling to gain altitude to cross the ice cap. The highest point listed is 10,700 feet, hundreds of miles north of our route. For safety's sake I climbed to 13,000 ft. and flew with the sun behind our backs. The sky above me was white; the snow below me was white; and only God knew where they met as I couldn't detect any horizon. I'm thankful my vacuum pump, which powers our attitude indicator, also known as the artificial horizon, didn't choose that time to fail.

Leaving the western coast of the misnamed island of Greenland behind and crossing the Denmark Strait to Iceland seemed almost a relief. Greenland geologically but not politically belongs to the

North American continent, whereas when we landed in Reykjavik, Iceland, we were in a part of Europe. What a contrast between the rustic pioneer tone of the Narsarsuaq airport and the modern urban environment of Reykjavik.

Flying from Iceland to Prestwick, Scotland, completed the Atlantic crossing all in fine weather. Then it was on to a small field outside of London where the Mooney was tied down for a well-deserved rest. The remainder of our European roundabout was conducted in a caravan. For those who don't know it, a caravan is the word used for what Americans call an R.V., or a recreational vehicle. The one I had arranged to rent by long-distance telephone could more accurately be designated a miniature R.V. We had no problem mingling with the Gypsies, particularly when Toni hung the laundry out the back to dry. After ten days in France, Germany, Italy, and the Low Countries, we loaded our caravan on a ferry boat and returned across the English Channel to our beloved airplane.

We would follow the same route back that had brought us here, but we elected to do something which is rarely done. We would stay a short time in Greenland. Most trans-oceanic aviators aspire to refuel and exit in the shortest possible time because the weather in Narsarsuaq is notorious for turning sour on a moment's notice.

Aviators are too often ranked by the quantity of their flying hours with little significance being attributed to the quality. Thus, the flyer that had accumulated 5,000 hours in the left seat of an airplane may be, in the reviewer's opinion, superior to one who had logged 3,000 hours. Judging by this mistaken tradition would have ranked me far above my rightful place because for seven straight years, I had exceeded three hundred hours as pilot-in-command. It is not my habit to boast, but when these numbers were revealed to two corporate pilots in my Pennsylvania hometown, whose full-time occupation and only source of food for the family table consisted in transporting executives in a Lear

Jet, they responded with "Wow, we don't get that much." The skill and knowledge of these professionals, of course, were superior to mine.

An employee will toil 2,000 hours during one year with a forty-hour work week. Somewhere I had spent 4,500 hours sitting in the left seat of an aircraft since being allowed my first flight with no one else on board in Belgium—the equivalent of two and a quarter working years. It is remarkable that my backside had not expanded more than it actually did.

In all of this time, aviation never became boring. The pilot is constantly wagering that his intellect and his skill will result in an inanimate piece of metal moving through the air from one place on earth to another and arriving without mishap. My hope was that now my prior experience would allow us to return home incident-free.

We refilled our tanks in Iceland and set off for Greenland. When heading west to Narsarsuaq, it is my habit when flying westbound to circumnavigate the southern tip of the island rather than cross over the ice cap. This allows me to fly northward on the western coast and locate the three fjords from which the pilot must choose one to enter in order to successfully arrive at Bluie West One. If I would attempt to cross the ice cap westbound, and should I be so fortunate as to identify the airport from above, I would have to descend from my cruising altitude of perhaps 12,000 feet and approach the airport between the high mountains which surround the landing strip.

We were approaching the end of my seventh trans-Atlantic crossing in Mooney N300MD. All previous voyages had ended successfully. I began to question, was I overconfident? Is it possible that I had used up my allotted portion of luck?

In 2007, aviators from all over the world had voted on the Internet. Narsarsuaq, abbreviated both UAK and BGBW, was named "The World's Most Dangerous Airport." Here is what tipster David wrote: "The approach is through a fjord, so it's necessary to make a 90-degree turn to line up with the runway while in the 'valley.' It's similar to flying down a city street with high rises on both sides with severe turbulence at all times except on the brightest of days; downdrafts are everywhere. There's the risk of icebergs drifting into the departure/arrival path.

"Unless the ceiling is at least 4,000 feet and visibility at least five miles, pilots without proper knowledge of the local topographical and meteorological conditions are advised not to attempt the approach to Narsarsuaq through the fjord. Strong easterly winds can create severe turbulence and wind shear in the vicinity of the airport. Takeoffs are limited to daytime, and the airport is in uncontrolled airspace.

"As soon as the weather falls below "great for flying" the approach to BGBW becomes a real hand humidifier. Going down the fjord, sometimes wind rushes in from the side and flicks your aircraft to the other side of the cliff wall; over-correcting can be as dangerous as not correcting. The procedure turn to line up on final is nerve-wracking. Before, or as soon as you finish the turn, there is usually a gust of wind either from the side, from the top or from the back, potentially giving you a not-needed-at-all speed boost all the way down."

We participated in the turbulence about which tipster David was writing. Anything not tied down got wings of its own and flew about the cabin. A man of my extensive experience should have known to firmly tighten his seat belt but I didn't, and the ceiling gave me a sharp rap on the head to remind me. But we bounced our way down to firm earth, and just for good measure gave it one more good solid bump on landing.

We checked into the Hotel Narsarsuaq, which began life as a U. S. army barracks. A degree in architecture is not required to deduce this. The area, however, has a rich history. It began when Eric the Red was exiled from Iceland for three years for murdering an old enemy in the Thingvellir, which was the ruling council of the Vikings. Erik the Red left with his son, Leif, to explore the lands reported to be west of

Iceland. He found Greenland and gave it this upbeat name to encourage other settlers to follow. He established a colony in Narsarsuaq, which endured for 400 years. Remnants remain and reconstructions of his buildings have been erected to encourage tourism. From this colony Leif Ericson, also known as Leif the Lucky, set sail westward on an exploratory trip and became the first European to set foot on the North American continent. Other Vikings returned and attempted to establish the first permanent European settlement in North America in Newfoundland, which unfortunately lasted only three years. A statue of Leif Ericson stands across the bay from the airport.

A second occasion when Narsarsuaq affected world history was during the Second World War. Vast quantities of war supplies and manpower were shuttled through here on the way to the war zone. A hospital with 600 beds for the wounded, which persisted until after the Korean War, was located in Narsarsuaq in an area known as Hospital Valley The hospital was abandoned in 1958 and burned down in 1972. The ruins can be visited.

We only spent one night in the hotel because in one long Greenland summer day, we were able to see most of the local sights. Then we departed for the last time to home from "The World's Most Dangerous Airport."

The End of the Mooney

The Mooney, 1965 Super 21, 200 HP, single engine, turbocharger added.

I was now the owner of a shiny twin—a 1984 Aerostar 700P—a pressurized turbocharged speedster—in fact, the world's fastest production piston-driven twin. But I also had the Mooney, which I had flown about 4,500 hours, crossing the Atlantic Ocean seven times, flying around the world, and landing on every continent except Antarctica. She had won as "Best Single Engine" at the National Aviation Awards in Reading, which in my mind made her the best single-engine airplane in America. Because it is not good for an airplane to sit too long without flying, I decided to exercise the Mooney a bit. Even though it had been several months since it was flown, the engine fired up immediately. I taxied over to the wash rack and scrubbed her down. She still looked sharp after all these years. After washing a plane, it is imperative that you drain the gas sumps to remove any water that may have gotten into the tank. Even though I had never had any water get into my tanks before, I drained all of the sumps thoroughly. I drained three times the recommended amount of fuel out and carefully checked for water. There was none.

I taxied to the runway end, and after a normal run-up took off. Everything was perfectly normal until about 400 feet off the ground, when I pulled the throttle back to climb power. The engine stopped! Well, it didn't stop—it went into idle power. Engine failure on takeoff is one of the most dreaded emergency situations for a pilot. It is generally taught that when this occurs it is best to land straight ahead, as the plane often stalls when attempting to turn. I had a lot of experience with the Mooney, and I knew I could make a 180-degree turn in a few seconds. I put the nose down, put the plane on its side, and reversed course in about one second. I dropped the gear and landed on the runway where I had just taken off.

Safely on the ground, the engine continued to run at idle power. I taxied to the end of the runway and played with the controls. I switched from one tank to the other. I tried both magnetos, I tried leaning the mixture. Nothing helped, so I began to taxi to the service shop. As I was taxiing, suddenly the engine revved up and began to behave normally.

It was a Sunday afternoon, and the fixed base operator was closed. I wrote a long note describing my experience in detail and asking them to check it out.

The shop spent days on the problem but could find nothing wrong. We consulted with the Lycoming factory, I spoke with the people who had overhauled the engine years ago, and we had several engine experts look at it. Nobody could find anything wrong.

I flew it once or twice and it functioned normally. But I didn't trust her anymore. There she sat, a pretty red plane that nobody flew. Eventually people began to pester me to buy her. I always related my story as soon as they asked. Finally, two young men begged me to sell her to them. Of course, they were completely aware of what had taken place; in fact, they were sent to me by the mechanic who had spent all of the time trying to find the cause of the engine failure. I took them for a ride and they fell in love with her, so I agreed to sell her.

One of the buyers asked me if I would take him and his wife for a ride about a week later and I agreed. I arrived at the airport an hour earlier to fly her around the pattern by myself to make sure that everything was functioning normally. Run-up normal, takeoff normal, but at about 400 feet, once again the engine failed. Once again I made a wing over and this time I lined up on the taxiway. This time I switched tanks, checked the magnetos, and leaned the engine in flight, but I couldn't get more power. I landed on the taxiway and over ran the end into the grass. Just before coming to a stop, the nose wheel went into a hole and the plane tilted up on its nose. I had stopped the engine so the prop was not damaged. She stood on her nose for a while and, if she had settled back on her wheels, there would have been no damage. But on that day there was a twenty-knot tailwind in the direction that I was landing and, after a short nose stand, she was blown over on her back.

The federal aviation Inspectors looked at it, and at first they said they would call it an incident rather than an accident because there was very little damage, but then they found an aileron was bent so it was classified as an accident.

The insurance company offered to call it a total loss, take the aircraft, and resell it. I jumped at this opportunity. They paid me $25,000. I had paid $12,700 for her. We had spent twenty years and had many adventures together. They sold her to somebody at Torrance airport, and I see her flying now and then.

The Aerostar, 1984 700 P, 700, HP, twin engine, turbocharged, pressurized, certified for known icing.

On American Airlines 5/31/96

Written on American Airlines *Someday, if I live long enough, I hope to write the story of my life. I will do this not to brag, but for the benefit of my children. Sadly, I have spent too little time with my children. Perhaps by relating my experiences, I will be able to convey and perhaps transfer some of the values which have brought me pleasure in life.*

Riyadh, Saudi Arabia, May 25, 1996 *Mr. Hassim, President of Obagi Plastic Surgery and Dermatological Hospital, comes into the operating room where I am doing a hair transplant procedure. He tells that tomorrow I am to fly to Jeddah to do a consultation for the brother-in-law of the King. He will get tickets and take care of everything.*

May 26, 1996 *Mr. Hassim gives me round trip tickets business class, Riyadh—Jeddah—Riyadh, departing Riyadh 6:30 PM and departing Jeddah 11: 30 PM.*

I dress in a neatly pressed grey suit and stripped tie. Dr. Max Sawaf tells me don't use my travel-worn black leather knapsack as a briefcase. I get a new clinic chart and put some extra pages in it. I'll take it without a briefcase. I look for a pen. Max advises me, "Don't use a cheap disposable pen. Better not to have one and they will give you one." I go to the shop and buy a $50.00 Cross pen. Now I am ready.

The car picks me up at the Intercontinental Hotel at 5:30 PM. It is approximately 25 minutes to the airport. I get there, go to the counter, and am told I will need my passport even though we are not leaving the country. I go to a cab. Can I go to the Intercontinental Hotel and return and catch a 6:30 flight? The cabbie says no problem. We agree on 100 Rial and leave. It's beginning to look very marginal to me. I tell the cabbie if we get there on time I'll give him 200 Rial. He brings me back to the airport about 6:30. I get to the plane, which is still there, but they won't let me board. I call Mr. Hassim, arrange to leave at 10:00 PM. The ticket is business class, but no business class is available. Must sit in economy. No problem on this short flight. Over the past several hours I have experienced much humiliation from the airport personnel. They tell me to "go down there and get your ticket stamped to be downgraded." I go in the direction they point, but see nothing. When I return he advises downstairs and to the left. I don't know where he wants me to go. Ask another airport employee. They point. Eventually I get to a desk with at least 30 people in front of me. I'll miss the second plane.

I eventually get through the crowd, get my ticket stamped, and just make the second plane in time.

The Boeing 747 arrives in Jeddah. Before anybody leaves the aircraft they page, "Dr. Paul, come to first class." In Jeddah the planes do not taxi to the terminals, but vehicles arrive at the plane to transfer you to the terminal. There is one vehicle for economy where everybody stands. There is a much more luxurious vehicle for first class and, I think, business class. This has rugs and seats and is quite elegant.

In Jeddah, three large black cars came out to meet the airplane. Their plans were that first I should exit to the limousine. The car in front and the car in back were security. After this, the first class could exit and later the economy class. They had to sit back down so I could get to the front of the plane.

With three large black cars, we drove to the palace. The personal physician of Sheik's family, the minister of health, and several other dignitaries rode in the limo.

From the air, as the plane approached Jeddah, I could see a huge white column about the size of the Washington Monument for miles away. It was the first thing one could see from a distance as you approached the city by air. As we got closer to the palace, I realized this was a huge water spout hundreds of feet in the air, lighted by floodlights on the palace grounds.

The royal family physician told me many details about the Sheik's health. He told me his red blood count, his platelet count, the history of his mild diabetes, the various medications that he took, what he had been on before, and what he was taking now for his hypertension. He must have run blood tests on him every few days.

At the palace, the armed guards checked my passport even though I was sitting beside people who were close confidants of the King. We passed the first gate and drove, maybe a quarter mile through extremely elegant landscaped grounds, to a second gate. There, once again, armed guards with tanks and weapons checked my passport. Remember, I was in the middle car of a three car caravan. We drove a while to the third gate. The physician explained that only a few people are able to get in here because this was where the King lives when he is in Jeddah, and he is here now.

On the way in from the airport, I noticed a second airport and said, "Oh, you have two airports in Jeddah." The physician answered, one airport is for the royal family. In Riyadh they only have a separate royal terminal at the airport.

A third checking of my passport and we were at the palace. As you can guess, it was unbelievably luxurious. I was taken through halls and rooms and elevators and asked to wait in a long room. I asked for a washroom. I didn't have to urinate, but I had left the hotel at 5:00 PM, had been hanging around the airport and rushing here and there. It was about 1 AM; I looked like I had been traveling for days.

Once again I was taken to still another large room. At one end was a large banquet table elegantly set with plates, silverware, and some fruit. At the other end of the room was a sitting area. The Sheik was sitting on a couch. The entourage entered and introduced me. The Prince motioned for me to sit beside him on the couch, while the remainder of the group stood.

In answer to my question, he answered he was 43, but he might have passed for younger. His skin was pale white and soft. He was overweight. His hair was about 1 ½ inches long, black, and didn't look too bad. He was friendly and likeable. He explained that he had been much heavier but had lost a large amount of weight on a Phen-Phen and apple diet eating 700 calories a day. I said, "Wow, you must get hungry!" He laughed and we talked. I talked to him just as I would have talked to my other consults. I felt quite comfortable. I told him he looked just fine and didn't have to do anything. He explained that he had had 180 grafts at the Mayo Clinic about two years ago. I planned to bring a clean comb wrapped in paper and open it so he could see I had a clean comb. I didn't forget it, but with the passport business, I didn't have time. First, I went through his hair with my fingers, but this didn't work too well, so I took out my own bent comb from my pocket and combed it through his hair. I kept the comb behind him so he couldn't see what condition it was in.

I told him he looked just fine and didn't have to do anything, and if he wanted his hair to look thicker, he should wear it longer. He was worried about a thin area in front where the hair changed direction. He did have general thinning over the entire top. I told him I could thicken his hair, but it would never be as thick as he dreamed about. I said, as I always do, I'm going to tell you all the good and all the bad about hair transplantation and spent most of my time discussing all the complications and probable hair loss.

He had hair loss after the operation at the Mayo Clinic, and I told him he would probably have it after my work too. However, in later years he would have more hair on top of his head than if he did no transplants. I told him he must make the decision. I talked to him exactly as I talk to my other consults, be they a businessman or a fireman. The other people in the room scurried around if he wanted something or they thought he might want something and barked commands at the servants. I talked exactly the same to the servants as I would the Sheik. I was in total command of the situation. The Sheik and I got along quite well, although everyone else appeared in awe of him. The Sheik said, "I am going to do it and I want you to do it for me."

I responded that we could either do it in California, in any one of three offices, or in Riyadh at the Obagi Clinic, or at the palace. There was no question the Sheik and everyone easily felt the palace was the place. The Sheik said he would do it after the summer because he didn't want to look bad for the summer. I told him I would send him some colored hair spray to use this summer so you couldn't see the thinning area. Also, I would send some Retin-A to add to his minoxidil, which he is now using. I told him this was my gift to him. We discussed how to use both in great detail.

The Sheik had to leave because the King was in the next room and calling him for dinner. (It was about 1:30 AM.) We parted friends. I'll never know if the table was set for me if I had arrived on time.

The limousine took me to a hotel and picked me up at 6 AM after a few hours of sleep. They took care of my return reservation, picked me up, and took me to the airport VIP lounge. I was taken by another car to the plane and returned First Class—courtesy of the Sheik.

Children, what I want you to learn is to treat everybody with respect. Don't try to fool anybody, just be yourself. Nobody is too low for you to associate with, and nobody is too great.

1998

My secretary interrupted my surgery; the Saudi Arabian Embassy was on the phone. "The Sheik is here to get his hair transplanted," the stern voice of the diplomat announced.

More than two years ago, in May 1996, I had been summoned to Jeddah. The last things the Sheik said, in spite of me advising him that it was not necessary, was he wanted to do it; he wanted me to do it; and he wanted to put in 1,000 grafts in September. His private physician had followed me out and informed me that the Sheik had forgotten that they were traveling in September, and the surgery would most likely take place in October or November. I had had no further contact with them for two years, and I assumed the Sheik had changed his mind and he had forgotten about me. The Embassy said he and his entourage were staying at the Ritz-Carlton in Marina Del Rey and commanded me to visit him that evening at 8:00 PM.

When I arrived at the hotel, one of his bodyguards was permanently stationed in the lobby. He carefully checked my identification and accompanied me to the top floor. It was not necessary to know what room number. He had the entire penthouse floor.

The Sheik had traded the white robe and red and white head scarf, which he had worn in Jeddah for a suit and tie. He greeted me enthusiastically and, as is the Saudi custom, offered me a cup of tea, which I took because to refuse is considered an affront. After I examined him, I saw his hair was thinner than it was when I last saw him, and now transplanting was definitely in his best interest. His private physician, Dr. Shaheed, was with him as was a large group of servants, bodyguards, and a "girlfriend." Dr. Shaheed is a very capable Indian doctor who is employed by the Sheik to provide medical care for the Sheik, the Sheik's family, and his entourage. Once again, Dr. Shaheed reviewed his health records with me in great detail and then made arrangements to do a hair transplant at my office a few days later. The Sheik wanted general anesthesia, so I made arrangements with Dr. Zaks, an anesthesiologist born in Russia, to give him conscious sedation for the five to six hours duration of the surgery. The day before, officials from the embassy and a few of his personal bodyguards came to my office to inspect for security. They inquired whether they could cordon off the entire building for the day, but I said this was not practical. The day of the surgery the guards stood outside of the building, in front of my office door and inside of my office as protection.

The surgery was uneventful. The Sheik slept through it. He was constantly monitored by Dr. Zaks and Dr. Shaheed. I put on a turban bandage, and with the help of about six of the men got him into his limousine. I followed in my own car to see that he got successfully into bed and was comfortable, although it seemed superfluous with all of the excess help and his own physician by his side.

Many Saudi's keep different hours than we do. In the desert, it is extremely hot in the daytime and cooler at night; they also like to telephone to America for business reasons, and nighttime in Saudi Arabia is the time when the businesses in North and South America are open. Therefore, they often sleep most of the day and stay up most of the night. My son would make a good Saudi. I made arrangements to come to his hotel suite the next evening to remove the dressing and clean his hair, which I did accompanied by my chief technician, Belinda Caldwell.

For the next ten days, Belinda and I made our evening trip to Marina Del Rey to shampoo the Sheik's hair. He was very accommodating to us, offering us dinner, tea, and dates, but always told us to arrive at eight and thought nothing of making us wait until ten or later while he talked on the phone or took care of other matters.

On the third day, we had a small earthquake. Dr. Shaheed called my office and left the message that the Sheik had moved across the street to the Marina International Hotel because he was afraid to be on the top floor of the Ritz-Carlton during earthquakes. That evening when we arrived at his quarters in the Marina International Hotel, we found carpenters tearing out walls and opening new doorways. They also were installing the largest flat screen television set I have ever seen. It covered almost the entire wall from ceiling to floor, and this was in the early days of flat screens. I asked, "How long is he going to stay here?" His doctor told me, "It doesn't matter. He owns the hotel. And he owns the Ritz-Carlton too." Later, Dr. Shaheed told me that the Sheik owned hotels all over the world but considered hotels to be a minor portion of his entire business ventures.

Later during the week, the Sheik felt better so he went to a car auction and bought about 15 or 20 cars. They were all old large American muscle cars. Some of them were in fair shape and others looked pretty beat up. I was told, "That doesn't matter. They will all go to the shop and when they come out they will look and run just like they did when they were new."

After about a week, the Sheik wanted to get some liposuction done. He made arrangements to have it done at Cedars Sinai Hospital. The day he went there, the car dealers sent two new Rolls Royce's and a new Ferrari for his transportation. They were hoping that he would take a liking to one or more of them and buy them. He drove to the hospital as a passenger in the Ferrari, and the entourage rode in the two Rolls.

Eventually, the Sheik returned to his homeland. Dr. Shaheed kept in close contact with me and called every week or so to report his progress. As was expected, he was very anxious because his hair looked thinner before thicker, in spite of the fact that I had told him to expect this. As is my custom, I had written this and other potential problems in my own handwriting and given the paper to him before surgery. After it grew out, his physician told me the Sheik was very pleased with the results.

Dr. Shaheed confided in me about his marriage, which was a marriage arranged by his parents in India; it was a happy union but they had, as of that time, been unable to have any children. Eventually he and his wife returned to Los Angeles for in vitro fertilization, which successfully resulted in a healthy child. Dr. Shaheed remains a close friend of me, my family, and office staff.

Operating in the Royal Palace at Riyadh

Dr. Shaheed kept in close contact with me, calling regularly from Saudi Arabia or anywhere else in the world he might have traveled with the Sheik. Two years had passed since the operation in Torrance, California. One day he called and said the Sheik wants to do another hair transplant, and he wants to do it in Saudi Arabia at the Palace in Riyadh. We discussed all the details.

"The operating room?"

"We will use the royal operating room in the palace."

"The anesthesiologist?"

"We will use the royal anesthesiologist."

"The time?"

"Four weeks from now."

"OK, that fits my schedule. I will have to take two assistants with me, and they will need passports and visas."

"Don't worry about the visas. The embassy will issue them if we tell them to do it."

"We'll have to put a rush on the passports."

There was no discussion as to the price of the surgery. Regular phone calls followed. He said they were sending one first-class ticket on British Airways and two coach class tickets for the assistants.

I explained that I wanted three business-class tickets so we could all travel together. Just before we left, he asked what I was going to charge for the surgery. I told Dr. Shaheed, tell the Sheik that the surgery was free, I would only charge for my time; $10,000/day beginning when we got on the plane in Los Angeles and ending when we got off the plane back home. I also said that each assistant should get $1,000/day for the same period of time. They had already said that we were staying in a five-star hotel in Riyadh.

The trip was an adventure for Belinda and Tarren. Tarren had never been out of the country, whereas Belinda was from Australia and more used to international traveling. However, traveling to Saudi Arabia for a female is cultural change, like throwing cold ice water in your face. In Saudi Arabia, the law says that all females must wear an Abaya anytime that they are out in public. This is a long black gown which completely covers their figure. They are also required to have their heads covered with a black scarf. Females except children before puberty may not go out in public alone. They must be with another female or their husband, or any male whom they may not marry. This includes their father, their brothers, their uncles, but not their cousins. They may not ride in a car with any other male than those listed above. Females may not drive a car or other vehicle. There is a separate section in restaurants and a separate entrance, including in fast food restaurants such as McDonald's, for females. This section cannot be seen from the section used by the men. The separate entrance is not adjacent to the men's entrance. Most Saudi women wear veils—it is considered polite—but the girls were not violating the law if they did not wear a veil. My assistants were in for a shock!

We slept in luxury flying overnight to London on British Airways. In business class, you sleep on a totally flat bed. From London to Riyadh, the closer we got to our destination, the greater the tension. The girls had to dress in their Abayas before landing. When they got out of the plane, their lives changed. Nobody can visit Saudi Arabia as a tourist. You have to have business there, and you have to have a Saudi sponsor to get a visa. We had the best sponsor possible, the royal family.

We were met by one of the Sheik's employees, who ushered us through immigration and customs. I had made many trips to Saudi Arabia to do hair transplants at the Obagi clinic. Entering the country as a guest of the royal family is much easier. We were ushered to a limousine and sped to the hotel. After an hour to shower and change, Dr. Shaheed arrived in another limousine to take us to the palace. I had visited the palace in Jeddah at night; now we would have a tour of the palace in Riyadh in the daytime.

In Jeddah, there we had to pass three gates with guards checking our papers at each gate to enter the palace. In Riyadh it was the same routine every time we entered.

Dr. Shaheed said, "The first time I'm going to take you through the main entrance to show you the opulence, on other days we will use the side entrance as it is closer to the hospital." I'm glad that he did because I cannot adequately describe the gold, the marble, the fountains, and the artistry of the three or four story entrance hall. Dr. Shaheed gave us a brief tour of the palace, but we were not taken to the residence rooms of the king or royal family. Gold was everywhere. I went to a lavatory. Everything was gold. Of course the fixtures such as the water facets, towel racks, and mirror frames were gold, but what impressed me was that even the brush to clean the toilet had a massive gold handle. All of the gold was 24-caret solid gold. No gold plate here. One might think that someone might just pilfer the toilet brush. Not likely. The punishment for stealing in Saudi Arabia is to cut your hand off. If you stole from the palace, you would get your head cut off. And justice is swift in Saudi Arabia. The trial is immediate and brief. The beheading occurs the first Friday which follows the end of the trial. In Saudi Arabia, you will have your head cut off for some things which we might regard as minor offences—for example, any narcotics possession, such as a small amount of marijuana.

Adultery for a woman has a special penalty. The woman is stoned to death. For years the women was tied down and the citizens had a pile of rocks that they threw at her, but now this is the modern age. In this advanced age, a dump truck dumps the rocks on the woman.

Every Friday is beheading day in the city square, and families take their children to see it. This is to impress them about what will happen to them if they do not behave. Riyadh had a traditional beheading place which they used for many years, but recently the city has been modernized and a new beheading site has been built.

Dr. Shaheed took me to see the royal operating room. It was very well equipped. Much of the equipment had never been used. When I asked for an electrocautery, I was shown a deluxe instrument which was brand new. I had brought all of the small specialty instruments with me. I was introduced to the royal anesthesiologist, a Saudi who had trained in the United States.

All arrangements were made for the surgery the next day, and we went to see the Sheik. He greeted me warmly and offered me a cup of tea, which I accepted as it is considered an insult to refuse an offered cup of tea. His grafted hair had grown well, but he continued to lose his natural hair. My two female assistants were with me continuously and remained respectively to the side. After my consultation with the Sheik, he invited us to dinner. It was nearly midnight. He motioned to a servant, who had been standing in waiting, and the servant opened a huge door to an adjacent room with a table in the center. Food covered the entire table I estimated to be 30 to 40 feet long. The Sheik sat at the head of the table. Dr. Shaheed and I sat nearest to the Sheik, and the girls sat next to me. I knew that this was a great honor because normally the Saudi men do not eat with females, even with their wives. One servant stood behind each chair and tended to each of the people who were invited to dine with the Sheik.

The surgery was scheduled for 2:00 PM the following day, which was considered quite early for the Saudi royalty. The surgery was uneventful. Bleeding was minimal; my assistants were efficient and well trained. Both Dr. Shaheed and the royal anesthesiologist were impressed. The Sheik was in general anesthesia during the entire time. There were a large number of officials and family waiting outside the operating room and at the conclusion Dr. Shaheed and the anesthesiologist gave the group a glowing review of my surgery in Arabic while I stood by their side basking in their praise. We took the Sheik to his room and saw that he was comfortable in his bed. Dr. Shaheed stayed by his bedside, but I had done everything that I could do, so the girls and I were taken back to our five-star hotel in the same limousine that had picked us up in the morning. We returned the following evening at 8:00 PM, which would be considered mid-morning according to the usual schedule of the Sheik. I had had several phone calls from Dr. Shaheed reporting on his recovery progress. I removed the dressings and my female assistants washed his hair. After meticulous post-operative care, the Sheik again invited us to eat with him. The spread was similar to the grandiose meal we had the day before. This time I silently counted the dishes. There were twenty-seven large platters, what you might call main courses, such as filet mignon, lobster, lamb, chicken, etc., and three times as many side dishes. All this for six people.

Each evening for five days, we visited the palace and repeated the experience. We would arrive at 8 PM, but often the Sheik would be busy, perhaps making phone calls or other business. He would often let us wait an hour or two before seeing us, but always the servants provided tea.

The last evening our plane departed at midnight, so we were under the impression that we would miss the daily banquet, which usually began about one AM. Therefore, we ate at the hotel before reporting to the palace. This was a mistake as the sheik had prepared a special going-away feast held by the side of his marble and gold indoor swimming pool, sitting cross-legged on plush cushions. It was an extraordinary royal honor for me and all the more rare because he allowed my female assistants to share it.

Running

"We ran a mile without stopping," we bragged to Bob McIlwain. It was the summer of 1972, and Chuck McIlwain, Bob's son, and I had, on an impulse, decided to take a jog. We ran the curving, slightly downhill, tree shaded, two-lane macadam road from my trailer in the woods to the bridge at the junction with the main road. It was one mile. There we sat on the bridge rail for five minutes, caught our breath, and ran back. A bubbling stream which followed the curves in the road provided the only sound except for the synchronous thump, thump of our running shoes. Our nostrils were treated to the fragrance of wild lilacs with dense woods on one side and a golf course on the other. It is said that an alcoholic loves his first sip of booze; perhaps this idyllic setting of my first jog led me to addiction.

I had run the half mile on the Somerset High School track team simply because nobody else wanted to run that distance. I don't remember ever finishing any race in any position other than last place, and typically I was the single last runner well behind the others running ahead of me in a group.

But I wanted to get in shape for skiing. My skiing had remained at the intermediate level for years. I just couldn't seem to move up to the expert level. I thought maybe if I got my legs in better condition, my skiing would improve. In retrospect this did work. My skiing did improve.

Chuck and I started running every evening. After a while, Chuck dropped out but I continued. In those years runners were rare, and people in cars driving by used to laugh to see a grown man running. I gradually increased my distance and soon was running ten miles with occasional runs of fifteen miles. I decided that I would run one marathon in my lifetime. Marathons are races modeled after the distance from Marathon, Greece, to Athens. They are all 26.2 miles. The story is that in 490 B.C., when the Greeks defeated the larger Persian army at Marathon, the Greek general, Mardonius, sent the runner, Phidippides, to Athens to bring the news. The exhausted runner announced, "We are victorious!" and dropped dead. I had no interest in dropping dead but did want to run one race.

In 1978 I entered the Johnstown, Pennsylvania, marathon. I didn't know if I could really run that far and I didn't want to embarrass myself, so I made a trial run of the course one month before the race. My time for the practice run was four hours; the time for the actual race was three hours and thirty minutes. I was 45 years old.

After I moved to California in 1979, I fell in with a crowd who greatly influenced my life. Dan Sheeran, a talented runner, introduced me to the Palos Verdes Breakfast Club. This group of about fifty men has been running together Sunday mornings for more than forty years. We meet Sunday mornings at 7:00 AM and for years ran fifteen miles, then had breakfast together. Now the runners are getting older and our runs are about seven and a half miles, and many are walking. About twenty-five of the members show up on any given Sunday. Each member hosts a breakfast in rotation, so each member provides the breakfast once a year. Some men have their golf or poker friends; we have our running friends. This is not only a place to get exercise; it is our primary social group. If you meet together for such a long time, everybody knows everybody quite well. For years, each member had the breakfast at their house, but in recent years more and more members are hosting their breakfasts at restaurants. What used to be an ordinary running club has turned into an old men's running club. In 2009 we had eight members over 80; twenty-three, 70-79, and nine 60-69. We are an amazingly healthy group. We have had only four deaths, one caused by a brain tumor, one by liver cancer, one by stroke, and one by Parkinson's disease; none by heart disease. Two things may have contributed to this—the regular exercise and the friendship. It has been shown that people who have friends live longer.

Everybody raced in the early years. When compared to my fellow club members, I produced mediocre finishing times, but at least I never quit. Later, many of the others stopped entering races but, consistent with my stubborn personality, I continued. I had the unusual habit of running my age in miles on or near my birthday. On my 50th birthday I ran 50 miles, on my 51st birthday I ran 51 miles, etc. I continued this ritual from 50 to 56. At age 57 I had an injury and ended this tradition. The embarrassment of no longer running my age was compensated by substituting a second obsession. For the next twenty years—that is, until the ripe old age of 76—I completed five marathons each year. This series made it easier to estimate in how many of these orgies I had participated. Twenty times five is, of course, one hundred. Prior to that, I didn't keep track. I simply would bring a participant medal back from Boston and give it to the children to add to their toys. I most likely have been silly enough to have run 125 marathons.

One of our favorite breakfast conversations revolves around our past running times. Many of the old codgers can brag about sub-three hour marathons, but I sadly but honestly report that my personal best is only three hours and twelve minutes. After that, I got slower and slower.

Always a middle of the pack runner, I persisted until the pack thinned down. In my seventies, I took third place in my age group in Los Angeles, second at Las Vegas, fourth at New York City, first at Big Sur, and first, second, and third at Death Valley, where I was the only runner in the age group. One advantage of getting older is that some of your competition dies off.

To train for these marathons, I often get up on Sunday at 2 AM and start running at 3 AM. This training run circles the Palos Verdes peninsula for a distance of 22 miles and climbs and descends 1,200 feet up and down our mountain. This I did for eleven consecutive Sundays before the Los Angeles marathon. My neighbors, who are awakened when I leave my house at 3 AM, think I'm crazy.

Two entities are of equal importance in distance running: being in excellent physical condition and having the proper mental attitude. I talk to myself like a schizophrenic before the event and play mental games during the competition. The sequence is, go to bed early, get a good night's sleep, and picture myself running past landmarks on the course while falling asleep.

The following day, during the run, I count my steps, counting to one hundred, then projecting one finger; when all five digits of my left hand are extended, I've made 500 strides with my left foot, and it's time to repeat with the right hand—anything to keep my mind off the "agony of de feet." When tiredness sets in I begin to set goals, telling myself that I will run to that tree in the distance and, when I get there, picking another point further away as my target. Thinking about continuing the many miles to the end would be discouraging. I also sing to myself and run the tempo of the song. Fortuitously I do not sing out loud, as I have no crooning ability, and I doubt my fellow runners and the spectators would appreciate my rendition of "Mama's little baby loves, mama's little baby loves, mama's little baby loves short'nin bread."

My weird way of breathing makes me a pitiable conversationalist. Your ability to run fast is proportional to your maximum oxygen uptake in your lungs. Your oxygen uptake increases as the pressure of oxygen in your lungs increases. When I used to fly at altitudes above 12,500 feet without oxygen, I used to pressure breathe in an attempt to keep mentally alert in spite of diminished oxygen pressure. The trick is to inhale normally but exhale through pursed lips, increasing the pressure in the mouth, trachea, and lungs. I reasoned that the increased oxygen pressure in the lungs would cause increased oxygen uptake. I had never read this anywhere; it was my own idea, but it seemed to work. I also used this breathing technique when mountain climbing at high altitude, and I adopted it to running. You can be nearly exhausted, just ready to quit, then adopt my pressure breathing technique and feel a new surge of power. I have never seen this technique described in any running manual, but it should be because it could make the difference between a win and a loss in a close race.

Running the Palos Verdes Marathon (26.2 miles) pulling Erik in my patented jogging cart.

When the children were little, baby joggers were popular. These are three-wheeled carts which hold the child and are pushed ahead of the runner. I realized that swinging the arms is an important part of the runner's stride. Just try running a while with both arms held ahead of you in the position they must be to push a stroller. For this reason, I designed a jogging cart that the runner pulled behind him in the manner of a rickshaw and was attached to his waist by a belt. I used a child's automobile seat and two wheelbarrow wheels with rubber tires. On July 18, 1989, the United States patent office issued me patent number 4,848,780 on my invention, but I never attempted to manufacture it. My son, Erik, and I completed two marathons with him in it, Jacquelyn, my oldest daughter, did one, and Morgan, my youngest daughter, did one.

The legacy runners are the competitors who have run all of the Los Angeles marathons. In 2010, we will have completed twenty-five of them. With each year, the number in this group grows smaller, and the membership is permanently closed. For this race I wear the permanent number 10281 on my chest. When I quit running Los Angeles marathons, this number will be retired and no other person will ever use it. I was interviewed for this club and was asked what advice I would give to beginners. I replied, "If you want to run twenty-five consecutive Los Angeles marathons, begin before the age of fifty-two."

December 7, 2008. At 76 years of age I have only two more miles to complete the Las Vegas marathon. At the finish I will have run five marathons each year for the last twenty years. This adds up to 100 marathons; each 26.2 miles. Before that I had run about 25 marathons for a total of about 125 marathons.

Appendix

Life on the Run ━━━━━━━━━━━━━━━━━━━━━

The Palos Verdes Breakfast Club
By Lanny Nelson

> "Never give up. Never, never, never give up."
> —Winston Churchill

One of them has run 239 marathons. Another fell into a crevasse at 23,000 feet on the slopes of Mt. Everest. Yet another flew around the world, solo. Collectively they have run over 2,000 marathons, they have run 100-mile trail races, they have swum from Catalina to Los Angeles, run triathlons, bicycled across the country, tried out for the Olympics, finished in the top five at the Boston marathon—all this while they have served their country and raised families and pursued careers.

Fifty men. They are doctors and lawyers, military men, insurance brokers, business owners, and family men. All but six of them live in and around the Palos Verdes Peninsula, a huge mound of rock at the western edge of California. They are unsung war heroes, and they are famous within their business careers. And yet they remain just a group of regular guys who get together every Sunday to run, eat breakfast, and talk.

What makes them unique is that they have been doing this for nearly forty years.

"I was the fifth guy," said Blair Filler, meaning he was the fifth person to join the unofficial Palos Verdes Breakfast Club. Note: the club has a roster and the roster is titled "PV Runners Club," but I was told rather pointedly by some of the more "seasoned" members that the club was called the "Breakfast Club." So be it.

Now 77 years old, Blair Filler is a practicing orthopedic surgeon who has run 53 marathons and still runs five or six days a week. His wife, Dodie, 74, also runs. They just returned from a trip to Peru, where they hiked to Machu Piccu.

"I was the fourth guy to join," said Reinhold Ullrich. In 1995, Ullrich found himself on the slopes of Mount Everest, at 23,000 feet, trying to scale the last of the seven highest summits on seven continents. He accidentally fell into a crevasse and broke his arm and was forced to turn back, a bitter disappointment. Ullrich, at 78, has not slowed down. He recently "walked" a marathon on the deck of the Queen Mary—enduring stormy weather and pausing long enough to shower, dress in a tux, attend a formal dinner with his wife, only to return to the deck and finish his walk.

The members of the Palos Verdes Breakfast Club have been together since 1967. Only two of the original members have passed away. Only one left the group voluntarily. Orville Atkins, a Canadian born runner who trained under the famous Hungarian coach Mihaly Igloi and who finished 5th in the 1962 Boston marathon, once moved to Florida for eight years. "I was miserable and depressed," he said. "I went to see the doctors and they could not help me. I moved back and rejoined the group and the symptoms went away."

Al Corwin, 81, recently came out of retirement and ran the Palos Verdes Half Marathon with his daughter and three grandsons. One of the grandsons, age eleven, won his age group. Al

Corwin won his age group as well. Of course, he freely admits that there was no one else in his age group.

What makes these guys tick? How have they been able to fend off old age, to fight back the normal array of problems we are so familiar with—arthritis, back pain, hip problems, cancer, poor circulation, etc.? And how did this group of ageless men all land in one basic geographical area? It makes one wonder if the fountain of youth might actually be hidden somewhere in the hills of Palos Verdes. Perhaps these men have found the mythical fountain and keep it carefully hidden in a secret glen high above the Pacific Ocean.

Or maybe it's something else. Maybe it is the simple fact that these men genuinely and unabashedly care about each other. Woven in and around all of their daring feats and remarkable accomplishments is something rare, so unusual, that it is almost dismissed as irrelevant—but it is the very thing that has kept them going.

These men are like brothers. They are family. They have a bond that unites them. It makes them stronger.

Kelsie is sixteen years old. She is a natural born runner with a smooth stride. She lives a few miles away from my home and attends the same high school as my son, where they both participate in cross country and track. My wife and I make it a point to attend the track meets, and we often sit with Kelsie's parents. One afternoon at a late-season track meet, I was introduced to Kelsie's grandfather. He was a tall, thin man with a certain sharpness about him. I noticed that he moved with ease up and down the bleachers. He wore running shoes that had obviously been well used.

"Hello," he said. "I'm Blair Filler."

I picked up Blair Filler the next morning, and we went for an eight-mile run. I had never run with a 77-year-old person before and I wasn't quite sure what to expect. My reaction was nothing less than shock and then complete admiration. We did not run fast ... but we certainly did not go that slow. We moved right along, and when we came to the downhill sections, Blair Filler ran like a man half his age, clocking sub-nine-minute miles. Together we crossed a stream, ran through the desert, ran up and down hills, and we talked the entire time. To my delight I found that he was a wealth of knowledge, and his story fascinated me. He had run all over the world, and in every kind of weather and climate. In China he had taken a wrong turn and ran into a group of armed soldiers, who formed a line across the road and shouted at him to leave immediately. Apparently he had stumbled across some secret military road while out on his morning run. As an orthopedic surgeon, he continued to see patients and gave lectures on a regular basis—not to mention that he knew just about everything there was to know about the effect running had on the physical body.

And then Blair told me about his group of friends—men he had been running with for nearly forty years. "Some of us have slowed down a little," he said. "A few guys only walk now, but most of us still run."

A running club that has lasted forty years? With the same group of men? Unbelievable. And the more I heard about some of the amazing accomplishments of these men, I knew that I had to meet these guys. "I would like to meet your friends," I said. I told him that I was in the process of writing a book called *Life on the Run*, and it would be an honor if I could interview him and his friends. "It would be the last chapter of the book," I told him. "Because you guys are *Life on the Run*."

Blair Filler agreed. "Sounds good," he said. "You can come out and run with us too!"

On a foggy Sunday morning in early July, my fifteen-year-old son and I ran six miles through the hills with the Palos Verdes Breakfast Club. A few of the runners were sixty years older than my son and thirty years older than me. Most of them wore cotton t-shirts collected from other runs, other races. A few wore hats.

Nobody carried water. Very few of them had eyeglasses on. No radios or walkmans or MP3 players. No specialized cling-free, ultra light microfiber running gear. Some had watches. Some did not. They reminded me of running as it was in my high school days—pure and simple, without the trappings of modern technology.

They laughed when my son took off down the hill in the first few miles. "There goes the youth of America!" someone shouted.

"The youth better save his energy!" someone shouted back. "He has to come back up the hill!"

More laughter. More jokes. Catcalls.

Up and down we went. The group led us over narrow trails and dirt roads that followed the rolling hills. Below us was the Pacific Ocean, powerful and endless guardian of the west. It felt as if the Palos Verdes Breakfast Club runners were really just boys in a giant playground of rolling hills and cool, foggy valleys, kept safe by the mighty Pacific. In this playground, these men ran and shared their lives with each other. There they ran and talked to each other and learned to trust each other and hold each other up. Out in the open air, safe among the hills, guarded by the sea, they grew closer than brothers.

"We know everything about each other," said Blair Filler. "We tell each other everything."

And that's when I realized that the Palos Verdes Breakfast Club runners had indeed discovered the fountain of youth. Only it wasn't a fountain as we thought it might be, a rocky pool of crystalline water in some lost garden. The fountain was actually inside each man—in the center of his heart. Together, the Palos Verdes Breakfast Club runners kept the fountain flowing. Together they navigated the hills of life and learned not only how to survive, but to thrive.

Scotty is a short, live wire of a man. Born in Scotland in 1927, Scotty (whose real name is Dan Sheeran) has run 239 marathons. He also served two countries in two different military organizations. He was a submariner in the British Navy and a paratrooper in the U.S. Army. Scotty (along with a few other members of the breakfast club) has run all twenty Los Angeles marathons. He has run the London to Brighton 54-mile run. Thirty-nine times he has finished a marathon in less than three hours. At the age of fifty, he ran it in less than two hours and fifty minutes. That's twenty-six miles back-to-back, each mile ran in less than six minutes and thirty seconds—at the age of fifty!

Outspoken, gruff, filled with energy, and quick with a joke, Scotty latched onto me when I visited the PV Breakfast Club runners, and he quickly became my official guide. He took me from man to man and introduced me. He made sure that I heard the stories. The endeavors. The tales of exotic adventure. If one person wouldn't open up and talk to me, Scotty did it for him.

"That guy over there (Paul Straub) is famous," he would say. "He flew around the world solo in a single-engine plane and got lost over the sea. Lights out. No contact. No radio. Now that's adventure."

"That guy (Bob Trujillo) just ran a 5K in 24:13. He is 74."

Scott sat next to Lt. Colonel Tom Jones, 84, a former U.S. Marine for 30 years, a World War II veteran, a man who wrote a book titled *A View from My Foxhole*, and a man who ran his first marathon when he was fifty.

"Ed and I ran the London to Brighton together," said Scotty. That would be Dr. Ed Berman, 75, a practicing cardiologist who drove a brand new red Corvette. Clear and precise, Dr. Berman looked and spoke like a man twenty-five years younger. He ran his first cross-country race in the fall of 1944, when he was fourteen. That is over sixty years of running. "I can still remember that day," said Berman. "That was a long time ago."

"Too bad John Hill's not here today," said Scotty. "Now that guy is crazy. He swam from Catalina Island to Los Angeles. He has biked across the United States. He has climbed all the highest mountains." Scotty laughed and nodded sincerely. "And a whole lot more crazy things, too, I'm telling ya!" John Hill will soon be 70.

And on it goes. Story after story. Adventure piled upon adventure. On the back porch of Blair Filler's home, on a Sunday afternoon, with good food digested and cold drinks in hand, time began to slip away, and I realized that I did not have enough time to personally meet every runner in the Palos Verdes Breakfast Club and to hear his story. I could have easily spent two hours just listening to each man tell me about his amazing life. Blair Filler was a good example. His home office is filled with trophies that both he and his wife have collected over the past three decades. Marathons. Half marathons. 10K runs. First place. Second place. Again and again. Dodie Filler ran her first marathon at the age of 42. She went on to run many more races, winning her age group in many of them. At the age of 69, she and Blair climbed Mt. Kilimanjaro. "I added an extra day to the trip," said Dodie. "I didn't want to rush."

Dodie Filler, now at the age of 74, still runs 20 miles a week, helps her husband run his business, drives, cooks (unbelievable pies), and moves around with more energy than most 30-year-old soccer moms. I spent a weekend in her house and watched her spend an entire day cooking. She did not sit down to rest until 7:00 PM that night.

"We used to sleep in," said Dodie, "until we started running." That was over thirty years ago.

What is a Life on the Run? I have asked myself that question again and again. But not until I met the Palos Verdes Breakfast Club runners did I truly understand the question. Not until my son and I ran through the fog-covered hills with men of another generation did I get it. These men, in the final chapter of their lives, gave me a glimpse of the life I was looking for.

Life on the Run is about a life of feeling. It is about standing shoulder to shoulder with family and friends, breathing deeply, and enjoying every moment of that life. *Life on the Run* is about feeling passion and love for the people in your life. It is about getting in touch with the simple things of life—like cool foggy mornings and homemade apple pie. It is about being thankful for a good set of lungs and strong legs and understanding that health is a gift, not a membership.

An Interview with a Veteran

By Jacquelyn Straub

The veteran that I decided to interview is my father, Dr. Paul Straub, who is a Korean War veteran.

He was born in Johnstown, Pennsylvania, December 2, 1932. My father put himself through college and medical school and finished with no debts. He attended the University of Pittsburgh, Pennsylvania, and was taking a full time program leading to a Bachelor of Science in physics while working eight hours a day at U.S. Steel Research Laboratory and was within six months of graduating. The Korean War never came to an official end. Hostilities remain today between North and South Korea, and there are armed guards at the border who still occasionally shoot at each other.

The United States government was easing itself out of the hostilities and announced that any man inducted into the military after December 31, 1954 would not get the G. I. bill. We had the draft at that time, and all young men who were in good health were required to put in two years of active military duty. A college student could defer this duty until he graduated, then he would have to enter the service after graduation. This would have meant that my father would have been drafted six months later but would not have gotten the G.I. bill, which he was counting on to pay for his doctorate studies. This news was made public about one week before the end of the year. Vast numbers of college students crowded the enlistment centers, attempting to enlist prior to the end of the year. On December 23rd, the day my father enlisted, the line snaked around the block, and the picture of the line was on the front page of the Pittsburgh Press. Because of the large number of college students attempting to enlist, all enlistments were stopped two days later. He arrived just in time. He was 22 years old.

My father took the general military intelligence test, and he was told that he was eligible for any school that the military had. He decided on the Language School in Monterey, California. The recruiting officer recommended that he enlist for the Army Security Agency.

One month later he was doing basic training with the 3rd Armored at Fort Knox, Kentucky. This lasted for three months, and as with all recruits, he was required to crawl through the obstacle course with live machine gun bullets being fired a few inches over their heads and explosions going on throughout the training field. This was his only exposure to live weapons being fired at him.

After Fort Knox he went to Fort Devens, Massachusetts, for introductory training in military intelligence. From there he was transferred to the Presidio of Monterey in California for six months of intensive training in the German language. At the language school, there was one native instructor for every six students. There was six hours of classroom instruction every day and homework every night. After a few days, all instruction was done in German. This method is called total immersion. Every Friday afternoon, they had German singing and they learned all the German drinking songs. Near the end of the course, they visited a department store and were to ask the word for anything they could see and for which they did not know the German word. After six months the students had a good foundation in the German language, and they were advised that if they wanted to perfect the language, they should mix with the German people. My father took this advice to heart and became proficient such that the natives would not believe that he was not a German.

After Monterey he was sent to Frankfurt, Germany, and was assigned to the Army Security Agency (ASA), where he spent two years. He tells me that when he was discharged, he was never to tell what he did in Germany; however, he said that he saw an article in *Time* magazine which told almost the entire story, so he felt that perhaps he was no longer bound by this. This was the height of the Cold War. Germany was divided into East and West. The *Time* magazine article said the ASA monitored the telephone lines of the Communist Party in East Germany. They stated that a tunnel was dug under the border. (This was before the Berlin wall was built.) And the telephone lines were tapped. The article stated that there were at least 3,000 spies in Berlin at that time. I guess my dad was one of them. He specialized in scientific conversations. There were many translators and interpreters, but most had liberal art backgrounds and he had a strong scientific background. He started a group which he headed called the scientific group; they were very successful and as a result of his discoveries, a new military base was established on a German mountaintop in an effort to intercept even more secret messages.

After two years, my father returned home. He was a changed man after his experiences. He completed the last semester at the University of Pittsburgh and got his B.S. degree. Then he returned to Europe. He enrolled in medical school at the University of Louvain in Belgium in the Flemish language. This is a dialect of Dutch. Dutch is a separate language, but geographically it lies between England and Germany, and for a person who spoke fluent English and German and knew how to learn a language, it was not too difficult to learn Flemish. He completed five years at the Belgium University on the G.I. bill. The G.I. bill would not nearly have paid for medical school in America. He returned to America to do his internship and residency.

There is no question that his military experience greatly changed his life. If it were not for that, my dad would not have become a doctor. If it were not for that, he would not speak four languages—English, German, Flemish, and French.

From this interview, I learned that my father is a very determined man. I would like to have the same goal orientation in my life.

Bob McIlwain

I will tell you about my good friend Robert McIlwain with a copy of the letter that I wrote to his six sons when he died.

October 6, 2001
Dear Robert, Chuck, Doug, Tony, John, and Tim,

I'm sure you know that your father was as close to me as a brother. He was a wonderful, giving person. He was an usher at both of my weddings. He was at my first wife's funeral and my mother's funeral. I would like to tell you the story of our relationship. I often felt that Bob did so much more for me than I was able to do for him.

Sometime about 1964 I met Bob at the Johnstown, Pennsylvania, airport. I had just completed my internship and gotten a medical license. As soon as I began to work and accumulated a bit of money, I bought a Tripacer for $4,500, but I had only a student pilot's license. Bob had a new Mooney, which looked to me like a Learjet. Years later, when I was able, in imitation of Bob, I bought myself a Mooney. Bob took me under his wing. He was handsome. He liked people and people liked him. Everywhere he went, people knew Bob and were happy to see him. He took me with him and introduced me to his friends.

One of the first of the many good things that Bob did for me was to take me on a trip to Florida in his Mooney with a WJAC sports reporter to visit the Pirates for the local television station. There were four of us in the plane. It was a marvelous trip. I was a Somerset boy, raised in a poor, but honest home, and had never had the opportunity to take such a long trip in a new plane as fine as Bob's Mooney.

After a couple of months of dragging along with my local flight instructors, Bob said, "Come on, they're taking too long here. We're going to get your pilot's license." We flew to Ohio, where he knew a flight examiner. We stayed a weekend and the examiner gave me some instruction for a few days, then gave me the exam, and I came home with my pilot's license.

Bob and I stayed close friends. One day he said we'd fly to Baltimore to get some clams and oysters and have a clam bake. With four people in Bob's plane, we flew to Baltimore and got 200 lbs. of clams and oysters. I'm sure we were over gross when we flew back. But we made it and had a great clam bake with lots of people at Bob's house.

A few years later when I married Margie, Bob, my best friend, was an usher at my wedding.

In the '60s we were scuba diving. We had located a motorboat which had been sunk in Deep Creek Lake, Maryland. We marked it with an underwater buoy that couldn't be seen from the surface; then we went to the insurance company and bought the salvage rights for $100. We then set about to raise the boat. It was quite a large boat, and the location was within sight of the main bridge. In those days scuba divers were rare, and we had a large crowd watching our salvage operation. Bob operated the rowboat at the surface while Paul Blackner and I dove. We filled several oil drums with water and sunk them, then lashed them to the boat. We then filled the oil drums with air using a compressor in Bob's boat. Most of the crowd of people were saying all day long, "You'll never be able to raise that big boat." They were laughing at us. But we did it. We raised, put it on a trailer, and hauled it to Bob's house. There is no question that Bob got great pleasure out of that day because he had to sit at the surface and bear the jeers of the crowd. When we raised the boat, he was ecstatic.

We hunted many times together. We went up to the farm many times, but the most memorable was when Doug, at age 13, shot the deer.

It was a bitter cold day, December 1st, the first day of deer season. Bob, Doug, and I hunted with Emmit and the boys the first day. All of us were cold and nobody had gotten a deer. We stayed in the cabin that night, and the second day we weren't as eager to freeze again. Emmit and the boys left before daybreak to hunt again, but Bob, Doug, and I stayed in the cabin to keep warm. About 9 AM we decided to go hunting and got into Bob's car. We were driving down the dirt road when a big buck ran right beside the car. Bob stopped. We all piled out. We scrambled up a small slope from the road to the field where the deer was. Bob took a shot and missed. I took a shot, but the safety was on my gun. By the time Doug shot, the deer was only a speck several hundred yards away. With one shot the deer fell dead. When we got to him we couldn't even find the bullet hole, but it was a huge buck with a huge rack. We loaded the dead deer in the car and drove back to the cabin.

Later, Emmit and the boys returned to the cabin. They were frozen and had had no luck. At Bob's urging, we said nothing. They said, "You guys are still sitting where you were this morning. Didn't you even go out?" Bob, of course, said no. After a while, Bob asked Emmit if he would get something from the trunk of his car and handed Emmit the keys. The boys were always polite and of course he did this. When he opened the trunk, he saw the buck.

Bob and I shared both the happy and the sad times. When Margie was killed in an airplane accident, Bob, who had been with me at the wedding, was with me at the funeral.

After Margie died, I was kind of lost. Once again Bob took me under his wing. He said, "Come and live with me." But I didn't want to do that. He said, "Get a trailer and put it on my property so you can have a place of your own."

I thought I'd buy a cheap, used trailer, but Bob had other ideas. He took me to a dealer that he knew and I bought a new, super deluxe, all electric mobile home. Then he took me aside and said, "You choose where you want to put it." I walked deep into the woods and found a flat area. Bob would have preferred it closer to his house, but what I wanted was OK with him.

A few days later, he took his bulldozer and Lester drove it through the woods to the spot. Behind the bulldozer was an unpaved road. Lester cleared out an area for the trailer. I was just amazed at what was accomplished in one day.

A few days later we hauled the mobile home up. The widow lady in the house leading up to Bob's property was opposed to having any mobile homes because she felt this would devalue her property. When we came up the lane with the bulldozer pulling the trailer, she came out with a shotgun. I think she was gunning for Bob. All of Bob's men found safety hiding behind the bulldozer while she waved the shotgun and shouted and cussed at Bob. Bob whispered in my ear, "Doc, I think she is more sympathetic with you. Go see if you can reason with her." So I crept out from behind the bulldozer and cautiously approached her.

Well, she was a bit hysterical and pushed the muzzle of the shotgun about two inches into my belly button and screeched, "You think I won't shoot?"

Lucky for me she refrained from pulling the trigger. Her son talked her out of it, and she spent a few days in the psychiatric ward of the local hospital. Eventually we became good neighbors for many years.

I lived many years on Bob's property and never paid him a cent of rent. I offered it to him, but he refused to take it. These were happy years. Bob picked up Paul Blackner, who, like me, was temporarily down and out because he was going through a divorce. Paul Blackner put a trailer on the other side of Bob's house by the lake, and we lived a lighthearted bachelor life. Bob was always building things. First he put a lake at his place. Then he put a small lake in back by my trailer. We put in a swimming pool. When we found that it was too cold out there because of the trees, Bob built a building to cover the pool. He built a garage with a room above. And we had parties. The enclave became some sort of a social center.

Bob noted that Paul Blackner was very experienced as a produce manager and working for a salary. He proposed that he and I put up the money to build a produce market and Paul Blackner could manage it. So we built the Produce Mart, and Paul Blackner managed it for more than ten years.

Bob and I did a lot of traveling. On one trip we toured the Soviet Union, including Russia, the Ukraine, Georgia, Armenia, and Azerbaijan. This was sponsored by the Pennsylvania Medical Society, and Bob loved it when they addressed him as Dr. McIlwain.

When my mother died and the weight of a heavy snowfall collapsed the pool building, I moved to California and Bob followed. He bought a house in Carpentaria, and we remained close friends. When I married Toni, once again Bob was an usher at my wedding. In reality, Bob was a part of my family, and I was a part of his. We celebrated together, births and deaths, holidays and birthdays. He was just as close to me as any of my family.

I last spoke with Bob approximately six days ago. I called and a fellow named Chuck answered the phone. I thought it was Chuck McIlwain and began asking what he was doing there. It was, however, one of Bob's caretakers. Bob was getting breathing therapy, and at first it appeared that I couldn't speak with him, but shortly they volunteered to break the therapy so I could talk with him. I'm glad that they did that. It was my last chance to talk to Bob. He appeared very good, alert, cheerful, and optimistic. He said, "I'm going to get better and come out to see you soon."

I won't be with you when you bury Bob, but, of course, you know I'll be there in spirit. It means a lot to me that I was able to talk to him only a few days ago. Burying Bob is to me no different than burying one of my immediate family. I owe so much to Bob.

Countries Visited

1)	Alaska	36)	Jamaica
2)	Antigua	37)	Japan
3)	Armenia	38)	Korea
4)	Australia	39)	Luxemburg
5)	Austria	40)	Macau
6)	Azerbaijan	41)	Martinique
7)	Azores	42)	Mexico
8)	Bahamas	43)	Monaco
9)	Barbuda	44)	Morocco
10)	Belgium	45)	Netherlands
11)	Brazil	46)	Norway
12)	Canada	47)	Pakistan
13)	Costa Rica	48)	Philippines
14)	Croatia	49)	Portugal
15)	Czechoslovakia	50)	Puerto Rico
16)	Denmark	51)	Russia
17)	Dominica	52)	Saint Kitts
18)	England	53)	Saint Lucia
19)	Fiji	54)	Samoa
20)	France	55)	Saudi Arabia
21)	Georgia	56)	Scotland
22)	Germany	57)	Sicily
23)	Grand Inagua	58)	Singapore
24)	Greece	59)	Slovenia
25)	Greenland	60)	Spain
26)	Grenada	61)	Sweden
27)	Guadeloupe	62)	Switzerland
28)	Guatemala	63)	Thailand
29)	Haiti	64)	Turkey
30)	Hawaii	65)	Turks & Caicos Islands
31)	Hong Kong	66)	Ukraine
32)	Iceland	67)	United Arab Emirates
33)	India	68)	United States
34)	Iran	69)	Venezuela
35)	Italy	70)	Virgin Islands

Paul Straub

- circled the world six times,
- made 19 trips to Saudi Arabia,
- made 15 parachute jumps,
- is a YMCA certified scuba instructor, deepest dive 144 feet,
- is a member of the party of four climbers who made the first successful ascent on the face of the cliff from which Angel Falls, the worlds highest waterfall originates. All previous attempts at climbing this cliff, three times the height of the Empire State Building, and overhung at points, were unsuccessful.
- is the **17th person to fly solo around the world,** not counting flights that shipped the plane over oceans by boat. According to earthrounders.com, the first person to fly solo around the world was Wiley Post in 1933. 17 people flew solo around the world in the 44 years between 1933 and 1977.

Personal Mission Statement---Paul Straub

1) "The only way to be is to be totally honest"—from my father Ralph R. Straub.
2) "Just practice good medicine and the money will take care of itself"—from Richard Zimmerman, MD FACS, my mentor during surgical residency.
3) Anytime I make a deal, with my patients, my employees, my family, or anybody else, they get more than we agreed on.
4) Medical practice is a profession, not a business.
5) I never have a bad day.—from Dave Gilbert. Since I am responsible to make my own day, why should I make a bad one?
6) I am responsible for my life, my day, my attitudes, my emotions, my success, and my failures. I blame nobody else and no circumstances.
7) I never let any chemical substance, such as alcohol, drugs, or other substance, be in control of me—from my father.
8) I don't need a budget because I always spend less than I earn.
9) I never buy anything if I don't have the money to pay for it. If I want something I first save the money, and then buy it.
10) I do not need to be amused. I can entertain myself. I read to learn. I watch little television, except to learn something such as the news or the weather. I seldom watch sports; instead, I prefer to exercise myself. I do not go to movies to entertain myself.
11) I center my life on principles, not on self, money, work, pleasure, or any other thing.

CPSIA information can be obtained at www.ICGtesting.com
Printed in the USA
LVOW121536070112

262631LV00001B/6/P